ANTONIO, ANTONIA

ANTONIO, ANTONIA

Joseph Howatch

HOUGHTON MIFFLIN COMPANY BOSTON

1976

The author is grateful for permission to quote from the following sources:
From *Collected Poems* by Edna St. Vincent Millay, Harper & Row.
Copyright, 1917, 1928, 1945, 1955 by Edna St. Vincent Millay and
Norma Millay Ellis. And from *Amers* by St.-John Perse, published by
Gallimard, Paris, 1957, and quoted by permission of Princeton
University Press.

Library of Congress Cataloging in Publication Data

Howatch, Joseph.
  Antonio, Antonia.

  I. Title.
PZ4.H8562An [PS3558.O8836]   813'.5'4   76-25010
ISBN 0-395-24769-1

Printed in the United States of America

C   10   9   8   7   6   5   4   3   2   1

To Susan

and, of course, to
Gina Sullivan
wherever she is

CONTENTS

Book One

ANTONIO

HARRY'S STORY

The Conspirators

EVERYTHING IS PREDICTABLE. There won't be any surprises.

I'll stand facing him, absolutely determined, incapable of relenting. He'll see from my face and know from my words that my resolution couldn't possibly be firmer. I'll tell him what I've told him before: that the two of us are through if he doesn't do as I say. (He already assumes that means disinheritance so there'll be no need to speak of that.) He'll know nothing can ever change my mind. I am prepared to hold out beyond the bitter end. Harry Rambulcek will not back down.

Equally predictable is the next part of the scene. We'll probably be on the big terrace, the one facing Sicily, standing about ten feet apart — no, farther; such a confrontation requires a good distance. Then Jeffrey will calmly inform me of his decision. And I'll stand there convinced that his determination is also complete, that there's not the slightest chance of his backing down. "Tough deuce, Dad," he'll say, or whatever the current equivalent is. We'll exchange one last hard look and then I'll sigh.

I'll hesitate a moment (embarrassed? or trying to hide my elation?), then shake his hand, tell him I love him, that he'll always be my son, and that nothing could ever stand in the way of our friendship.

HAPPINESS IS MERELY a matter of perspective.

Our fortunes change, from good to ill and back to good and all again. In the midst of good fortune, the view is exhilarating. Life, after all, has meaning. Everything has been for the best. Our past adversities appear as but challenges overcome, steppingstones to victory. Hurriedly we search for the Beethoven, start the record at the fourth movement, take a deep breath — then with tears of gratitude filling our eyes and the Ode to Joy filling the room . . . Of all living creatures, who, so much as man, pauses to celebrate triumph?

But if we turn the page, next year, next week, or perhaps even before the Beethoven has finished: the phone will ring, the letter will arrive, our dearest friend or lover or enemy will speak the words again announcing the end of the world. Once more insurmountable sorrow surrounds us. We find ourselves still awake at three in the morning and, whether on a double or a single bed, the knowledge of our hopeless isolation overwhelms us. In desperation we reach for the ultimate painkiller: the Scorecard of Praise and Blame. Of all living creatures, only man seeks refuge in such fantasy.

If there is a moral, it may be this: begin at the beginning, go on to the happiest part, then stop.

AS BEGINNINGS GO, mine probably couldn't have been better.

I came into the world, usurping Valeria's place as the baby of the family after she'd enjoyed that position for almost nine years. The interval is probably a good one since I was met, not with resentment, but with unceasing attention and love. I can remember Valeria only with her eager smile and eyes of devotion. And the same can be said of Frank, Janko, Kashia, Joe, Cyril, Marisha, Paul, Helen, and Richard; in my memory it now seems none of my brothers or sisters ever looked at me without smiling.

Anywhere I wandered in those six tiny rooms, I was never out of reach of the patting hand or the enthusiastic kiss. Or the extra bit of food saved specially for me, though my brothers with their miners' appetites never had enough for themselves. As for clothes, I should have had the usual rags of my contemporaries, except the boys kept a jar into which their (rare) spare coins were collected so that I might have one of the bright-colored jackets or shirts that lit up the racks of the company store.

My parents were not especially extraordinary, but they did have one wondrous talent — despite the thirteen bodies housed in that tiny shack in Wersend, Ohio, my parents somehow managed to maintain a family atmosphere which contrasted with that of most neighbors. I can never think of a time in 9 Warsaw Street when the atmosphere was not one of tranquility and serenity. If there was an outburst, it was of song or laughter, especially during the holidays. The flimsy walls shook as the polkas and *cardas* from Frank's accordion enticed my brothers to dance even with my sisters if no other girls were present. Father prohibited stamping (the man thwacking the floor solidly with his free leg as he leads his partner out of a corner turn), but only because the house would have fallen down. Whatever noise or boisterousness there was in that house, it seems it was always joyful. Even when the Depression came and things got even tougher, the atmosphere at home became no less civilized.

I remember Dad sitting in the round wooden tub in the kitchen, the steam from the scalding water indistinguishable from the smoke of his cigarette. (Father's one privilege seemed to be a leisurely bath; all the boys were rushed through theirs or else the kitchen could never be cleared in time for supper.) Joe and Cyril were acting up in my parents' bedroom, which served as the parlor during the day. "Cyril," my father called and immediately Cyril appeared in the doorway. "Please," Father commanded, whereupon Cyril and Joe made their way through the steaming kitchen and out the back door. They could fight as often as they pleased, but it had to be done behind the outhouse. (The sight of a brother entering the back door with a bleeding nose evoked only a wearied look from my mother and no sympathy whatever from my sisters. Nor was the victor ever congratulated.) Another rule was that no fight could take place without another brother supervising.

Once Janko broke Frank's nose, but it was Richard whom my father reprimanded. Even though Frank and Janko were giants, it was Richard's responsibility as supervisor to stop the fight when it had gone too far.

"How?" Richard pleaded.

"I'll tell you how," Dad said, rising from his bath and putting his hands to his shoulders to take the big towel which one of the girls would be holding behind him. (He rose from his bath and took the towel to his shoulders with all the dignity and grace of a king receiving a cloak or Father Hrichka taking the golden cape over his shoulders at Benediction.) "You say 'stop' and if they don't, you walk into the house and tell me. Understand?"

Richard nodded. Stopping a fight between two giants was as simple as that in our house. Everything was simple then . . . simple as in "the gods take care of everything." And so they did.

It's one thing to find security and joy in the warmth and love of one's own home, but what happens when a pampered boy ventures out into the cruel world. The problem was answered in the most satisfactory manner by my being half an inch taller than Joey Stecz.

The wonder and excitement of my social debut was interrupted on my first morning at school by the clanging of a hand bell swung with supreme authority by a ferocious Mrs. Mann. We were to form lines, one for the boys and one for the girls, each two abreast, smallest up front and tallest in back. After much confusion and giggling we were finally assembled and Mrs. Mann was again about to ring her Pavlovian bell when she stopped, rushed to the end of the boys' line, plucked out me and Joey, stood us back to back, then promptly inserted us back into the line. Now, however, I was standing at the very end with Bernie Kaminowicz, whereas Joey now stood in my former place with Carl Daskin as his partner. Thus it was that my happy childhood was determined.

Mrs. Mann had a peculiar system of "chums." Our partner that first morning in line became our "chum" and everything in the classroom was done with one's "chum." We sat together, completed projects together and eventually became identified with each other.

Among the first of my classmates to assume recognizable identities were Bernie and Carl. Bernie was the tallest and biggest, and while not a bully, his tolerance and humor were limited. Early on he spotted Carl's timidity, exploited it, and gave us Carl as the class sissy and himself as the class tough guy.

Bernie then began to go after Joey, who (being Carl's chum) must also be a sissy. Poor Joey was at first confused, but finally asserted himself and freed himself from the sissy stigma only by turning on Carl. Joey wasn't a bad guy at all and it was sad he had to become somewhat cruel to save himself.

By the time all this had been accomplished, I, as oblivious as ever, had become identified with my chum, Bernie. The respect he'd fought for early on was also given to me. Then it became apparent that one of the two tough guys (me) had a nicer disposition than the other (Bernie). Before long, and no doubt mostly because I must have expected it, the adulation I accepted as my birthright from my brothers and sisters was also forthcoming from my classmates.

If I continued as I'd begun, there's little doubt that I should now be a successful businessman, a major figure in Wersend politics, and president of the chamber of commerce at least. The gods, however, apparently thought such a career too modest for their favorite; anything short of a worldwide reputation was out of the question. But there was one problem.

Take a healthy child, give him nothing but love and attention, make him so secure that he never has to be mean, spare him from all afflictions, watch over him in the desert and on the mainland, protect him from the pain, shield him from the ecstasy . . . and what do you have? A pleasant, content, perhaps even likable young man, but essentially a dummy. Such a one could make it to the presidency of Wersend's chamber of commerce, but there would not be the ambition necessary to face the squalor and violence of the big time and to rise to the top of the world. The gods therefore found it necessary to awaken (as painlessly as possible, of course) the mind of their darling. This they achieved by creating two additional characters.

The first appeared on a morning when the fog blended nicely with the gray of the company houses, in an alley off Warsaw Street, just as I was taking a lard sandwich from the pocket of my new pea coat. He was sort of screwed around a pole, much like a small child embracing the leg of a protecting adult. He hesitated when I offered half the sandwich, but finally took it and, now propping himself against the pole, began to devour the unexpected treat. We ate in silence, never taking our eyes off each other. (Only young children and soldiers in a Hemingway story are capable of such prolonged mutual appraisal.)

He was shorter than I, but more muscular and though he looked tough, I could tell he wasn't a bully like the twins Piss and Shit. His size was that of a first grader, like me, but his face looked older. I wasn't worried; I'd already had two fights with second graders and won both. Besides, I didn't know what fear was then.

"*Ako sa voláš?*" I asked, but he looked blank.

"*Kol'ko máš rokov?*" But he shrugged his shoulders.

"*Kde byvaš?*" Again his shoulders went up. He didn't know where he lived? It was exciting. "*Pod'me domov,*" I commanded.

I'd always had a way with stray dogs and cats and now I'd found
a stray boy. How pleased everyone at home would be! "*Nuž teda,
pod'. Čo ti je?*"

I tried to take him by the arm, but he resisted and then I saw
the fear in his eyes. I put my hand on his shoulder and smiled to
reassure him. Perhaps he couldn't talk. "Don't worry, you can
live with us, but we'll have to give you a name."

"My name's Antonio," he said resentfully, though he allowed
me to lead him down Warsaw Street toward my home. I tried to
hurry him along, unable to wait for everyone to see him.

"*Je veru pekná,*" Mother said after she'd fed him and sent him
home. "But he must go to his own mother and father."

"Why can't he understand me?"

She laughed and I think she must have realized I had no idea
when I was speaking Slovak, Polish, or English. "He understands when you speak English. Just remember to speak English to him all the time."

"But what's the matter with him?"

"Nothing, darling. His people came from Italy where they
speak Italian, just like Baba and Zeda came from Slovakia
where they speak Slovak. And you must be very nice to him
because he'll be the only Italian boy in the valley. He's not in
your school?"

"No," I said, still crushed at having failed with my first stray
boy.

"I figure he goes to Father Hrichka's school then. He lives
near the old breaker by Auntie Betka. You can play with each
other after school."

Either Piss or Shit alone could have beat the hell out of me,
and together they would make more of a mess of me than they
were making of Antonio one day in the alley near Genkovick's
Groceries. I heard the noise before I turned the corner and
when Bernie saw me he called "Hey, Harry, we got the dirty
dago." I made my way through the circle of my friends and saw
Piss (or Shit) sitting on a bloodied boy while Shit (or Piss — they

were identical) was clobbering the boy across the face with a book.

I was surprised because it was unusual for us to gang up on just one boy, and then I saw the boy was Antonio. I screamed and jumped on Piss. Then I was into it with both twins, taking turns punching at their faces. I was a wild animal, but their stupefication more than my blows was defeating them. Then one picked up his books and started to walk away, but that wasn't good enough for me. I grabbed him by the neck and started pounding his face. "Let him go Harry," his twin cried. I turned on him and soon both were running off.

As I turned back to the group, Bernie was walking toward the still prostrate body of Antonio. I snarled at him like an animal defending its young and he jumped back, though probably he had only been trying to get a closer look at Antonio.

What was best about the incident was that afterward I thought of it only in terms of Antonio having been put upon unfairly. Never once did I even briefly consider that demolishing the twins simultaneously was an unprecedented feat, that I'd finally got the edge on Bernie (we never fought each other), and that in a few minutes I'd stopped the prejudice against Tony from taking root and growing. Only years later in high school, when we were scrimmaging and Shit (eventually called Chris, though Piss always remained Piss) decided to get me, did I realize how physically superior the twins were and how lucky I'd been. (Those whom the gods cherish they bless with invincible ignorance.)

Also, I don't think I felt any disappointment at Antonio's seeming lack of gratitude as I cleaned him up and led him toward his home.

Tony lived on Milbre Street, on our (the wrong) side of the tracks, but he attended the parochial school on the other side, Brodericks, where many houses were painted. (Except for a small clan of Irish, the town elite, Brodericks was also inhabited by Slovak and Polish miners.) From the start Tony was an outcast in his school because of his nationality and was daily

forced to defend himself. When he began winning most of the
fights, the taunts subsided and eventually he would have been
left alone. But it was about this time I began "waiting up" for
him after school and when it got around that he was associating
with the scum (us), the antagonism was renewed, even more
fiercely than before.

He had two expressions then, the grim, determined one when
he was with his classmates, and the more benign though blank
one when he was with us. My friends eventually accepted him
— their initial reluctance caused more by his perpetually
solemn face than by his being a "foreigner."

"Why d'ya bother with the wop?" Staszek, my best friend at
the time, asked, evidently meaning I was getting little reward
for my efforts.

I looked at him, not realizing what the question meant,
though I'd learned what a wop was. "Sorry," he said. "Just
askin'." If I understood the question, I should probably have
answered something to the effect that stray boys require more
patience than stray dogs or cats. As oblivious as I was, I could
recognize shyness and insecurity when I saw it.

Near the end of winter I paid my first formal visit to the
Contiorli house and announced myself in the best Wersend
fashion by taking up a position in the middle of the back yard
and called "Hey, Tony." Actually it was a chant with a prescribed rhythm, stretching the three syllables into ten.

A bright sun was beginning to soften the edges of the frozen
mud which carpeted our side of town. In most back yards wild
grasses were coaxed into something resembling a lawn, but the
spring would come to the Contiorli back yard with nature not
having a chance to make any impression. Lumps of coal, rusty
nails, rags, millions of pieces of glass . . .

After my first chant I realized that all along a growling had
been emanating from the house. Then as I got through my
second and even louder "Hey, Tony" (we knocked on doors only
when sent on adult business), the back door opened and crash-
ing through the rubble on the porch came a boy in his early

teens, his face red with anger or frustration. My calls probably weren't heard amid the noise inside and the boy didn't even see me until he was off the porch and heading round toward the front of the house. He stopped and greeted me with "Get the fuck outa here, shit." I began considering if he had mistaken me for *the* Shit when the flat of his hand pushed through my face and I went down backward. Apparently the form was for me to jump up immediately and run off, but the gods were off duty and I just lay there, not aware of what was happening. Most likely I was still considering how he could have mistaken me for Shit when he kicked me hard in the crotch. Before the pain came, I was able to watch him continue toward the front of the house, having put me completely out of his mind.

If one is to suffer intense physical pain only once in fifty-five years, then perhaps it's best to have it out of the way at an early age. That's the nicest thing I can think to say about Carlo Contiorli.

And the rest of his family wasn't much better, except the eldest, Philip. How he and Antonio came to be part of that ill-spirited, frustrated lot is a miracle. (The Contiorlis were "banned" in Pittsburgh whence they came to Wersend when Tony entered the first grade.)

In the company store one day I saw a huge man with a small boy, both with curly black hair and the same strange grey eyes. I should have known Antonio immediately — we were only twenty feet apart — except a smile had transformed his face into that of a trusting, happy child. He was looking up at Philip, who was making a funny face at him. Both of them obviously should have been Rambulceks and not Contiorlis.

When we were in third grade a mine dam burst and as its waters rushed down the hills, they crossed the highway, from where they carried a huge wooden billboard to down along the sulfur creek. The billboard came to rest at a forty-five-degree angle, from near the water's edge to the top of the bank, which created a tentlike shelter. The paint had long since peeled from the billboard, except for PRAVO in yellow letters against a flaking blue background. The *pono* vines along the bank were just beginning their spring growth and in a few weeks they spread over the entire surface, almost completely concealing the billboard.

We used planks for a floor, closed off the back, and put in a couple shelves and a hiding place for our treasures. Even from the beginning it wasn't very comfortable standing upright inside, but there was plenty of room to sit and listen to the purring of the sulfur creek and watch the parade of cattails that lined the stream all the way down to the sulfur pond. Behind the pond a grove of sumac trees hid most of the gray houses. Beyond the town we could see the hills rising toward Slaughter Mountain, far away from Wersend.

The Pravo (Slovak for "justice," though we never knew what the billboard had said originally) became the center of our world during grade school. On weekends when our friends joined us, the Pravo was our laboratory where we experimented with insects, cigarettes, "dirty pictures," and, later on, beer and ourselves. But essentially it was Tony's and my exclusive property, especially during the week. On rainy days we spent hours talking and slowly chewing the potatoes we stole from the barrels of Genkovick's Groceries.

In his school Tony remained an outcast, though a respected one. No one bothered him and he maintained a businesslike relation with his classmates about school matters. A boy named Freen was the closest thing he had to a friend in Father Hrichka's school, and though they exchanged information about assignments in the classroom, they never spoke out of school, and would pass each other on the street as strangers.

Of course it wasn't his nationality that kept him ostracized, but his involvement with us; he was definitely a friend of the enemy. Even so, when we had a skirmish with the Brodericks boys, Tony took a neutral position, remaining on the sidelines. However, the times Bernie, Staszek and I found ourselves outnumbered, he did join battle on our side.

Among my friends, however, Antonio not only was accepted, but eventually enjoyed leadership status with me and Bernie.

Bernie was not stupid, but his sense of humor was minimal, causing everyone — even the smallest boys — to make jokes about him, but never in his presence. Only Tony could make jokes about Bernie to his face; if others were present, Bernie would threaten Tony, but if the three of us were alone, he said nothing. I suspect he enjoyed Antonio's jokes, recognizing them as signs of affection rather than challenges.

Outwardly, then, Antonio was just a normal Wersend boy, but more and more I began seeing that he, unlike anyone else, had another side which remained a secret to everyone except himself and me.

I see him now walking alone through the tall grass of a field in the early morning, giving an impression of ease, looking serene and confident. But if a camera would zoom in for a prolonged study of his face, behind the façade one would detect the disguised alertness. It had become his nature to be prepared for anything, especially the worst. Whenever I picture him, the initial calm of the scene is eventually destroyed by that underlying tension I know was always there.

He is poised with a basketball, his attention completely focused on the old rusted hoop sans net which hung behind the school. There is the special October sky before twilight which makes even the most desolate setting seem poignant. Antonio looks unusually calm and untroubled; his effort was not something immediately apparent to others. There wasn't that excess motion, the strained expression or foolish movements of one who is trying too hard. He looks so casual and unconcerned only because he is perpetually poised, as no child should ever be forced to be.

Bit by bit I began seeing things as he did. I continued to see my world and its sweet pleasures as usual, but bit by bit it was dawning on me that there was more than one way to look at the world. The day we discovered Carson's Ledge — I can still hear the excited voices of my friends as we realized we had found the best view of the valley. They spoke of building a hut near the edge of the cliff. (It was never built since the only practical way up was scaling the face of the cliff.) But I can also hear, in the midst of the excitement, the silence of Antonio and me. We probably were more excited than the others about the glorious view of the river below and the flat treeless top of the ledge covered with huckleberry bushes, but it seemed that words would be distracting.

Even when Tony and I discovered Fern Marsh and were alone, we didn't speak, but simply spent the afternoon wandering about and swimming, all the time moved by the beauty of the place. When I was with him there was a special significance to places and things, as if their beauty were magnified and overpowering.

We were conspirators almost. There was no need to name the conspiracy just as there was no need to talk about anything but the most trivial things. When our friends got excited about leaving Wersend (the great dream, since staying meant spending one's life in the mines), Tony and I rarely joined in the fantasy. We knew it was a fantasy, except for us. We know we would leave and there was no need to speak of it.

Our conspiracy was acknowledged only at parting. When joining up on a Saturday morning, we silently fell in beside each other and set about the business of the day (which often began by picking coal on the culm banks — otherwise known as filling potato sacks with the anthracite discarded in the slag heaps near the collieries). But when parting at evening, Antonio would stop and give me a special look, almost as if saying that because we saw more than the others, then it had to be that our destinies lay outside Wersend.

By comparison to the cozy complacency of my early years, my mind had been somewhat awakened, but apparently not enough to assure the gods who saw fit to make things foolproof by introducing another force.

It was a late Saturday afternoon, shortly after we entered high school. (There was only one, so Tony and I finally shared the same class.) We'd scrimmaged against the sophomores that morning and done badly. I'd stolen two bottles of beer from my cellar and Tony had bought four cigarettes.

The area around the Pravo had once been a reservoir which was transferred farther uphill, leaving a creek, a pond, and a vast desert of slate coated with sulfur deposits. (Was it really sulfur? We always called it that.) Under the sun the desert was sparkling gold; in the moonlight the vast field of crystals gave a silver glow. (Children find beauty wherever they are; only as an adult did I 'learn' that all of Wersend was ugly.)

We'd been sitting in the entrance of the Pravo, sipping our beer and watching the deepening drama of the late afternoon skies. Tony began talking about joining the Coast Guard as a means of escaping Wersend. I attributed his unusual enthusiasm to the beer, though he usually just sang when he drank too much. I announced that as soon as he finished his bottle I was going to run home and put the empties back in the case. I was already taking a big risk that someone would recognize the ratio between full and empty bottles wasn't what it should be, but if there should be two empty slots . . .

He asked me not to go and began talking wildly — at least I couldn't understand what he was trying to say. I stayed a while and then again attempted to go, but still he urged me to stay.

"Sure," I said, "it ain't your ass that's going to get smashed." Dad rarely hit any of us, but I was committing a capital crime.

I reached to collect the bottles and then looked at Tony. He looked surprised; he wasn't looking at me, but just over my shoulder, and I thought there must be something strange in the sky. I turned and found myself facing a girl. The sudden confrontation was startling, but I assumed the obvious — that we had a trespasser on our hands. Then I realized they knew each other.

He introduced me and I edged past her with my beer bottles and hurried home in the twilight. I decided that Tony had tried to delay me so I could see her, but later I learned this wasn't so.

Rosalind had surprised Antonio at first in much the same way she'd surprised me that evening (he was later to confess). He'd been wandering toward the Pravo, looking for me. It had been a rainy afternoon and quite dark. He had been singing "Pridi ty, Suhajko," which I'd taught him, and as he approached the Pravo she had stuck her head out into the rain to discover the source of the song. He said he hadn't been surprised. It had seemed natural to see those light-brown eyes peering out into the gray day.

> *I would to God I were quenched and fed*
> *As in my youth*
> *From the flask of song, and the good bread*
> *Of beauty richer than truth.*
> *You go no more on your exultant feet*
> *Up paths that only mist and morning knew;*
> *Or watch the wind, or listen to the beat*
> *Of a bird's wings too high in air to view, —*
> *But you were something more than young and sweet*
> *And fair — and the long year remembers you.*
> [Edna Millay said these things.]
> *So is no warmth for me at any fire*
> *Today, when the world's fire has burned so low;*
> *I kneel, spending my breath in vain desire,*
> *At that cold hearth which one time roared so strong;*
> *And straighten back in weariness, and long*
> *To gather up my little gods and go.*

Rosalind lived in Brodericks, in the best part, where not only were the houses painted, but also there were sidewalks and gardens. Through all their years in grade school together they'd never spoken, and even when we all joined together in high school, Antonio never paid attention to her until he discovered her in the Pravo.

He had with him a potato stolen from Genkovick's and used a knife to cut half of it for Rosalind. This surprised me since raw potatoes seemed too grand for a girl from Brodericks where, it was rumored, meat was served more than once a week — and meat did not mean only chicken. (I never tasted a steak until I was well into my teens.)

"Did she eat it?" I asked.

"Sure."

"So how's come you never told me about her?"

"None your fuckin' business, shithead." The last was Antonio's term of endearment for me which he used only when I needed cheering up or when he was nervous.

"Do you see her a lot?"

"None your fuckin' business."

But he had seen her, or heard her, rather, as he later confessed. Several times he'd attended "concerts" given solely for him. They took place on Tuesday nights when the men were off to the union meeting. Antonio would wait near the outhouse of Rosalind's back yard until her parlor light went off; then he quickly stole to behind the bushes below the parlor window. Soon the light came on and for an half an hour or so he listened as she played the piano.

We'd all heard a little classical music (all called "opery") and knew it belonged to the world outside Wersend. But the night of the first concert Rosalind's playing the first movement of the Grieg Concerto was a milestone for Antonio. For one thing, it was the first live piano music he'd heard (accordians and harmonicas abounded on our side, but pianos didn't exist, not even in the school). Another thing was that Philip had his grandparents' love for opera and had held the young Antonio on his lap and sung "Cielo e Mar" and "M'Appari" to him. As Philip was the only one in his family whom Antonio loved, it was not surprising Antonio was drawn to Rosalind's music. (He assumed all "opery" was in fact opera and later asked Rosalind to sing the words of the Grieg.)

Late into the night after the first concert, Antonio says he stayed in his back yard, too excited to sleep. He was intoxicated by Rosalind, her music, and the forbiddenness of the entire evening. Rosalind had told him she wanted to be a concert pianist and give recitals all over the world. Some young men might make the break and escape Wersend, but it was inconceivable for a girl even to think such a thing. Rosalind's audacity thrilled Antonio and in his back yard that night he

saw his own escape as a necessity. No longer was it something
highly desirable that might require a miracle to bring off, it was
a simple necessity and that made all the difference. "It's a
necessity," he kept repeating. It was in fact this same realization he was trying to communicate to me in the Pravo before
Rosalind appeared when I thought he'd drunk too much beer.

"You guys better watch out. An' just give me the word if you
want any help, especially at night."

When I asked Bernie what he meant, he said he'd overheard
some talk among the Brodericks boys. "They're plannin' on
layin' for you."

Across-the-tracks friendships were tolerated in high school
(since we all shared the same classrooms), but when Tony and I
began spending all our time with Rosalind, the old antagonisms
flared up again.

I repeated Bernie's warning to Tony and Rosalind. Rosalind
said, "We're going to spend the night on Carson's Ledge and
watch the sunrise. We'll have supper there and bring things for
breakfast."

How was a fourteen-year-old girl going to arrange to spend a
night on the mountain top with two boys from the wrong side of
town? In answer to my question, Rosalind asked, "Can you bring
a pot? About this size? I'm going to make some *pagačky* and
holubky and we can just heat them. But you and Antonio will be
in charge of breakfast. And we'll need some old carpets and
blankets for sleeping."

When I was alone with Tony, I repeated Bernie's warning, but
again he ignored it and asked if I could bring some eggs; he
would get the bacon. How could anyone steal bacon from
Genkovick's meat case?

The night was as mild and balmly as midsummer, though it
was only late spring. Rosalind heated our supper on a small fire
we built and when we had devoured every scrap, we dangled our
legs over the edge of the cliff and watched the town lights as the
stars (every one of them) joined in our celebration. Finally we

lay down on an old carpet, spread a blanket over us, and sang ourselves to sleep.

The cracks of lightning gave us only a few minutes' warning before the rains began. There was no shelter on top of the ledge and the few small trees would be dangerous in an electrical storm. An hour later, completely soaked, we arrived at the Pravo just as the skies were lightening in the east. We planned cooking breakfast in the Pravo, but discovered it was already occupied, by Rosalind's father who had arrived a few minutes before us.

Mr. Yurkon was a fierce man whom we'd always avoided, but short of simply running away, there was now no escaping him. He was sitting inside, hunched over, and Rosalind went in to join him. Tony and I remained outside, the heavy rains suddenly more inviting than the dry but dangerous darkness of our refuge. We could barely see him, but his eyes somehow reached us and without a word being spoken we knew we were meant to go inside, where we squatted, breathless and trembling.

He lit a cigarette and surveyed me and Tony mercilessly. Obviously he'd just finished the night shift, as fresh layers of black dust hadn't been washed from his face and the sharp smell of carbide from the lamp on his cap filled the Pravo. "Tell me where you been and what happened." His voice was rough, but he spoke softly, almost matter-of-factly, but with such command we knew we had to tell absolutely everything, leaving no question unanswered. It was a moment of truth, much more absolute than any confessional. Fresh in our minds was the story of a few months back when Mr. Yurkon had hurled a Brodericks boy from the front porch, breaking the boy's nose and shoulder. The boy had been calling on Diane, Rosalind's older sister, and apparently his attitude did not please Mr. Yurkon. Tony began, telling all. I interrupted only when I felt an important detail had been omitted.

"Where did you get the eggs and bacon?"

I told him my mother gave me the eggs and Tony said he'd stolen fifteen cents from Carlo to buy the bacon.

"You *stole* the money from your brother?"

"Yes sir."

"Rosalind, you put this over your head and start on home. Your mother's waitin' for you. I'll be home in a couple minutes." When Rosalind was gone, he said "Here's what now. First if you wanna go out with Rosalind at night, you ask me. Now promise that."

We both promised.

"And then you never go sleepin' together like that anywhere. Now you promise."

Again we promised.

"You unnerstand now? You know why it's dangerous?"

"We didn't . . ." Tony began but couldn't finish.

"I know. I know what kinda boys you are, so do as I say."

We promised and after several more promises he left.

We remained silent and shaking till Tony said, "I'm not hungry, but we might's well cook up this stuff. I can't take it home." We built a fire and fried the bacon and eggs and, as we were about to eat, Tony stuck his head out into the rain and looked around, just to make sure we were alone. Then finally he looked at me and said, "I think he likes us."

A similar observation would be the answer to Bernie's warning. There was resentment against Tony and me for monopolizing Rosalind, but it was short-lived. To the three of us, being together was as natural and unquestionable as leaves on summer trees, but to others apparently there was something unusual about our relationship. We never did anything spectacular or even vaguely special, but the exuberance of our feelings for each other must have been throwing off magic fireworks. The resentment changed to puzzlement, then to wonder, until at last classmates from both sides of the track were flocking around us.

By the time we entered our second year of high school, an invitation to join us on a picnic or an expedition apparently was a sign of status. Rosalind's concerts were no longer covert and Tony and I sat on the front porch swing as friends filled up all available spaces on the porch and steps. If Mr. Yurkon should appear during a concert, his fierce eyes would beat down anyone who dared look up at him (a "Good evening, Mr. Yurkon" would go unacknowledged), but when he looked at Tony and me, there was a softness and warmth to his look. The Paraclete hovering over us in golden clouds and saying, "These are my beloved sons in whom I am well pleased" would have been more dramatic, but not necessarily more satisfying.

After each concert, when everyone had left, Rosalind would sit between us and tell us the names of the composers and their nationalities. It was a dream world, sitting on that front porch swing and talking about Chopin as night came and the shouts of children playing down the street faded and the crickets took over.

Through Rosalind's influence, Tony began reading books from the school library and when I began to feel left out, I too started to read novels. I think I became an avid reader primarily because of the excitement of discussing books with Rosalind and Tony (who often had to tell me what the books meant and why they were wonderful). Eventually I became hooked and wondered one day how anyone could go through life without reading a few books each week. It might have been at that point that the gods nodded wearily at one another: they could now relax a while. Their favorite had not only begun to think and feel; he had also begun to dream.

I went to sleep one night shortly after the colliery whistle began an interminable wail; when I awoke the next morning I learned that among three dozen miners killed had been Antonio's father and brother.

"Not Philip!"

My mother nodded, and warned me away from the Contiorli home. "The last thing they need at a time like this is a kid pestering them."

Rosalind and I didn't see Antonio, but when he didn't show up for school on Wednesday, two days after the funerals, I went to the Pravo that afternoon instead of returning to school. After waiting an hour I decided to call on him.

He came out the back door and told me to wait a minute. I cleared myself a place on the back porch, pushing away boots and coal. Coal was called by names according to its size: chestnut was the largest and most expensive, then came buckwheat, barley, pea coal, and rice (I think). Only pea coal was called coal, the others were simply barley, rice, et cetera.

"He's gonna finish school first," I heard Mrs. Contiorli say.

"Fer God's sake, Ma," Al said, "we need the money now. And what did it do for Carlo to finish school? Ya lost money for all that time. Am I right?"

"He's right, Ma," Carlo said. "It'd be different if the kid played ball."

"I do play ball," I heard Tony protest.

"That's ball? Second-string tackle!" Carlo said. "Shit, I'm talkin' about playin' . . ."

I heard a slap and then a tense silence. At last Carlo spoke again. "I'm sorry Ma, that slipped." (Apparently one was given two seconds to apologize after being slapped by the tiny Mrs. Contiorli. If no apology came, a second slap would be on its way. Even Phil, the biggest — who had earned more than the father — had been subject to the mother's slaps, though near the end he'd asserted himself by walking away without apologizing.)

"He finishes school," Mrs. Contiorli said, and I gave a silent cheer.

Without turning to look, I knew it was Carlo coming out the back door. I moved well out of his way as he passed. From inside I heard Antonio say something like "Thanks, Ma," but this was suddenly followed by another slap.

Silence. Then his mother's shrill voice. "You're what?"

"I'm sorry, Ma." Antonio said. Then he too rushed outside.

After Phil was killed, Antonio began telling Rosalind and me about his home life. Except for Philip's arias, Italian was rarely used and the family tried to adapt the Slovak and Polish customs, language, and dishes. Breakfast and supper were served at specified times and if you missed supper, that was it; you simply didn't eat till the next morning. None of us had much food then, but in Tony's home it was unthinkable for a child to take a piece of bread or some lard on his own. We all stole from the stores, and Antonio was particularly good at this, but he never dared take any food from home, even if he were absolutely certain the theft would go undetected.

Antonio had two sisters and I think he wanted to feel protective toward them, but they treated his affection with the same indifference as the nagging of Al or the cruel jokes of Carlo. "It's like they just can't see any difference, like to them Phil was the same as Carlo or Al."

And of course Antonio talked mostly about Phil and that the only love he'd known had come from Phil and not from his parents or sisters. "When I was a little kid, the only time I'd get a bath would be if Phil gave it to me." And only Philip seemed interested in Tony's having decent clothes for school. Most arguments in the house had been about Phil's spoiling Antonio.

One rainy afternoon the three of us were huddled in the Pravo and Tony suddenly began crying, a real out-and-out cry. I looked at Rosalind, but she gestured it was all right. He cried a long time and never said a word. Then Rosalind put her delicate hand on his arm and I saw that she was also crying. Antonio put his arms round both of us and I wondered if I too was expected to cry. Finally he stood up and went outside. Rosalind followed him and he kissed her on the cheek. When I joined them, he shook my hand and hugged me once more, then set off alone.

"It's because we're his only family now," Rosalind said.

Carlo was really a bastard. Despite the mother's proclamation that Tony would finish school, Carlo continued to harass him. Late one evening Tony and I were talking in the alley behind Hrivnak's Bar when Carlo appeared behind Tony and grabbed him by the shoulder muscles. Antonio struggled to get free, but Carlo's hands were dug in firmly and his strength was such he might have ripped Antonio's muscles right out. Tony should have leaned forward and with his hip or leg tried to hit his adversary in the groin, and Carlo, standing behind Tony and not much taller, should have been prepared for that obvious move; but he seemed confident Antonio would not try anything like that. I had the feeling afterward that they'd been through the same scene before and Antonio had fought back, only to find himself worse off. Carlo was capable of killing rather than backing down.

Carlo looked at me. "Me and your buddy are gonna have lots of fun together. I'm gonna take good care of him." The reference was to Antonio's eventually going down the mines. Antonio simply stood there, completely submissive and humiliated by Carlo's grip and the fact that this scene was no doubt for my benefit.

In the end it was only Al of all of them who seemed somewhat human. It was the beginning of our senior year, in the same alley where Carlo had surprised us, that Al appeared out of the evening. "I gotta be going now," I announced loudly.

"Stick around," he said. "I wanna talk to you guys." His manner was not threatening, so I stood and waited. "Come on," he said, bringing us into a huddle with him. He seemed completely civil, but I was frightened and determined to swing my knee into his groin if he tried anything with me.

"Great play," he said to me, referring to our narrow victory over Maltby Township the previous weekend. We'd both been undefeated and there was no score until the last quarter. We won 7–6 when I blocked Maltby's kick for the extra point. I was the man of the moment in Wersend. "I bet you can get anything you want, huh?"

I blushed and grinned and said, "I do okay." The closest I'd come to losing my virginity had been after the game when Patsy Shelorski, the head cheerleader, blew me.

"Tony's got a girl too, am I right? From Brodericks!"

He stared at me, waiting for an answer. Even though he'd washed, I could see the coal dust engrained in his face, making him seem much older than he was. "Yeah, sure," I said.

He reached in his pocket and took out a rolled but unwrapped condom, held it to Antonio's face, then ceremoniously placed it in Antonio's shirt pocket. "I don't care what you do with her or any other girl, but I'll honest to God kill you if you get her or anyone knocked up. Ya hear?" Then he blushed. I avoided looking at Antonio. "With Pa and Phil gone, we gotta stick together. We're a family and we gotta pull together like a team. We can't afford any kinda trouble. Ya know what I mean? I don't ever wanna hear ya got some girl knocked up. I'll kill you, Tony, I will." Then he gave me a quick, almost embarrassed look, as if asking for my help. His voice got deeper. "When ya want a rubber and can't get one, you ask me. I'll give ya a fuckin' gross if you want, but don't get us into trouble." Then he slapped me on the back and hurried into Hrivnak's saying, "That was beautiful playin' Harry."

Tony and I finally looked at each other, trying to suppress our laughter until Al was in the bar. "I'll bet it's a recap."

"Recap, hell," he said. "He probably didn't even wash it off."

"So you got a girl in Brodericks! Anyone I know?"

"None your fuckin' business."

"Glad to hear it. You see, I got a girl in Brodericks too. I'm taking mine to the Prom. How about you?"

He smiled and his voice became normal again. "Look, it's simple. We both take her. Who gives a fuck what anyone says."

Life's rewards were given early in Wersend. For the boys lucky enough to stay in high school, it was those few years of glory on the football team before one disappeared into the mines. Then the games became part of the town folklore, like legends of famous battles. Billy Grosnock had been killed in the mines before I was old enough to know him, but I can still hear his song — it was perhaps a true folk song, for although it was spoken, the retelling eventually acquired a prescribed rhythm. "Then Billy knew they weren't expectin' a line run; no fool would try that again." The title could have been No Fool Would Try That Again. But Billy had and gave Wersend its one and only chance at the state semifinals. Even now I can remember the score, 27–21.

For girls the big moment, before fulfilling God's will as decent wives and mothers, was the Prom. Except for weddings and

funerals, it was the only social event in Wersend. Wedding
gowns were recycled into prom gowns which were recycled into
wedding gowns. Somehow even the poorest girls managed a
gown for that one big night. Probably the Prom was more
important to a girl than her own wedding, possibly because the
girls had only to look round their own homes to realize what
happened after the fleeting glitter of the wedding. But Proms
were talked about by the women all through the year and, just
as with the men, certain Proms were remembered just as
certain games were. And glory to the family whose daughter
was Prom Queen.

Each year the senior class voted for the Prom Queen, but the
vote was little more than a ritual since the head cheerleader, as
far back as anyone could remember, had always been selected.
As head cheerleader, Patsy Shelorski was miles ahead of the
senior girls in looks and everything. She was "stacked," vi-
vacious, ever-smiling, and her mass of curled blonde hair could
be spotted blocks away. She smiled a bit too much — I can't
think of her without picturing that mouth full of perfect, pure-
white teeth — but she really was a nice girl, if not somewhat too
bouncy. Probably right from the first grade the mothers must
have known Patsy was destined to be Queen.

By contrast, Rosalind was thin and fragile, with only a hint of
plumpness on her upper arms and breasts. Her skin never
tanned and in summer only a few freckles accentuated the
translucent quality of her pink-ivory skin. Her eyes were the
same light brown as her fine hair, and when she smiled it was
her eyes that dominated. She was exceptionally pretty in her
delicate way, but certainly not a Prom Queen type. And yet —
perhaps as early as the end of our junior year — it was taken for
granted that Rosalind, and not Patsy, would be chosen.

There *was* a controversy about the Prom, but it concerned me
and Tony and which of us would take Rosalind to be crowned
Queen. Only when our friends began trying to get some hint
from us did we realize just how important this question was to
everyone. It was this interest which made me realize what
important public figures we'd become in Wersend High.

"Anyone ask you to the Prom yet?" we'd tease Rosalind.

She shook her head. "Wouldn't it be wonderful if the Prom Queen turns up without any boy?" She had absolutely no interest in being Queen and we both loved her for that.

Spring came and Rosalind was chosen Queen. By May everyone seemed to know, without our having said anything, that the three of us would go together. Even the teacher in charge prepared for this by buying two carnations for the jackets of the Queen's two escorts.

Two nights before the Prom, I was in the Pravo making love to Rosalind. We both had been virgins, we hadn't planned it, we didn't even know how it happened.

> Whatsoever things are true,
> Whatsoever things are honest,
> Whatsoever things are just,
> Whatsoever things are pure,
> Whatsoever things are lovely,
> Whatsoever things are of good report;
> If there be any virtue,
> And if there be any praise,
> Think on these things.

I thought for one moment there was someone standing in the entrance, but I looked up again and could see only the few lights of the town showing through the sumac trees beyond the pond.

Rosalind didn't turn up for school the next day and I was in the daze of love. Tony seemed normal when I saw him, but then when I waited for him after classes he came up to me and said, "I'm not going tomorrow night" and began to walk off. I caught his arm and he looked at me, his eyes dull.

He offered his hand, saying, "No hard feelings."

I just stood there, trying to find in his eyes that familiar look of our friendship, but it wasn't there.

"Look," he said and shrugged his shoulders, "this is the way life is. Will you shake hands with me or not?"

I shook his hand. "Won't you go with us tomorrow?"

"No, Harry, I won't do that. Sorry. We're big boys now and this is what happens. I hope you and Rosalind will be happy forever."

Through fifty-five years the gods have watched over me and protected me. I should have no reason to complain. Even this morning, as I set out in a small boat down the Strait of Messina toward the island of Rimara when I will do my fatherly duty by trying to persuade my son to see the world as I do — even with such a confrontation at hand — I know the gods will do everything for the best.

What isn't predictable is my meeting with Antonio. I'm sure to see him. It's nineteen years since we last met and many fine people would be alive today if we hadn't. What shall we have to say to each other now? The land and sea around here are littered with graves and the dead have been dead such a long time. The wisdom of my fifty-five years tells me it's too late for a grand reversal.

Rosalind would not go without Antonio. I could not go alone.

At about seven I went to the Pravo and waited the whole night, but neither of them turned up. From time to time I could hear hints of music coming from the town hall where Patsy Shelorski was being crowned Queen. The traditions of Wersend remained intact.

CRAFT'S STORY

The Partners

"EVEN MORE DEPENDABLE than you, Craft," she said, stepping down onto the balcony with a bottle of wine. Was her name Camille? At any rate, we were just friends and it was her sister I dated, though I can't remember her name either.

What I can remember are the deep blue skies, perfectly clear in the late afternoon, unusual for New York, even in June. I remember that Camille had poached some fish for an early dinner, which we were eating on the stone balcony of her Wyndham apartment, directly across from the Plaza. Between the wars (W.W.II and Korea), New York was the place to be for young people, especially young people from small towns trying to make their way in the world. And making one's way including being a wine "connoisseur." (Today we would say "wine freak," I suppose — much more accurate and certainly less pretentious.)

"What's so dependable?" Was she referring to the Chablis?

She placed the bottle before me and pointed above the regular label to a small white oblong, trimmed with red, on which the words "An Antonio Contiorli Import" were printed in bright green.

"Try it."

It was extraordinary. Much better than a *premier cru* and possibly as good as a *grands Chablis,* though the label said only Chablis.

"One dollar ninety-nine," she announced proudly. "Makes you wonder if you've ever tasted a true Chablis before, doesn't it?"

"It is good. Where did you find it?"

"Everyone's buying up anything he does." She pointed again to the importer's label. "You just can't go wrong. His label's as dependable as the Pope's imprimatur, or do I mean *nihil obstat?*"

And so it was. The smarter New Yorkers were indeed learning that anything imported by Antonio Contiorli was a dependable bargain. An *ordinaire* for ninety-nine cents would be the best ninety-nine-cent wine in the city. *Ordinaire* it would be, but with a clean taste and distinction often lacking in even three-dollar wines. If it should be a classified Pauillac, one could be confident that not only was it the real thing, but that it had traveled the Atlantic without being subjected to destructive temperatures.

"Antonio Contiorli." In saying the name I found it had a familiar ring. "Jamie Grahamn."

"You mean your boss?"

"No, his son. I think he told me about this Antonio Contiorli."

"Fine, Craft, fine. I let you in on the most important secret in town and now you tell me you already knew."

"No, really. I think I know him. Not for wine. For manganese."

I think we were having dinner early so Camille could drag me off to *The Great Gatsby.* She loved Alan Ladd who was (in her words) "the best thing since sliced bread."

*

"Who's Anthony Contiorli?" I asked Jamie when he made a
rare appearance at the office sometime later.

"An*tonio* Contiorli. He was my father's favorite son before
you showed up." Jamie and I got along despite my being, as he
said, his father's favorite son. Mr. Grahamn, head of Grahamn
& Engle Imports-Exports, had given up hope of Jamie ever
becoming interested in his business and made it known that I
was his shining star. I was only about twenty-five then, but I
was assured the position of chief accountant would be mine
whenever I felt ready for it. And it was merely a step toward a
vice-presidency, Mr. Grahamn once told me.

But according to Jamie, this Antonio Contiorli had also been,
if only for a short while, the fair-haired boy at Grahamn &
Engle. "I guess you don't remember old man Whissel," Jamie
said. "A small export business, mostly molybdenum, but really
small time. Tony worked for him and was made manager,
whatever that meant. Whissel died and Tony found he'd been
named to run the show. A couple months later Whissel's wife
died and since they didn't have any kids, Tony woke up one
morning to find he'd been made sole heir. I think it was only
about two years from the time he first came to work for Whissel
until he owned the place. Tony doesn't waste time."

"And I'm meant to infer he was — how shall I put it —
responsible for their journey to box city?"

Jamie laughed. "No, he's just a charmer. We served in Italy
together and after the war I brought him here. Of course Dad
fell in love with him; nothing was too good for Tony boy. He
stayed here a year or so before going off on his own."

"Really fond of him, aren't you?"

"No, Tony's not a bad guy. I liked him, actually. He uses
people, but then what else do you do when you want to get
ahead?" This was disappointing since I'd come to have complete
faith in the Contiorli label and had become fond of the sound of
his name.

Jamie also told me how Contiorli got into manganese.
Grahamn & Engle dealt primarily in cotton, wheat and rice, but
also imported tungsten from which tools and drill bits are

manufactured in the United States and then sent abroad, to take advantage of drawback tariffs. After the war shipments to Russia were banned and the Russians retaliated by stopping their export of manganese to the West. There's no good substitute for manganese as a deoxidizing agent for making steel and Nikopol was the world's chief source. (When the Germans invaded Russia, they headed straight for Nikopol and not Moscow. When they had to retreat, Nikopol was one of the last places they abandoned.) But new sources were found in Mexico, Brazil, Australia and Africa. Using the small Whissel inheritance, Antonio Contiorli got into manganese at the right time as a broker and doubled his capital.

A couple weeks after my talk with Jamie, Mr. Grahamn stopped by my office, inviting me to join him, the three directors, and Senator Witing for lunch. "I'm afraid it's the old 'Cheese Amendment' business," he said, "but Mr. Contiorli will be joining us. You'll like him."

A light rain was beginning as I hurried from the taxi into the warm security of the Colony. Paul winked and then disappeared to get me my vermouth on the rocks as I sat down, late as usual, to join the meeting.

"Begging your pardon, Mr. Contiorli," Senator Witing said peevishly, "there are those who consider a vote for Section 104 their patriotic duty."

"Even though Truman doesn't share their view." The words were said quietly. Was this Antonio Contiorli? It had to be; I knew everyone else around the table.

"Then let him veto it," Senator Witing said, turning to smile at me and extending his hand.

"And veto his mobilization powers for Korea?" Contiorli said, and then Mr. Grahamn introduced us.

Antonio gave me a broad, open smile and a firm handshake. When talking to Witing, he'd looked the confident, hard-nosed businessman I'd expected, but when he smiled at me, he looked almost boyish. I realized he was not much older than I, probably in his early thirties.

No doubt Jamie was right: the smile was too open, too friendly. It made him seem vulnerable, which didn't fit with his powerful build and huge hands. Also, he was doing things backward.

Mr. Grahamn often invited me to important meetings where I would be greeted with a look that meant "What the hell's this kid doing here?" Mr. Grahamn, purposely I think, never explained my presence and I must have seemed no more than a glorified office boy. But during the discussions I would speak up more and more, giving Mr. Grahamn the figures and calculations he needed. I was an accountant, but had worked closely with all the directors and analysts, which gave me a good grasp of fine points of law and pending legislation. I could instantly put together any FOB, FAS, CIF & C scales along with minimum profitable units and tariffs and duties, and come up with quotations Mr. Grahamn could accept as faultless. I also knew when to remain silent or pretend data were not immediately available. It was not for nothing that I was the fair-haired boy. By the end of lunch the new client, competitor or Congressman would never fail to give me the warm handshake and thanks which were as important to me as my salary. (Oh how I needed to be loved, on my own terms.) Being ignored at the beginning made the acknowledgment at the end all the more satisfactory. But Contiorli was doing it all wrong.

"Either we're worried about the Communists or we're not," he was saying to Witing. "We dawdled so much with the Bari almonds until the Russians finally stepped in and bought the whole lot. Now who do you think the Bari farmers consider their friends? The Marshall people tell everyone to produce as much as they can and 'strengthen themselves against Communism' and then we slap quotas on their goods because cheese is 'necessary for the protection of essential security interests and economy of the United States in the existing emergency in international relations.'"

Don't take that tone with Witing, I thought, though pleased at the prospect of Witing putting him down. Besides, the Cheese Amendment was so quoted and parodied, we all knew the exact wording.

(Looking back now to the postwar years, it does seem we were a nation half-hysterical about the Red Menace. After all, we did let McCarthy come to power. But it was a different world then; Hitler had not been just a name. What Hitler did and what he planned to do were almost beyond comprehension. And he had almost succeeded — it had been a very narrow escape. Then within the next five years the impossible was being repeated. Hungary, Poland, Czechoslovakia — country after country was being sealed behind the Iron Curtain. Back then, when these things were becoming realities, it seemed more than possible that western Europe was again about to lose its freedom. The Communist votes in Italy and France were shocking to us.)

"Craft," Mr. Grahamn asked, "what's the total involved?"

"Less than fifty million pounds for six months."

"That's less than five percent of the cheese produced in the States, isn't it?" Contiorli asked me. It was, but I was not eager to help him against Senator Witing. Danish and Italian cheese were not very important for Grahamn & Engle, but apparently they were for Antonio Contiorli.

"Is it, Craft?" Witing asked. I nodded.

"And less than ten percent of American milk is used for cheese, isn't it?" Contiorli again looked at me.

"I'm not sure," I lied.   **1926059**

"Well, it is," he insisted.

His arguments were correct. We were giving billions through the Marshall Plan to keep the world free from Communism, saying we wanted our allies to be self-supporting and to increase trade with us. We accused the Russians of rhetoric and challenged them to prove their words by concrete deeds. At the same time, however, we were establishing quotas and tariffs, making it almost impossible for our allies to sell to us. The magic title of the Buy American Act of 1933 still played on our emotions. All this was true. It was just that Contiorli . . .

"What sense does an eleven percent tariff on manganese make, Senator?" he was asking. "It's high on our list of essential defense materials; we went into a panic when the Russians cut us off; we know we can't produce any here in the States — "

"But we are producing — "

"Fourteen percent iron is not usable. We're stockpiling sub-grade junk that we're never going to be able to use."

The devil quoting the Bible for his own purposes. And he was handsome as they used to say the devil was. Most of all I envied his skin. If he weren't Italian and dark, you would have called it baby skin. Not a blemish or pore was visible. Just healthy, firm flesh as if he'd never had a troubled thought in his life or spent all his time studding. He could machine gun an entire village without being capable of wondering about right and wrong. A mass of curly black hair fell over his fleshy forehead, giving him a look of pure health, like a free animal.

"Why not use the world's supply and save our limited resources only if the enemy cuts us off? That's the way we should be thinking if we are really worried about national security — not the other way round!"

That's the way we should be thinking if we want to make the Mafia rich, I thought.

Lunch was a disaster as far as I was concerned. It wasn't only that Contiorli had begun by being too friendly and in the end seemed to disregard me; it was that Senator Witing had fallen in love with the enemy. Witing took Contiorli by the arm and led him from the table, saying he'd think it over. That meant he'd vote against Section 104 (though it wouldn't matter, since it would pass anyway). As they walked to the door, Contiorli turned back and waved at us, smiling broadly with the innocence of a schoolboy. I was signing the check and looked across the table at Mr. Grahamn. His eyes were sparkling as he watched his former protégé disappear into the street. I couldn't have been happier seeing him disappear forever.

But during the next two weeks he was in and out our offices, meeting with Mr. Grahamn and the directors, digging into our files and asking questions of everyone, and finally, early one morning, asking if I would please get together some data for him on *our* molybdenum schedule. He was standing in the doorway of my office. I was looking at him and deciding whether to say I'd have to check with Mr. Grahamn or simply say "no."

Then Mr. Grahamn was standing behind him, suggesting that maybe Tony would also like to see our tungsten projections.

I gave him what he wanted and also did several other projects for him during the next week. He never came into our offices without sticking his head in my doorway and giving me a smile. I told myself not to get upset; he was going back to London the following week. He had a small waterfront office in New York with a staff of ten, but his principal office was in London.

It was a Friday afternoon, the last day he would be in New York. Mr. Grahamn took him to lunch at the Colony and invited me to join them, but I excused myself, saying I was behind on the quarterly report.

At four that afternoon the smiling face of Antonio Contiorli made its last appearance in my doorway. I didn't smile back, just looked up at him. He crossed the room and stood before my desk.

"Craft, Mr. Grahamn says it's all right if I ask you to join me in London. Would you be interested in working with me?"

"Yes, Mr. Contiorli, I would. Thank you."

A Reynold's Rocket for your pocket — they were the most miraculous thing to appear after the war. A lifetime supply of ink in the cartridge. Twelve ninety-five. They were becoming something of a collector's item as cheaper ballpoints were flooding the market. He took a Reynold's Rocket from his pocket, bent over my desk, and wrote an address on my calendar.

Then he shook my hand and smiled again. "Come as soon as you can. I'm looking forward to working with you, Craft."

It was even more absurd than it first seemed. Although I could digest, assemble and calculate a mass of figures in my head and blurt out the results in two seconds, I was painfully slow in making decisions about my own life. I was incapable of buying a sweater, even when I knew it was perfect, without allowing myself a night to "sleep on it." But without a thought I had said, "Yes, Mr. Contiorli, I would. Thank you," to a man I strongly disliked.

*

Well, you've done it now, I said to myself as I surveyed the shabby corrugated metal building near the docks in Southampton. A small sign proclaimed "Contiorli International-American Enterprises." This was the "London" office.

Inside, a pretty girl regarded me indifferently as she said, "Good morning." Behind her half a dozen young girls were typing invoices and bills of lading with various degrees of enthusiasm.

I introduced myself and the girl pointed to a wooden chair badly in need of new varnish. She fumbled with some papers, opened and closed drawers, and finally picked up her telephone. "He's here, Bernard," she said, and then to me, "Mr. Brown will see you in a minute."

The building probably had been a small warehouse. Paint wouldn't have improved it much, but the windows badly needed cleaning. Along the back several small offices had been partitioned off from the main area. One door was open and two young men about my age were bent over a desk. Then another door opened and a young red-haired man emerged and made his way to the "reception area." I thought of the plush security of the Grahamn & Engle offices with their magnificent views of the Wall Street area and the New York harbor. Mr. Grahamn had said it broke his heart to see me go, but it was only because he cared about me so much that he gave his blessing. If I wanted a great career, well, I just couldn't lose by joining up with Tony. Watching Bernard Brown approach, I said to myself, well, I'll say this for you Craft, when you lose, you lose big.

"Good morning. I'm Bernard Brown, Mr. Contiorli's partner. Mr. Contiorli's in our Stockholm office this week. Let me show you around."

He was American, though affecting a subdued British accent. Still, he was pleasant enough and made the polite inquiries about my journey and offered the use of his flat until I got settled. He was pleased I was joining them as the books probably weren't up to scratch. He needed a good accountant to keep things in order so he could be free for more important things. He would help me as much as he could and I shouldn't worry about interrupting him with questions until I knew my way around.

He was bright and cheerful as he introduced me to the others, but more and more he put across the message that I was his new assistant and should receive full cooperation from everyone.

I was shown to a ten-by-ten windowless cubicle, my office, and by midafternoon my desk was piled high with manila folders and envelopes which he brought at intervals from his office.

I dislike anyone who uses obscene expletives as a matter of habit, not because I am shocked, but because I feel cheated. There come now and then into everyone's life some moments when the wretchedness of circumstances are beyond one's powers of articulation. It is for such moments, and those moments only, when an obscenity can have the most salutary effect. Excessive use, of course, deprives one of the satisfying release. Whenever Bernard Brown appeared in my office with yet another mess of papers, "the books," I would give a faint smile, then to myself say something from my perhaps limited repertoire of obscenities. I thought them rather than spoke them, of course; I was saving my verbal outburst for Antonio Contiorli.

It was Gina Timley who enabled me to get through that first week without losing my mind. She and I were the last leaving when the first workday was over. As she locked the doors of International-American, I surprised myself, but not her, by asking her to join me for dinner. I've always been too shy with girls, but my fury that afternoon was such that, after a fair meal and some drinks at the Three Crowns, I ended up in her flat where I spent the night.

And each subsequent night that first week. I was one of the few Americans she'd slept with and she made the most of me. "American men are wonderful. You just kiss a girl; you don't ask her first. Mind you, England's full of chonks who start to undress you before they say hello, but I mean men with manners. You Americans have manners, but you don't hem and haw about girls."

I laughed. If she found me aggressive, what must the Englishmen with manners be like? I felt like Alan Ladd when I was with Gina.

During the day I waded through masses of contracts, agreements, and note receipts. In addition to New York, Stockholm, and 'London,' I-A had offices in Bordeaux, Paris, Milan and Geneva. It seemed — one could never be certain from the "books" — that I-A employed about fifty people, excluding part-time agents and brokers. And cheese, wine and manganese were hardly the limits of I-A's field. There was a contract with an American cake mix firm naming I-A as consultant; a contest was to be held in several German cities where housewives were to submit their favorite cake recipes (other American firms had failed trying to establish a cake mix market because they incorrectly assumed German housewives would buy what Americans bought.) In most agreements and contracts, I-A was named agent, consultant or broker, but rarely distributor. There was one agreement with an American corporation in which Contiorli (and not I-A) was named consultant. He was to receive one percent of all net profits for the first four years from bowling alleys set up and operated in several Italian cities.

But these were things I could decipher. There was a mass of notepaper sheets filled with illegible writing. By the end of each day I reached the point where I began muttering my obscenities aloud. Each night Gina calmed me. I mustn't explode yet. I disliked Bernard Brown, but it would have been futile to waste my rage on him. I patiently awaited the return of Contiorli.

"Love, I hope it doesn't upset you," she said on Sunday night, "but Hal's coming back Wednesday. It is his flat, you know." Hal was Gina's boy friend.

Gina had taught me to make love to her sitting upright, my legs under me, yoga style. Her head was propped up on three pillows and in that position we would talk an hour or so, just as casually as if we were facing each other across a table at the Three Crowns.

"Don't worry. I won't be in Southampton long." I had begun to

confide my disenchantment with I-A and she knew the next
day, if Antonio showed up, I was going to verbalize the
obscenities I'd been practicing all week.

"What you going to tell him?" She was eating a peach and
from time to time would rub the juice on her nipples for me to
lick off.

"I'm not planning anything; it's got to be spontaneous, but I
don't think I'll be at a loss for words."

"You just may be surprised," she said smiling. "Why do you
have it in for him?"

I sighed. "The truth is I had a great job. I had my whole future
laid out for me, and I came over here where I'm to be nothing
but a shit, if you'll pardon the expression please."

He took me to lunch at the Running Horses. He was extremely cordial and apologized for not being there to greet me
when I arrived. Then he got down to business.

"I'm afraid, to begin with, I'm going to have to ask you to get
the books squared away. Bernard and I operate out of our heads
mostly, but it's getting too complicated for that."

I smiled at the understatement; then he smiled to acknowledge my meaning.

"We need a system that's flexible enough to handle one-time
shots and the small deals. Have you discovered yet that often
we're operating with money that's due in the next day or next
week?" I nodded.

"We're putting everything into expansion. Now once the
system is set up, hire the best people you can find to operate it;
then I assume you'll need only spot-check from time to time.
The important thing is that, no matter where we are, we've got
to know exactly how much leeway we have, how much we can
afford. Last Thursday I had a chance to handle some Italian
wine for Germany, for vermouth, but I didn't know what extra
money we could count on over the next two months. Probably I
was right in turning it down, but I would like to know just where
we stand."

"And then?"

The eager smile appeared again and his grey eyes asked what I meant.

"After I've set it all up?"

"You mean what happens to you?"

"That's what I mean."

"What do you want to happen?"

"Really laid into him, didn't you?" Gina teased as we walked to her flat after work. She'd seen us return from lunch with his arm round my shoulder.

"All that beautiful hair," I sighed. She'd had most of her long black hair cut during the lunch hour. Short hair didn't suit her.

"Tweedle. You're not meant to be around Liverpool much longer anyway," she teased.

"Gina, let me tell you, it's quite a shock to be twenty-five and learn you find another man irresistible."

"I knew he'd get to you. Truth to tell, love, I can't imagine anyone calling Mr. Contiorli down. Not that he needs calling down, mind you."

"But the son-of-a-bitch is so smooth."

"Now you sound like Bernard. Mr. Contiorli's a gem of a man."

"What do you think about Bernard?" I asked when we got to her flat.

"Don't know as I ever have."

"He told me he was a partner, but it's not true. At least Antonio said it wasn't true. Whom should I believe?"

"Craft, love, I feel peckish for some pasta. There's a nice Italian restaurant up the hill. Do you think we could go there tonight?"

"Sure, but answer my question first."

"Was that a question? The way I see the world, Craft, is like I said. Mr. Contiorli's a gem of a man. Bernard's the son-of-a-bitch, besides being a chonk, I mean."

A year later Antonio and I were having lunch in M. Ginorde's garden, just outside Vougeot. We'd been to the annual banquet of the Confrérie des Chevaliers du Tastevin the day before and were still celebrating. Lichine has just acquired Le Prieuré, and it was the first year Romanée-Conti was producing a vintage since the war (though it would not be until 1959 that a wine was made comparable to that of the old days).

Starched white linens were spread on the lawn tables and M. Ginorde had personally gone to fetch the 1869 Lafite we were to be given the honor of tasting. It was to be the first time I would have a chance to taste one of the truly ancient Pauillacs. Ginorde had decanted it himself and we all stood up as he tottered across the lawn with a plain crystal decanter. Between the trees there was a moment when the sun caught the ruby-red color and the wine looked closer to eight years than eighty.

I watch Antonio as he took his glass and sniffed deeply.

It seemed much longer than just a year since I'd come to work for him. My system was all set up, though we still had some problems. In fairness to Bernard, the standard accounting ledgers he and a part-time accountant maintained were not so bad as I'd first thought, though a far cry from the integrated accounting-retrieval system Antonio wanted.

We'd been forced out of manganese, but only because we thought the capital investment needed to match the new competition could be utilized more profitably in other fields. Antonio's reputation as a wine importer had spread through most of the larger American and Canadian cities, and while the profits were fair to good, it was the prestige of his name that attracted our real business. He'd been elected to the Board of Trustees of the American Chamber of Commerce in London, and American companies stood in line to get him as consultant when opening up subsidiaries in Europe.

It was the little details that could spell success for American products, like knowing that American labels and instructions should be included along with the Italian when selling toasters in Italy, but that a similar scheme was wrong for the French market. And when Antonio acted as negotiator for United States companies acquiring European businesses, or merging with them, he always knew the right approach, like knowing that no Italian takes you seriously if at some point you don't shout and bang the table. With the British one had to remember that details were for underlings to work out; just come to an agreement of general principles and get to the golf course before lunch. I'd been shocked at first when I accompanied Antonio to Munich to negotiate with the Germans; he acted as if I were an inefficient messenger boy and he some kind of prince. ("Don't you know," he laughed afterward, "that for Germans the boss must know everything? A bright young man who shows how smart he is gets axed by the boss who feels his job threatened. They wouldn't have had much faith in me if I let you show how smart you are.")

Then there were the French. It was amazing how Antonio suddenly could carry off the atmosphere of *grandes écoles*. He was precise and almost painfully calm. ("I just pretend I'm a librarian," he confessed.)

In M. Ginorde's garden I watched Antonio raise the '69 Lafite to his lips, draw in a big mouthful, then suck in some air before chewing the wine. It fitted the early image I'd had of him as a great wine expert. But he was no more an expert than I and he readily admitted this. "You have to grow up with wine, fine wine, and live it every day. Besides, I smoke too much."

International-American's success with wine was due to Antonio's expertise, not in wine, but in people. He realized the wine-buying public knew only a dozen or so names in wine. Of course there was Romanée-Conti, the great Pauillacs, Clos de Vougeot, Grands Échézeaux (which never fared as well as it should because people are afraid of the name), and Clos de la Perrière. But these wines were all spoken for and commanded great prices. What the public mostly bought was Pommard, St. Emilion, Chablis — despite the fact the world drinks in one day more wine labeled Chablis, for example, than is produced in a season. The greatest frauds are always with the lower-medium-priced wine — a sad fact, since France and even Italy produce hundreds of fine and good wines that can be had at a reasonable price. The problem is that (back in the fifties) one could spend two-fifty for a Chablis or Pouilly-Fuissé that in reality might be a palatable but undistinguished blend or a VDQS from Provence. On the other hand, a bottle of true Chablis could also be had for the same two-fifty or even less, if one knew whom to trust. And the Americans were discovering they could trust Antonio Contiorli. All Brouillys are not created equal, and if Antonio Contiorli imported something simply labeled Brouilly, it was because there was something distinct and clean about it. Modest as wines go, but for two dollars a bottle there would be more character and pleasure in it than in an elaborately labeled bottle selling for twice as much, which in reality might be a run-of-the-mill Beaujolais. One of Antonio's great successes was his ninety-nine-cent Entre-Deux-Mers. From the great quantity entitled to that name, Antonio selected only the nicer ones and solved for New Yorkers the problem of an everyday white.

Of course he didn't select them himself. Even the great *négociants* would not be so presumptuous to claim they know it all, but depend on local *courtiers* who specialize in certain communes or districts. Antonio's great expertise was in knowing the experts.

I remember the first time I accompanied him on a buying trip to Beaune. Andre Prevert brought out a bottle of Bâtard and we sat down to discuss business. Antonio began by inquiring after Prevert's family (he knew all their names). They discussed the grandson who had just cut off half his hair with his mother's manicuring scissors. This went on for at least half an hour, though it seemed much longer. I was enjoying the Montrachet, but thought Antonio mad. He seemed to relish each detail of Prevert's family life, as if there was nothing more important in the world. His grey eyes twinkled eagerly and one could almost believe he was not acting. From time to time they would speak in French and I thought at last they were getting down to business — but no, not yet.

Then Prevert brought out another bottle and began inquiring after Antonio. "I'm a little nervous because everything goes so well." Antonio's pronunciation remained American, but his grammar seemed to get more and more French. "Craft has been a great blessing to me. He is very strict and won't let me speculate so foolishly now. Everything must be done properly, like a proper business. But he is a great friend and I am fortunate to have him.

"We are becoming quite successful and Craft thinks it's time

we went public — selling shares in the business to anyone who
wants to buy them. But that would mean a proper board of
directors and all that nonsense of which Craft is so fond.
Anyway, it's a very fortunate time in my life, so I try not to be a
fool and miss it. I still have not found a wife, but I have
confidence, Andre. I used to look very hard for her, but now I
don't. I know I'll find her when the time is right, but there is
nothing I can do about it until that time comes, so I enjoy myself
anyway."

"And you, monsieur," Andre said to me, "I can tell you have
found a wife. You are so serious." Then he and Antonio laughed.

"No," Antonio said, as if I were a three-year-old, incapable of
speaking for myself, "Craft is an American, but a very good
man. But too young yet. With Craft the smile will come when he
finds a wife." Antonio began to sound more and more like a
grandfather or great-uncle at least.

Then they talked about the new vines at Romanée-Conti.
Andre said not much must be expected until the vines were
more mature. Romanée-Conti had been the last to hold out
when the phylloxera struck, but during the war chemicals were
hard to come by and the vines deteriorated until they had to be
uprooted in 1946. After they let the soil rest a few years, new
vines were grafted onto phylloxera-resistant stock.

Just when I'd given up hope, they finally got down to business.
Andre specialized in Beaune whites, especially the Montra-
chets. He said he had found some nice *premières cuvées* Chas-
sagne and a *têtes de cuvée* that might be the best since 1949.
Antonio said he'd like twenty *pièces de Beaune* of the former
and ten *pièces* of the latter. The business took a minute and a
half.

Later, as were walking down the Rue des Tonneliers, I said,
"You were great. For a while there I actually believed you
couldn't live unless you knew every detail of Andre's grandson's
life."

"Yes, I was fantastic, wasn't I," he said quickly but coolly.
Afterward he was subdued until we were at the airport.

"You're breaking my heart Craft. You know that, don't you?"

"What's to break?" But I didn't sound as breezy as I'd wished.

"You see, from the beginning I assumed you could work only with the good guys. But if you can work for someone rotten, you mustn't be too nice a person yourself."

I must have made some reply, but can't remember what. When we were over the Channel, however, and beginning our descent toward Heathrow, the truth about myself and Antonio became clear.

I'd always worked hard and tried to be clever and useful so people would like me, which is okay — feeble, but not too bad. The sad thing was that I never cared much about the people themselves. They were useful to me only insofar as they admired me and made me feel special.

Antonio used people too, but not as Jamie Grahamn had said. Business was almost just an excuse for Antonio's being with people. I thought of Andre Prevert waving good-by at the curb, twice as full of life as when he'd first welcomed us. Two hours with Antonio was better than a sack of vitamins or a long holiday. Antonio used people to exercise his affections and vitality, but foremost was his enjoyment of them, and his true concern for them — that's what made it work so well. Back then this simple revelation was shattering to me, making me realize how narrow and cowardly my life had been.

In M. Ginorde's garden on that bright afternoon I had tasted the Lafite. The 1864 was better known, and there was more of it, but the 1869 was the first that had been chateau-bottled.

Over eighty years old and still there was the slightest hint of sweetness. And it was miraculously smooth and gentle. I was later to taste other old wines and discover what is called the trace of dead leaves. The taste is just slight and not really objectionable; it just signifies the wine is nearing its end. But the '69 Lafite had no such trace. It was extraordinarily pure and simple. Great character, great nobility, and all that, I suppose; but to me it mostly was pure and simple. And unique.

With the end of the Korean War, the Department of Defense stopped stockpiling tungsten and the price fell drastically. I-A was not affected since we were out of minerals, but Grahamn had invested heavily and when the mines closed he found himself in a financial bind, so much so that the FCIA threatened to cut off his credits. We loaned him what we could and then Antonio went around securing the rest of the money Grahamn needed to pull through a difficult time. It was only one of several times we were able to pay back Mr. Grahamn for his earlier help.

As for ourselves, things couldn't have been better. Trade was easier, thanks partly to Eisenhower. "Unreasonable costs," the differential between American and foreign bids was finally reduced to six percent instead of twenty-five. Then there was the famous Foster Memorandum by which foreign and domestic bids were to be considered on a common basis. The Schuman Plan, which had blossomed into the European Coal and Steel Community, would eventually lead to the Treaty of Rome and the Common Market.

We'd set up respectable headquarters in London on Poultry from where Brown managed and coordinated all operations. I found no fault with him professionally; he was obviously a born manager and a brilliant one at that. He could keep fifty projects in his head at once, and not only keep them in order, but use the combinations to great advantage. There were always great sums of money crossing the Atlantic and Bernard had the almost infallible instinct for knowing when to swap long- and short-term commercial papers to take advantage of devaluations and fluctuations in currency. His only professional shortcoming was that, once things left his head, they could be lost forever. But that's where my system came in. Our abilities complemented each other perfectly.

But I didn't like the man. And that was because he didn't like me. Which in turn was understandable since at one time he'd considered himself Antonio's partner and must have resented the change when it was I who accompanied Antonio on his travels.

Antonio was clever in choosing men like Bernard and me. I could never allow myself to be outdone in my area of systems and accounting. If someone somewhere devised a technique or concept superior to mine, Antonio knew I'd never rest until I

not only mastered it but also improved it. And the same for
Bernard and his work. He and I had the same strong egos and
ambitions, but — Antonio must have recognized — only as
number two men. Neither of us would ever want to be chief,
simply because there would be no one to feed our vanities by
seeing how well we were doing and praising us. Leadership
would have been too lonely for us.

However, what Antonio may not have realized was that
although we felt strongly about never becoming the top man, we
also felt as strongly about not being content with a number
three slot. To become number two was to triumph; to be number
three was to fail. Antonio had two number two men. From time
to time he would make a special trip to London just to mollify
Brown, telling him what a great job he was doing and how
indispensable he was. And that was what I didn't like: Brown
was too indispensable. Antonio encouraged me in my efforts in
trying to put everything in the new computers, but he never
took kindly to my suggestion that perhaps we should have a
couple young men in the wings who would be capable of running
things in case Brown was run over by a double-decker.

"You know Craft, I think you're jealous of him, to tell the
truth."

"To tell the truth, I think he's jealous of me. And having such
a man running things doesn't make for sound business operations."

"Look, I know Bernie. I know what he's like. Sure he wants
his head patted from time to time, but don't we all?"

"Yes, but it's my opinion that he depends too much on you —
which again is not a sound business policy."

He laughed. "Craft, this business wasn't built up on textbooks.
It was built on working with people. Real people who have real
feelings. The day your computers can do it alone is the day I get
out. Then again, if I remember correctly, when you first joined
us you were mightily upset when you thought you'd be working
under Bernie instead of me."

"That's true. I was upset. But I've changed since then."

And I had. Certainly my abilities had developed to the point where Antonio trusted me to handle the complete negotiations between American Fabricating and the Brazilian government when they set up several plants in Brazil.

I had become more confident, more sure of myself. Back with Grahamn & Engle I had viewed some men (like Foster M. Corey) with awe. But then came the times when I could sit across a green-felted table from Corey and feel I was dealing with an equal . . . almost.

I was also loosening up a bit, not taking myself so seriously. I never knew when I was being solemn and it was usually when I thought I was making a joke that people thought I was being pompous. But Antonio's sense of humor had brought me round a bit.

There was one area, however, in which I seemed to make no progress whatever. I was still shy with women and could have satisfactory sexual relations only under one of two conditions: either I had to get to know a woman over a period of many weeks or months before I had the confidence to make an advance, or else I had to buy her — not with drinks and dinner, but with cash, paid in advance. (Gina Timley had been the one glorious exception in my life — because she had taken the initiative.) I marveled at the ease with which Antonio could walk into a respectable bar, begin talking to a respectable woman, and then within an hour walk off with her on his arm. And I never heard him say anything in the least suggestive. They'd chat like two former schoolmates meeting accidentally in a foreign city.

I tried to imitate him, speaking of the sights of the city or the latest tennis results, mustering as much charm and wit as I could. So far so good. Then, using Antonio's identical words, I would suggest dinner or dancing or a small place where real gypsies did the flamenco. Zero.

I had just about decided I should say to Antonio, "Look, what's the secret?" when our business brought us to San Diego.

After three and a half days of hard work, I decided to put off my flight to St. Louis (a social call on an old friend) until the next morning and just relax at the Del Coronado pool. I was

beginning to realize I needed a long vacation and began considering where I might go.

On the lounge chair next to me was a young woman whose
bathing suit and long hair were almost the same soft tan color of
her skin. It was extraordinary, like those love sequences in some
films where a special lens is used to produce a lush monotone of
color. She was very pretty — beautiful in fact — and I wondered
if behind the sunglasses were a pair of tan eyes. When she took.
off the glasses I turned and saw her eyes were blue.

"You're Foster Corey's daughter," I said. "We met up in
Boston a couple weeks ago." Funny how I remembered her eyes
but hadn't noticed then how striking her hair was.

We talked a while; then after a swim I suggested a walk along
the beach. On the beach I suggested dinner and somehow
wasn't surprised when she gave a bright smile as if she'd never
been asked to dinner before. "I would like that very much."

Only when I was in my room dressing for dinner and heard
my heart frantically thumping away did I begin to suspect
something unusual was happening.

We were overdressed for the brightly lit restaurant I chose
down the street from the Del Coronado. Men and women
continued to look our way as we ate at a corner table covered
with red-checkered plastic, but if Helen had been wearing
ordinary slacks and a sweater, she wouldn't have been less
striking.

"If you've been asked more than a hundred times how you got
your name then you needn't tell me."

"You know, I've never been asked before. I guess I must just
look like my name should be Craft. Actually I was named after
my uncle, in Kansas, where I grew up, but I don't know how he
got the name."

"Are you much like him?"

"My God, I hope not!" I almost shouted.

"Was he such a villain?"

"The last I saw my beloved uncle, he was raping my sister." I
had never told that to anyone before, not even to Antonio, to
whom I had revealed most of my childhood experiences.

With Helen it literally was as if I were breathing for the first time in my life. Or maybe like an elaborate clock that's been wound up tight for years but has never run because a bolt or something is wedged in the gears — and finally the bolt is removed and suddenly the clock starts working.

At the door of her suite I kissed her good night and asked if I might call at her home when I got to New York the following week.

"Please call, Craft. I would like to see you again."

I kissed her once more before she entered her room. The lock had almost clicked when her door opened again and she was smiling. "I can talk to you so easily," she said. "I'll be waiting for your call." Then the door closed.

Antonio and I kept an apartment at the Wyndham — in fact, the same apartment with the stone balcony where Camille had shown me the Chablis with Antonio's label. It was the nearest thing to a home either of us had in America and we were often in and out. But when I arrived from St. Louis I was surprised to see Antonio's suitcases in his room as he should have been back to London by then.

Helen was pleased that I'd not forgotten to call her, but said it would have to be for lunch the next day that we could meet as she already had a dinner engagement. Then she hesitated a moment. "Craft, could I call you back? Maybe I can make dinner tonight. Can I ring you back in five minutes? Would that be all right?"

Within two minutes the phone rang. "I can see you for dinner after all, if you'd like, but I'm afraid it must be at Lutece at about eight."

"Fine, actually I was going to suggest Lutece myself, to make up for that place in San Diego. Shall I pick you up at eight?"

"No, I'll meet you there. At eight."

There was no fire and music, no lightning flashes, no ecstacy in their eyes. There was nothing to be seen by an outsider that would show Antonio was trying to win Helen or that she was being swept off her feet by him. But before the appetizers came I saw what only the greatest fool would fail to see: their rapport. They acted as a devoted husband and wife might on their golden anniversary. How it could have happened in that short time since they'd met in San Diego, I don't know, but everything was settled between them.

Looking back, it was no doubt for the best that it happened so quickly. There was no doubt I was falling in love with Helen and if she hadn't met Antonio (the same morning I was taking my flight to St. Louis) it's likely I would have soon proposed marriage. I also like to think that she would have accepted.

But given the reality that there was an Antonio, that he had met her, and that so quickly he had won her, it was for the best. There was much less pain that way.

Foster M. Corey's wedding present to his daughter was the villa Consente on Rimara, a tiny island twenty miles south of Reggio di Calabria on the tip of Italy's toe, and the same number of miles due east of Sicily.

Helen and Antonio spent their honeymoon at Consente but then, when the three weeks had gone by, I received a call from Antonio asking me to join them.

"You want me to join you on your honeymoon."

"Craft, you've never seen any place like this."

"Is Helen aware you're inviting me to join you on your honeymoon?"

"Craft, I'm talking to you from the new headquarters of International-American and ordering you to report to work *tout de suite*."

A week later I arrived at Reggio di Calabria (Regg' to the southerners), where I was met by Antonio and Tommasdo Vicari, a tall, heavy man who was chief of the Rimara *carabiniere*. They'd come over to the mainland in Vicari's launch and hurried me down to the harbor as a storm was coming.

Once we were in the Strait and headed south, Antonio pointed to a dot on the horizon, my first view of Rimara. But as the seas became rougher and the skies darker, the island blurred. Finally, when we were less than a mile from it, a heavy rain began and I could see nothing. "As you said," I shouted to Antonio, "like nothing I've ever seen."

"It is the American atomic rays," Vicari said, laughing. (Just as in the States, all bad weather was blamed on the bomb.)

The wind was howling and pelting rain from all sides as Antonio drove the car up the hill from the village and soon we were passing through enormous bronze gates into a large courtyard. Consente looked like a yellow Greek temple surrounded by a mixture of architectural styles. Through the heavy rain I caught glimpses of Moslem turrets. I had never seen anything like it.

Inside, however, I found myself in rooms reminding me of my trip through Versailles. Then I was sitting before a fire roaring in a baroque fireplace as Antonio handed me an enormous martini. My hair was dripping and my suit thoroughly wet, but after that boat crossing a drink seemed most important.

Helen was curled up in a small Louis XIV chair near the fire, wearing a simple white dress and looking warm, dry, soft and cozy as could be.

"There aren't any substantial ruins on Rimara," Helen was saying, "not like Sicily — "

"Sicily has more Greek ruins, and in better condition than all of Greece and the Greek islands, except for Athens of course," Antonio said.

" — But some of the stones in Consente date back three thousand years. Mussolini had it built — "

"One of his captains built it, fortunately, and modeled it after the Temple of Minerva in Syracuse, which was originally Greek, but altered by the Romans, and then the Normans and then the Saracens. Why are you laughing Craft?"

I didn't know these people. Both were beaming like teenagers who have just learned what love is. They were acting the way I thought they should have acted months ago.

By late afternoon all traces of the storm were gone and I had my first tour. The property covered almost a hundred acres and consisted of two villas, the original house, Sontern, in which some servants lived and which was separated from the newer Consente by a high wall, several thousand feet in length, behind which the flowers and bushes for the main villa were cultivated.

The grounds and gardens of Consente were spectacular. We watched the sunset from one of a dozen terraces, this one surrounded by manicured orange and lemon trees, all heavy with fruit. Unlike Sontern which had a lot of brick, all of Consente, including its walls, terraces and countless steps, was of yellow sandstone — which Antonio quickly pointed out was the material of most Greek and Roman buildings in that part of the Mediterranean. "Except for Catania," he said, pointing toward Sicily. "Catania's all black; you'll love it. All the buildings are of black lava and Catanians wear nothing but black. It's fantastic."

"Tell him about Charondas," Helen urged.

"I don't remember what century he was, but it was B.C. He passed a law that anyone could get divorced, a man or a woman, but they could never after marry anyone younger than the person they divorced."

"And this was in Catania?" I asked, trying to find the story as hilarious as Helen and Antonio did.

They became silent as the sun descended toward the hump of mountain they identified as Etna. The sun was bigger than any I'd seen and it fell directly into the mouth of the volcano. It was spectacular, but Helen and Antonio remained silent as if the show were only beginning. The sky and sea exchanged pinks and blues and yellows, and then, as it grew darker, a marvelous thing did happen. The bright pink glow where the sun had set on Etna remained. I realized at last that it was the volcano glowing, but it had looked as if the sun had fallen into the mountain and set the top on fire. "It's been a different color pink every night," Helen said. "Sometimes it's red or even purple."

For dinner we were joined by the occupants of Sontern, the housekeeper and her husband, the gardener. They had been managing the villa since the Allied occupation, obviously doing a good job, as Consente was in immaculate condition.

Joachim, the gardener, was in his sixties and had an enormous head and the frame and hands of a decent-sized giant.
It was incongruous for him to be dressed in a dinner jacket and
tie (fashionable perhaps a quarter century earlier, though
they looked new), like an illustration in some children's book
of a bear dressed for dinner. Great tufts of brown and pure
white hair protruded here and there from beneath the smooth
cloth of his shirt and jacket. He was avidly engaged in
conversation with Helen about the bergamot, a highly prized
fruit essential to all good perfumes. It grows nowhere but the
southern tip of Italy and Rimara. As with truffles, attempts to
grow it elsewhere have failed. "And two hundred years
ago it was unknown," Joachim said half in English and half in
Italian.

His wife Paulina seemed at first not much older than Antonio,
especially when she spoke excitedly and smiled as she leaned
forward, intent on her conversation with Antonio. But when
she sat back, listening, all expression disappeared and she
looked like an ageless prophetess — a prophetess in a sur-
prisingly voluptuous body.

They talked away as if they'd been intimate friends of Helen
and Antonio for years. At first I was pleased, but then began
wondering about servants not knowing their place. At the end
of soup I admitted to myself I was jealous.

"I am anxious," Paulina said, turning to me just as I admitted
my envy, "that the dinner will be satisfactory. Our new chef is Jozef and this is his first meal for us. He is a happy man and — how
do you say in your country? — serious in the proper manner."
She had been including me in her conversation with Antonio,
but they spoke mostly history, which had never interested me.

Again, just as I said to myself that I hated history, Paulina
smiled at me. "On Rimara you cannot escape history. It has
been one procession, a wonderful procession and also a horrible
procession. The Phoenicians, Greeks, Carthaginians, Romans,
Saracens, Normans, French and even the Spanish. Does that
surprise you? Then the Mafia, the Germans, and the Americans, but we were never bombed. The people here speak of the

Greeks and Romans as you speak of your grandparents. They
are a very old people."

A few months before I was falling in love with Helen, only to
have Antonio take her before I could catch my breath. On the
wedding day as I stood in for the best man, I felt saddened at the
prospect of losing them both. Then the reprieve, the invitation
to join them in the middle of the Ionian Sea. And now two
meddling servants shutting me out.

But they weren't servants of course. After a month at
Consente I was to lie in bed one night, completely relaxed and
content. I'd become enchanted by the beauty and strangeness of
the island, and though it was so foreign from what I'd known
before, I felt at home. I felt a warmth and security I'd not
experienced since early childhood, as if I'd finally found my
family. Like Antonio and Helen, I'd come to regard Paulina and
Joachim as intimate friends of long standing. Paulina was an
enigma. Her management of Consente was a marvel of
efficiency and understated authority, which gave her the time
and freedom for "real life." Besides her profound knowledge of
history, she enjoyed all forms of twentieth-century art and was
au fait with most artists and performers, having met and even
dined with such people as Chevalier, Bruno Walter, Kodály, and
Edward R. Murrow. Among ourselves we often referred to her as
"the Lady Paulina," which was as right as the blue and white
she always wore.

Originally we planned Consente would be our base, and of
course also a home for Helen to raise her family. But once
settled in, we were reluctant to leave and took only those trips
that were essential. After the years of living in hotels and
business offices, we were in great need of the serenity and
stability which Consente provided.

Anyway, business was coming to us, we no longer had to go
out after it. Bernard was capable of managing all operations
from London. He had a staff of twenty-five and our computers
were finally operational. Counting the staff at our other offices,
I-A employed almost a hundred people, just the right number to

handle the amount of work. For myself, I was quite content to let it stay that way for a while; I'd spend the morning on the telephone and often that would be it for the day. I was having the first real vacation of my life.

For his part, Antonio, who had seemed happy and content before marriage, had now truly found a home and his perpetual ecstasy during the first years at Consente made me think how wonderful it would be to be married. Antonio apparently also thought I should be married. (Newly married men, provided they have been blessed with good wives, are as avid proselytizers as reformed alcoholics.)

Guests were frequent at Consente, but no matter who was visiting, there usually was some attractive single woman or divorcée or widow whom I surmised had been invited solely for my benefit. Once he imported (sight unseen obviously) Constance, a French starlet who not only was quite stupid, but also an aggressive Lesbian, or so she proudly announced during drinks the first evening of her stay. I, however, had not been present for the confession and when Helen told me about it later, I had an idea.

The next morning we all went to the village for the Festa di San' Delfio. The corso was lined with booths and yellow carts, some whose spokes and panels were intricately carved and freshly painted. I took Constance by the arm and led her past the venders selling everything from tambourines, fortune-telling devices and perfume to heaps of garlic, water jugs, and octopuses. Families and children strolled past the booths at a slow pace, but we found most of the Rimarans in the *duomo,* a dark cavernous place with dogs running in and out the doors. With my arm around Constance's waist, I led our group through the throng towards the shrieks and calls coming from the front altar. Old women, men and even children were shouting at the wooden image of Saint Delfio. There was no priest visible and no service was in progress.

"How nice!" Constance said. "They are talking to their saint!" She was right, of course. It was the most direct and homely religious rite I had ever seen.

Saint Delfio stood in white and yellow robes in the center of the altar, peering somewhat blasély at his audience. Gold rings and precious stones ornamented his robes and hands. On both sides of the altar hung crutches, artificial limbs, crudely painted pictures of hospital operating rooms, wax reproductions of various parts of the body, including some surrealistic genitals — all mementos of the cures Saint Delfio had wrought.

Constance appeared to enjoy my attention and friendly familiarities during the day, though not so much as I enjoyed the hint of a worried look on Antonio's face as he watched us.

We returned to the village that evening for the procession and saw Saint Delfio carried on a huge yellow wooden throne, preceded by some two dozen men, each carrying a thirty-foot pole from which hung long narrow banners, all pure white. The people were hysterical and called out to their saint for miracles. "*Evviva San' Delfio! Evviva!*" One man had been following close by the saint's side, holding a small baby up to Delfio's nonchalant gaze. The man must have been screaming, but his voice was indistinguishable from the cries of the crowd and the *castello di fuoco* fireworks which were continually exploding overhead, lighting the sky with silver, pink, blue and orchid. We watched the procession until it disappeared out of sight down the Viale Agam Spano. The man was still holding his child and screaming at the saint, but others had edged in closer to the throne.

"Last year," Paulina said when we'd retreated to the calm of Consente, "they stripped Delfio's robes and hung him by his neck over the cliffs. No, not thieves or vandals, the people. The same people you saw tonight. And why? Because he had not brought enough rain. You are shocked? It is wonderful, I think. Religion is always a business — how do you say in your country? — proposition? Here the people understand this. I think it is wonderful."

The next morning Helen said, "He believes you're serious about Constance. He feels terrible. You must tell him it was a joke."

I did, but not until the next day after Constance had left. It was the only time I saw Antonio blush, but he was soon laughing with us.

"It makes no difference at all, the people are ungovernable." Baron Elesco was talking about Rimara being under Italian rule. The Separatist Movement had recently brought about a regional government for Sicily, which enabled it to decide its own economic fate, but Rimara was still considered part of the mainland. "Of course we belong to Sicily; we always have; we have nothing in common with Italy. Do you know why we are considered Italian? The only reason they can give is that we're not volcanic!"

His short fat fingers scooped up half a dozen canapés. "But it makes no difference. *L'Italia che cambia!'* *'L'Apertura a Sinistra!'* Mere words! The people are ungovernable, always have been. Italian or Sicilian, they're all animals."

"But you do consider yourself Sicilian then, Baron?" I asked.

"Most certainly, but I'm sure you'll agree there are Americans who care about history and the important things and devote their lives to civilization, while there are also Americans who are merely animals. No offense please, but certainly this can be said of all countries. In Italy now the only question is when does the next war begin."

Elesco owned most of Rimara. His villa was a huge baroque *castèllo* at the eastern tip which he visited once every few years. He had been an ardent Fascist during Mussolini's reign, but now he was equally as ardent about the Christian Democrats. He was the sort of man who can thrive under any regime. Eighty percent of the olives, grapes, almonds, wheat and hemp produced on the island came from his land, worked by *mezzadria* and *contadini* under the watchful eyes of Elesco's overseers. "The only reason Rimara is free of *banditi* is thanks to our Inspector Vicari here."

At this compliment Tommasdo lifted his glass and smiled at the baron.

Antonio and I had once been invited to dinner at Tommasdo's modest but cheerful and well-kept house. His wife, Serafina, was delightful and had a remarkable figure for a mother of five. Her large brown eyes had a look of innocence and wonder, like those of a child. I had by that time come to have great respect for Tommasdo and, seeing his wife and family, I found him completely understandable. I had been warmed by the joy of the Vicari household and reluctant to leave. But now, this scene with the baron struck me as incongruous: either Tommasdo was in league with Elesco, or else completely obsequious. Either way it was strange and not to my liking.

A week after the baron's visit to Consente, Tommas invited Antonio and me to come with him for some swordfish; we'd been curious about the strange boats like huge letter *L*'s skimming the waters. "You must try it, but it is a little late in the season." Antonio and I took turns as *guardiano* on top of the tall steel girder from where we tried to spot the *pesce spada* and direct the boat while Tommas went out to the tip of the other steel girder, projecting horizontally from the bow, where he would spear the fish. But we had no luck, even when Tommas became the lookout and Antonio and I took turns as the *allanzaore.* "*E tròppo tard'!* But maybe we try again next year." Then he put into a cove where we could have our lunch.

Antonio and I went in swimming and then Tommas finally joined us. Apparently he had never exposed his chest to the sun as his arms, face, neck and legs were tanned a dark brown while his truck was a soft white.

"What happened there?" Antonio asked when we were sitting on the narrow strip of sand. Tommasdo's back was almost all scar tissue.

Tommas smiled. "It is only because I am an animal."

"What do you suppose he meant by that?" I asked Antonio later.

"I don't know, but I think he isn't very fond of Signor Baron."

We were on an excursion to Enna, an incredible town perched on a mountain in the middle of Sicily, when Tommas told us his story. He'd been born in a village halfway down the mountain, in the heart of the Yellow Country where sulfur had been mined since the time of the Greeks. When he was eight his parents sold him to the mines for seventy dollars.

"I never blamed them; it was what everyone had to do. Every family sold one or two boys as *carusi.*" They worked fourteen hours a day carrying sulfur up to the surface. "About fifty kilos at a time, sometimes more, all day long. Some boys were younger than me." He was paid ten cents a day, but never saw the money as it went to pay off the seventy dollars his parents had received. "Plus interest, of course. Many boys died before they were able to buy their freedom." The scars on his back were from beatings and burns from the lamps of the overseers. He escaped when he was ten and went to Palermo where he begged, stole and sometimes hired himself out to English and American men for a night.

In his late teens he made his way to Rimara where he worked as gardener and handyman at a villa on the north shore. "A widower lived there then, Filadelfio Gengo. What could I think that he hired me for except to work me to death or else for his bed? But it was not so. He was a good man and he taught me to read and write. He took me once to Florence and to Rome. But it was not for a year or maybe more that I learned to trust him. He let me sleep in the house and each night for the first year I waited in my room for him to come in and beat me or kill me. I could not believe anyone could be nice to me. I had no experience with such a thing. I mean from people who had money, from the people who were not *animali.* Then one day I woke and cried for the whole morning. I understood at last that Gengo was a good man and wished me no evil.

"Later he brought to the villa a young girl who had been a prostitute in Palermo. She cooked for us and took care of the house and our clothes. Here one marries only virgins, and they are all real virgins. They have never even spoken to a man without their family keeping watch. And this happens only when the young couple is engaged. But I liked this young girl and I fell in love with her. She is my wife now, you know.

"There is nothing special about Elesco. He is a tyrant like any

other tyrant. If I hate him more than other tyrants it is because
I know him."

When Helen was in her seventh month of pregnancy, I went
into our offices early one morning and was tearing off print-outs
from our teletype when some figures on the summary sheet
caught my eye. "We've been sabotaged!" I shouted to Antonio
when he came in. At first I thought of Bernard Brown, but it
turned out to be a malfunction on the feed from Stockholm into
the main computers in London. After a few days the computer
people had it cleared, but somehow the "bug" was disrupting
our Bordeaux-London line and our data were getting hopelessly
muddled. I had to go to London to keep things straight. When
we thought the problem was solved, a malfunction appeared on
the Milan-Paris line. I wanted Bernard to be the one responsible
— that somehow he was sabotaging "my" computers — but
after a few weeks, when *the* expert from Newark came and set
things straight, it was obvious that not even Bernard could have
persuaded some mysterious cathode or whatever deep inside the
equipment to behave perfectly during the day and then go
berserk at sundown. The man from Newark fixed it, though
even he couldn't explain it. "Ionospheric changes?" he suggested dubiously.

It was the way Bernard behaved during my stay on Poultry
that irritated me: he never once made even the most abstruse
remark about "my" computers, even when he sometimes stayed
late in the evening with me as we desperately tried to keep our
data straight. But at least once a day I would see the instan-
taneous flicker in his smiling eyes and I knew he was thinking,
"Your goddamned computers are fucking us up royally, Craft." I
might have come round almost to liking him if just once he had
said the words aloud.

I was away more than a month and returned to find great
excitement as Helen's time drew near. Antonio was even more
esctatic than before, singing all the time and unable to sit still.
It seemed he danced everywhere instead of walked. But the
impending new addition was not the only cause of his joy. He

was also happy about something else. "I've done a ruthless," he finally confessed.

"It's unlikely you won't expand on that."

He told me how much he was loaning the Italian government.

"Ruthless? Impossible! We just don't have that kind of money lying around Antonio!"

"*Ci penso io.* A mere detail. They want to make Agrigento into a tourist town and have asked for money from the World Bank and from America. Part of *Casa per Il Mezzogiorno.*"

"Well, it's just awfully nice of you. I hope they'll at least put your bust in the square at Agrigento."

"At three percent they should put all of me, and you too, don't you think?"

"Three percent! You're crazy!"

"Possibly Craft, possibly. But other crazy things have happened while you've been visiting the strip joints of Soho. The Italian government has acknowledged it made a mistake on the Mezzogiorno land scheme. Even more unbelievable, they're going to correct their mistake. After all, Rimara *is* part of the mainland, isn't it?"

"Elesco's land?"

"*Sisignor.* And the final touch is that he'll be reimbursed on the value declared in his tax returns!"

I was delighted. It was no secret Elesco was a first-rate tyrant, to use Tommasdo's word. But I suspected Antonio hadn't told me everything.

"I said it was a ruthless, didn't I?" he said smiling.

He never told me then, but I believed it was nothing worse than a bribe, though I never found any International-American shortage, so he must have used his own money.

What it all meant was that most of Elesco's lands on Rimara were to be broken into twelve-acre plots and given to the *contadini* and *mezzadria* who had always worked the land as slaves. Out of their profits they would pay off the mortgage to the state. The scheme was part of the Reconstruction of the South taking place on the mainland; there was no reason why Rimara shouldn't have been included in the beginning. Part of Antonio's deal was for us to export the

produce, something I guessed would really cost us money
(which it did), but we brought to the Rimarans a prosperity
they couldn't have dreamed of. There was the danger of
Elesco's overseers' bringing in the Mafia, so we paid the overseers off, including expenses to Sicily. Except for the petty thievery of the *Scassapagliara*, Tommasdo saw to it that
the island stayed free. He knew the people and they respected
him. If there were three *carabiniere* in history who were never
referred to by the people as *sbirri*, it had to be Tommas and his
two men.

And it was nice to contemplate Elesco being reimbursed on
the basis of his tax returns since it's usual to declare one-third
value or less, since one knows the collectors will automatically
double or triple that amount. But the loss was little to Elesco,
who owned land everywhere in Sicily and Italy. He would return
to his villa every few years, but he never again paid a visit to
Consente.

The morning was clear and sparkling, the sea looking like the
Aegean and not the Ionian. One could almost believe the dark
line of the southern horizon was indeed Africa. It was the first
time Paulina invited us all to her "quarters" for breakfast.
(Anna and the other servants stayed at Consente.)

Sontern occupied the extreme southwestern tip of the island,
and from its terrace we overlooked the dozens of acres where
Joachim developed the hundreds of trees, plants, and flowers for
the main gardens. The yellow stone wall cutting this section off
from Consente made it possible for Joachim to spend months
bringing red-orange flowers and other treasures into bloom
without our being aware of the great mass of startling color
until we'd walk out one morning and find our gardens being
transformed — something like a child waking up on a Novem-
ber morning to find his world transformed by an early snowfall.
Portions of Sontern itself had been converted into greenhouses
where Joachim nurtured his tropical prizes.

It was a revelation to go beyond the wall to what one assumed
was a decent-sized house on a small plot and discover instead
the curious mansion perched above an extensive world of

manicured vegetation. (I have no doubt Joachim knew each of the countless trees and plants individually — they had that look.)

On the terrace Helen was nursing Alexander, who was about three months old. Every day she became more beautiful. Paulina was at her side and Antonio and I were lazily looking over some papers as we finished the last of our breakfast coffee. "Can you believe I feel so good I don't think I'll have my cigarette — at least not yet," Antonio said, then walked over to the women and crouched down to look at his son. It was an idyllic scene with the almond trees at their peak of bloom. There was no sense of time passing, as if we were in some tableau, listening to the defiant cheer of the birds and feeling the gentle coolness of the morning air.

"When are you going to get a family, Craft?" His tone as much as his words threatened to shatter the mood.

"I have a family."

After a while Antonio smiled and then turned to Paulina. "Is it good for a young man to be alone?" he asked more earnestly than seemed proper. After our tennis the previous afternoon I'd said something about how good it would be when Helen could play with us again and how special it was when the three of us did things together. Did he think my love for Helen (which was great indeed) was improper?

"What answer do you want?" Paulina asked.

Antonio sat down and folded his hands in his lap. "Whatever answer there is."

"And you will be content with my answer?" She pronounced each word slowly and distinctly, as if practicing her English.

"I'll be content."

"Then look to the water and tell me what you see."

Antonio described the water and beach and almost as an afterthought added, "And Joachim's collecting sea grapes for his garden."

"Do you think there is not enough help at Consente that Joachim must go down each morning and gather fertilizer himself?"

Antonio looked astonished, as if he'd been negligent. "I thought Joachim enjoyed gathering the sea grapes."

"Look at him and tell me if you think he enjoys it."

Helen also turned toward the sea, but, unlike Antonio, her face was completely serene, except for a slightly amused smile. Like me, she enjoyed the confrontations between Paulina and Antonio. Antonio brought out the mystical side of Paulina and Paulina was the only one capable of getting the better of Antonio in friendly debates.

"Yes, I do think he enjoys it."

"Do you see how slowly he moves? But is he not graceful? It is not the slowness of age." Joachim had always fitted so perfectly into the landscape that I'd never realized how graceful he was.

"When I met Joachim I was governess in Nancy." Again Paulina was surprising us; we never knew where she'd been born, but occasionally she'd tell some story of her youth and it seemed there'd been no European country in which she'd not spent some time. "He was a gardener of the neighbor. When playing with the children I could see Joachim working. There was only a low hedge separating the properties. We often looked at each other, but never spoke or smiled. We watched each other in a lazy way under the hot sun of the afternoon. But we never looked away when our eyes met. I was a shy girl then and it would have been bold of me to keep looking at a man who was looking at me. But even then, when he had the body of a young man and I watched the sweat shining on his peasant muscles, he moved as he moves now. Slowly, but not slowly. The rhythm of his movements gave me confidence in him. Without ever having smiled at him or exchanged a word, I knew him completely.

"One afternoon he was bent over some flowers and he looked up and I could see only his head above the hedge. Then he stood up and continued to look at me for some time, until at last he went to the peach tree where his shirt was hanging. He put on his shirt without hurrying and still without hurrying walked over the hedge.

"I have seen once in a film African animals leaping over bushes, but the film was slowed down — how do you say in your country — slow motion? The animals seemed to move very slowly and the grace of those animals was the same as Joachim slowly lifting one leg and then the other over the hedge. As if in real life he were leaping swiftly, but a camera had slowed him down to show his grace.

"His face and body are old now, but in the years I have spent as his wife, his movement has not changed.

"There is only one other man I have seen in my life whose movements can compare with Joachim's. Not in the slowness, but in the grace. In my life I have seen only one other man who is as content as Joachim. You call him your friend; yet you want to take away his peace."

Antonio looked at me, impressed by Paulina's words, but probably not completely convinced I could be so content. Then quickly he turned again to Paulina. "But you mean you don't think I'm content?"

Smiling as if she were a portrait by a medieval master suddenly come to life, she asked, "And what answer do you want this time?"

He stood and grinned like a nervous schoolboy. "I want a good answer."

"Then you must have one. Your happiness, Antonio, exceeds by much, by very much, that of other men. You have, Antonio, a capability for joy which most men would not understand. You have extraordinary capacity."

His shoulders relaxed, then he turned to the sea. "But yet you said I'm not as content as Craft or Joachim."

"Did I say that? I think not. Antonio, a beautiful morning can last a long time. And it may be followed by another beautiful morning. And perhaps another. And perhaps even more. The number does not matter. Then there might be an earthquake and everything changes and never again will it be as it was. To a content man, number does not matter."

"Is that a riddle?"

"A riddle is nonsense spoken by someone we respect. Do you want it to be a riddle?"

*

"Good grief! You're really not going to do it?" Antonio had been chosen as one of the twenty men to carry the Virgin's throne for Ferragosto, the August *festa* second in importance only to Christmas.

"Oh, you're amused. It's an honor, you know."

"But you don't believe any of that business, or do you?" I was amused.

"What 'business'? How do you know what I believe? Besides, Paulina says it's really pagan, going back to Augustus. His Fèriae Augustales to celebrate his victory somewhere in the east. Then in the tenth century Leo the Fourth . . ."

"The Fourth," Paulina said, "in the ninth century."

". . . changed it to the feast of the Assumption. You jealous because you haven't been asked?"

"Possibly. But if you're going to play the native, you can bet I'll become the *forestieri* and get every bit of it on my camera."

"Remind me someday Craft to give you a lecture on love."

With bare feet and wearing only white trousers and a yellow sash across his chest, Antonio and nineteen other men carried the Virgin on her goldplated throne through every street and alley in the village. "It was no mean chore, let me tell you," he said afterward.

We all came to watch, though Helen had an uncomprehending look as she saw her millionaire husband glistening with sweat among the *contadini*. But it was too much for her that evening when, after perhaps two gallons of *mezza montagna*, Antonio challenged Tommasdo to the net race. Taking positions on opposite sides of a twenty-foot circle, they each grasped one end of a fishing net and began running round the perimeter, all the while attempting to pull the net in such a way that the opponent would be forced inside the circle. After ten minutes Antonio's face grew dark red and I saw Helen's worried look. I held her hand to assure her just as Antonio stumbled, ending the contest. He was as much cheered by the crowd for his efforts as Tommas was for winning. Amid the screams and fireworks and dancing, Helen managed a nervous smile.

Unlike Antonio and me, it was not possible for Helen to know the villagers. We were invited into their homes for meals, but the Rimarans would have felt too presumptuous if they invited La Grande Signora di Consente into their humble dwellings. And, unlike northern Italy where the entire family turns out for the evening parade, the *passeggiata* in Rimara was strictly a male affair; the woman's place was most definitely in the home and her social life limited to the market and church, which was too bad.

If I have one regret about those years on Rimara, it was for not letting myself go as Antonio did. I became good friends with Tommasdo and his family; Evandro the shoemaker and his wife Rosa; Vincenzo and his goats (each morning he went from door to door and milked his goats directly into the housewives' jugs); Cristoforo the shepherd, with his talent for sketching the sea and cliffs; Agostino and his illegal tobacco plants; the Bonfantis, who could offer only artichokes boiled in a kettle over charcoal; and poor little Enzo in his wooden clogs, who always begged me to take him to America.

These people became my good friends and shared with me everything they had. And they even respected that reticence I was never able to hide completely. But Antonio was able to let himself go so naturally that they truly loved him.

"These people know how to love," he once told me.

"I may assume we are here concerned with other than romantic love, or if I fail to make myself clear, you're not talking about sex."

"You may so assume, shithead. Look, what usually happens is you work with someone, or become their neighbor or some circumstance occurs by which you see them fairly regularly. After a couple years if your trust and respect increases, a great affection may develop, but this happens only after a number of years. *You* could probably do a study on the frequency and intensity of exchanges of trust and respect needed to achieve various levels of affection.

"Anyway, the Rimarans cut through the preliminaries and the first or second time you meet they're ready to make a commitment. I guess they've been so poor for generations that the only comfort they have is one another. When you've had nothing for so long you aren't shy or coy about exchanging affections. Mankind's greatest curse has been the pursuit of happiness, and these people know it. They know that happiness, like romantic love — sex to you — always comes in the back door, and always uninvited. They know the only thing to do is make peace with people; exchange the simple acknowledgment that you're both nervous souls put here by nature for some worthy but not very apparent purpose. Once you've found peace, then everything else follows; happiness pursues *you*. This would all be nonsense except it's true.

"People here know you can bear just about anything if you feel you've got others who really care about you just as you care about them."

"No stopping you Wersend boys," I said, handing Antonio a copy of *Time* whose cover was a black-and-white picture of Harry Rambulcek.

"So the old bastard's done it again!" Then after he'd read the article he said, "We've got to get him out here."

That was the problem, trying to get Harry to come to Consente. I'd met him perhaps a dozen times, usually at airports between flights, but always hurriedly. Once, before we moved to Consente, Antonio routed our return from Vienna to New York through Cairo, just so he could meet Harry at the Cairo airport for one hour. Except for one full day the three of us spent together at an inn outside Brussels, Antonio had not had a leisurely reunion with his old school friend in years. When Harry married, Antonio flew halfway round the world to be best man; but a year later Harry was having his appendix out, so I had to stand in for him as Antonio's best man.

I was a fan of his long before we met. In fact, I had seen his first full-length film a year before I met Antonio. It was playing at the Fifth Avenue Cinema, just above Washington Square. This was long before the underground film movement and before experimental films became popular. In those days the

Fifth Avenue Cinema was the only place where one could regularly see films by unknowns. Probably as a relief from the precise and highly organized nature of my work, I went frequently to see these somewhat abstract, often irrational works. But after seeing *A Modern Man*, Harry's first film, I felt I had stumbled onto something special.

Though Antonio's reunions with Harry were few and brief, they phoned each other often and we all followed Harry's progress in the magazines (twice he made the cover of *Life*). And the great treat of course was when we'd receive a print of his latest film, usually before it was released. We set up the projector and screen in the almond courtyard and had our own outdoor movies.

"Somehow it's appropriate that Mary should write in gold, and especially in such perfect Latin," I said.

We'd all gone over to Messina for the feast of La Madonna della Lettera, one of the few *feste* Paulina had never seen. "Can we trust you to know perfect Latin?" Paulina asked as we examined a letter reputedly written by the Virgin to the Messinians. "It is of course not the original. Mary wrote in Hebrew. This is a fifteenth-century translation made of Paul's Greek translation."

"Do you really believe that?"

"Craft, is it so important if you believe or do not? It's the story that is important. Paul was preaching here and the Messinians were so impressed by what he said about Mary, they sent deputies to her, asking her to pray for their city. She wrote back a note of appreciation. What could be more logical? Do you think we are the only ones who have manners?"

"She may have had manners," Tommas said sardonically, "but I am grateful she was not the protectress of Rimara."

The short letter ends with Mary saying, "Wherefore we bless you and your city, whose Protectress we will always be. Given in Jerusalem in the year 42 of our Son. Mary, the Virgin. Who moreover confirms this writing with her own hand."

It was indeed fortunate that Mary was not the protectress of Rimara. Messina had been sacked by Richard Coeur de Lion and through the centuries it suffered from naval bombardment, the plague, a cholera epidemic and three major earthquakes. The last, in 1908, killed over eighty thousand within the city limits alone. It was the Americans who provided the greatest aid, building hundreds of temporary shelters for the misplaced and helping to rebuild the city. But, ironically, in 1943 American bombs destroyed large portions of the city and killed five thousand inhabitants. The cathedral, restored many times, is the only old building in the city.

As I rang again for the elevator, from behind me a woman's voice whispered, "You looking for some fun mister?"

I took a deep breath and was turning around slowly when I recognized her laugh. "Gina Timely!" Her hair was long again.

She came close and presented her cheek for a kiss. "Mrs. Carter, if you please, mister, and don't get smart."

"You're looking great! How are you doing? You're married?"

"Matthew and Mark much prefer it that way. They're my boys. Twins."

"Congratulations! What are you doing here?"

The lift opened and she went in. "I don't know quite how to tell you this, Craft, but I work for you now, as I have for the past month. We live in London now and the boys are in school. I needed something to do and one day I ran into Louise." Louise was Bernard's secretary-administrative associate-girl Friday-mother, the manager's manager; she'd been with I-A since the beginning.

"Did you marry that — I forget his name, I'm sorry."

"Not to worry, I have too, almost. No Craft, I found myself a super man. He looks very much like you, as a matter of fact, though I'm probably the only one who would see the resemblance."

"Well, I am flattered — if I'm meant to be."

"You are indeed, Craft."

Bernard was on holiday, which was why I had come to London, just to check that things were in order. Gina and Louise

and I had lunch at the Savoy Grill, my traditional treat for
Louise when I was in town.

"Craft, is there any reason why Bernard should be keeping
his own files?"

I shrugged.

She went on about how he kept one drawer of his desk always
locked ". . . which is curious since he has no secrets from me.
Never has. I'm the one who has to remember to send flowers to
his mistress and candy to his wife."

One of the wonderful things about working at Consente was
that I was free from the petty traumas of a regular office.
However, I listened sympathetically and then she mentioned
the name Elesco.

It was the next morning that the calls began. The story broke
in an American magazine and the London papers had just got
hold of it.

Two weeks later we were certain that Bernard's sabotage extended only to a shipment of VDQS from St.-Pourçian-sur-Sioule
labeled as one of the best *grand Chablis*. Even the labels had
been done poorly, with ink that ran at the first drop of water, to
make sure the deception would not go unnoticed. Even the most
misguided fly-by-night would not have attempted so blatant and
foolish a deception. Our investigators found the small plant in
Hoboken, New Jersey, where the wine had been bottled and also
a printer in Jersey City where the labels had been prepared.

"Of course I remember him," the printer said. "You don't
forget someone who makes you use cheap ink for such a fancy
job." The printer identified Bernard from a photograph and had
records showing when Bernard had been there — even Bernard's signature on the order, with his peculiar *w* though he
used the name Maxwell Knopp. The owner of the bottling plant
also identified the photograph of Bernard Brown and even his
speech. "I knew he was American even though he tried to talk
funny." Bernard had personally supervised the labeling of the
bottles; the workers remembered him well.

Antonio and I missed no opportunity to be interviewed,

always carrying with us copies of the thoroughly documented report of our investigators. The *Times* kindly carried our full statement, which included excerpts from the investigator's report. The story in *Life* began with a full-page photograph of Bernard Brown and pictures of the workers and printer who made the identification. Bernard was supposed to be having his holiday in Switzerland, but we were not surprised when we couldn't find him.

Antonio worked nonstop and most of the press was taking our side. We were about to leave New York and return to Consente when a banner headline in the daily paper announced CONTIORLI SELLING U. S. TRACTORS TO COMMUNISTS.

The story went on to report that the United States Bureau of Foreign Commerce was holding special meetings to consider censure of International-American for shipping American-made tractors to Rumania. What the story did not report was that we were in fact selling the tractors to Lebanon and that it was a Lebanese firm that was immediately selling them to Rumania.

Our investigators couldn't find any connection with Bernard, but they did find that Baron Elesco had a plush villa in Beirut, the port where the tractors were received and then immediately reshipped to Rumania. The owner of the Lebanese firm was occupying Elesco's villa.

In the end, the Bureau of Foreign Commerce put I-A on six months' probation. (What added insult to injury was that this decision was made a week before the Bureau gave special permission for the shipment of five hundred Chevrolets to Bulgaria!)

Within a few weeks the name of Antonio Contiorli changed from being the epitome of trustworthiness to a name linked not only with the Mafia, but with the Communists as well. But Antonio in adversity was even more admirable than Antonio in prosperity. He never wasted a minute feeling sorry for himself, moaning, or even cursing Bernard. All Antonio's energies were focused on what must be done; he always approached the

problem as something which could be remedied because it *had*
to be remedied. At times, almost, it seemed the disaster was
nothing more to him than an inordinate run of bad luck.

However, one afternoon en route from London to Rimara,
we'd just settled in our seats and were taking the first sips of our
much-needed drinks when I said, "I told you so."

He smiled and said "Well, I'm glad that's over." We laughed a
bit more, but Antonio's cheerfulness was not completely con-
vincing.

From the time I first met him, there had never been any
difference between the face Antonio wore and what he was
feeling inside, which probably is why I mistrusted him initially.
I couldn't believe any man could be so bold and unafraid to
reveal everything. Even when he was banging the table and
being excited with the Italians or being droll with the British,
there was no dichotomy between his actions and his inner self.
One would not speak French to the Italians, and speaking
Italian meant banging the table, part of the language.

But now I was beginning to perceive, behind his matter-of-
fact expression and his cheerfulness, the presence of something
else: a fierce determination, an unnerving alertness — he was
perpetually on guard.

A message was waiting for us at Consente: our London
lawyers had just been informed that Bernard Brown was suing
Antonio for defamation of character, slander, and whatnot. The
amount of the damages petitioned was ten million American
dollars.

Of course it was ridiculous. Bernard Brown was guilty as sin
and we could prove it. We knew he had made short trips to
America — ostensibly because his mother-in-law in Brooklyn
was critically ill. The first trip was to take his wife to her
mother. A short time later he made a second trip and brought
his wife back to London with him. Her mother had recovered.
Louise remembered it well: she'd phoned BOAC for the tickets
and reservations, and of course there was a record of I-A's
having paid for the tickets. The dates involved coincided per-

fectly with the dates the workers in Hoboken and Jersey City
met with Bernard Brown, or at least a man who looked and
talked like Bernard Brown, though he had given the name
Maxwell Knopp.

But then *Life* magazine continued its coverage of the great
wine scandal by showing a picture of Bernard's passport, clearly
stamped at Orly the very day we said he arrived in New York.
The day Maxwell Knopp first met with the printer, Bernard
Brown was meeting with Andre Prevert. There was a picture of
Prevert who had to admit, yes, Brown and his wife had dropped
by. They had said they were taking a short holiday in France
and just came by to say hello and have an informal chat about
business. Prevert had dealt with Brown before and he had no
doubt it was the real Bernard Brown. The hotels where Mr. and
Mrs. Bernard Brown stayed in Paris and elsewhere in France
would of course not have registered them without seeing their
passports, and certainly Mr. and Mrs. Bernard Brown had been
registered on the dates in question. Moreover, BOAC could find
no record of the Browns flying to New York during that month,
but BEA did have them on flights to and from Paris. There was
no end of evidence that Brown could produce showing beyond a
doubt that he had never been involved in the wine fraud. I had
greatly underestimated just how clever Bernard was.

"All we have to do is find this Maxwell Knopp, or whatever his
real name is, and get him to admit he was hired by Bernard and
Elesco," Antonio said confidently. "After all, we do know what
he looks like." But two months later we were still unable to find
a trace of him. Then Bernard himself called and asked to meet
me, but not Antonio. He arranged an elaborate farce by which I
met him at Whyte's in Brighton, then changed into bathing
suits (so he could be sure I had no recording device on me) and
we sat on the beach. His only purpose, he cheerfully admitted,
was to see the expression on my face when he admitted
everything. "And the man's name was Maxwell Knopp, really.
But I wouldn't tell you that unless I was certain you'd never find
him, would I?" He pointed to the boardwalk, where two heavies
(his bodyguards?) were taking photographs of the two of us. God

knows what use Bernard could have found for such pictures. I
think perhaps it was only to keep his bodyguards busy and
maybe intimidate me.

"But all we have to do is prove some conspiracy with Elesco;
at least that would weaken his case," Antonio said desperately.

"What was involved when you had Elesco's lands taken from
him?"

"Two bribes. But it was obvious he had made bribes in the
first place so he could keep his land."

"Never mind the morality, if there is any. Bernard and Elesco
are sitting back somewhere just waiting for the grand finale to
begin. Bernard is far more clever than we've given him credit.
All through this we've been doing just what he wanted us to. He
wanted Louise to be suspicious and to remember the name
Elesco." (The secret files in the locked drawer were a collection
of our wine labels. And the day before he left for his holiday, he
gave Gina a special notebook in which she was to record any
messages from Baron Elesco; but would she please, under no
circumstances, let anyone see them. No messages came, but
Gina had a notebook with Elesco written on the cover.)

"He wanted us to link him with Elesco and now he's waiting
for you to take that bait. Antonio, I tell you, I just know they've
got some grand scheme cooked up about those two bribes that's
going to top everything."

The lawyers believed that whether the case went before a
judge or a jury, the verdict would be the same: we didn't stand a
chance. Only after much pleading did they get Antonio to agree
to settlement discussions.

One million dollars was the price and I thought it was a
bargain. We could barely afford it, but it was possible.

Two weeks later, after we'd browbeaten Antonio into agree-
ing, our lawyers, after a very short meeting, returned with the
news that of course the one million dollars had to be accompanied by a statement from Antonio saying he sincerely believed Bernard Brown completely innocent of any wrongdoing.
Antonio would be free to make any other statements, such as

insisting the fraud had been perpetrated by someone else, but he must make it crystal clear to the press that he believed Bernard innocent.

Again two more weeks and our lawyers returned with our prepared statement rejected. We'd said the obvious things — about Antonio knowing Bernard could not have been in Hoboken, et cetera — but managed to avoid saying explicitly that Antonio believed Bernard completely innocent of any wrongdoing. Bernard's lawyers did not like this at all. If we wanted to settle without making a proper statement, the price was five million.

One way or another it's going to cost something near that figure, our lawyers pointed out to Antonio. A trial judgment was sure to be in excess of three million, and a year more of publicity . . .

The wine business was finished; that was definite. Our cheese would probably survive, as would most of our business with men who had known and dealt with Antonio for years. Many newer contracts were canceled, and I-A stock dropped to twenty-three cents a share, but all was not lost, if only we could get the thing settled as quickly as possible. But raising five million was clearly impossible. And Antonio would not make a statement saying Bernard was innocent.

The final compromise was three million with a statement saying Bernard obviously had not been in Hoboken, et cetera; therefore he had been slandered, et cetera. People reading the statement quickly would get the impression that Antonio was declaring Bernard innocent on all counts, but of course a careful reading revealed the statement had been carefully prepared just to avoid making that point.

Helen Corey, Helen's mother, put up most of the three million. Foster Corey had died shortly after Alexander was born and soon afterward Helen Corey had a stroke. But from Boston she phoned Antonio each day and finally got him to accept the money and make the settlement.

"What should I do?" Antonio asked me when we were alone and nothing remained but to sign the statement.

"I can only tell you what I'd do. I would sign it. There's no choice."

"Sign it and give up the fight."

"What fight, Antonio? There is no fight. Brown and Elesco have us down on the ground with knives at our throats. It's not a fight anymore. You either decide to live or die. We have to pay a price to live; we don't like the price, but it's better than dying."

"I should sign it, then?"

"You have no choice."

"If you were I, would you sign it?"

"I would."

Before the scandal there was no difference between the way Antonio presented himself to the world and what went on inside. And then this changed. Was it that Antonio maintained a façade for the world but began withdrawing more and more inside himself, keeping his own council? Or was it that a new Antonio was secretly developing inside? Academic, I think. He was just being manly, keeping up appearances. But after we gave up the fight with Bernard and Elesco, not only did the difference between the observable Antonio and the man inside intensify, but the man inside began to change character, his job no longer merely to govern the keeping up of appearances, but primarily to be perpetually on guard against enemies, whoever they might be.

During the next four months Helen, Paulina and I acknowledged Antonio's deteriorating condition and sought ways to help him, but we were not overly worried; after all, a man of integrity who has his reputation and business nearly destroyed is entitled to a goodly dose of withdrawal, self-pity and even paranoia.

I closed our Bordeaux and Paris offices, appointed Louise general manager, and helped her train two new young men as her assistants. Helen and Paulina reported that when I was away Antonio went to his office each morning, but from the amount of work undone I suspected he was mostly shuffling papers. Once I insisted he accompany me to the board meeting where for two days he participated in discussions and made suggestions. He could function normally for short periods, but it was obvious to me he had no interest in what was happening. "My God," Louise said after the meeting, "what's happened to that man?" I said we'd just have to be patient. She nodded, then began crying, and that really worried me. Louise could be accused of anything but sentimentality or soppiness, and she had known Antonio longer than any of us.

One day at Consente I was filing some papers in his office, in the alcove just round the corner from Antonio. Anna put his lunch tray on his desk and a bit later I heard him muttering. I poked my head out and saw his face distorted by rage or pain. He continued muttering, obviously having forgotten I was there. Then his arm swept out and across the desk, sending the lunch tray and a lamp flying. The noise of the crash echoed through the halls, but Antonio's face remained distorted, as if he hadn't heard. Anna reappeared in a minute and Antonio's face instantly became normal as he smiled at her and apologized for the "accident."

Only with Alexander was his smile more than a façade. But then there was the time Alexander became fascinated by elephants and I promptly sent father and son off to the Sudan to look for elephants. A week later they returned and Alexander asked me when his father was going to get better. Then a month later Alexander ran into my office, a red mark on his face still visible from where Antonio had slapped him. From time to time Alexander might get his bottom slapped, but this was different.

After this incident (which I never reported to the women), I saw that Helen, Paulina, and I were becoming less candid with one another. As Antonio got worse, we each tried to assure the others he was getting better.

Finally I decided to see Harry in Lisbon where he was shooting *Incidental Music*. During the scandal he had phoned often, saying how rotten it all was and how angry it made him and offering any help he could give. I went to Lisbon to take him up on his offer.

"Why doesn't he see a psychiatrist or something?"

We had dinner early, in a small, one-flight-down seafood

restaurant just off the square. We were the only diners and the three waiters took positions about the room, leaning against the rough plastered walls and silently changing places like some modern ballet troupe.

"He'd never agree."

"Look Craft, I am in favor of homemade everything — except medicine and psychiatry. Well-meaning, full-of-love amateurs can really screw things up. There's no substitute for professional help if Tony's as bad as you say, though it's hard to imagine that. He's a tough boy, you know, and no one knows better than Tony how tough the world can be. I wonder if you're giving him enough credit?"

Without asking, one waiter whisked away our empty glasses as another waiter silently placed fresh drinks before us.

"Sure he's tough and a fighter, but only when there's something visible to fight."

"What does that mean?"

"Look, Antonio's smart and a damned hard worker, and he's had the best breaks, but it wasn't his toughness that got him success. He's really a dreamer, you know, and he's always believed in certain inevitabilities and they've always worked out. Magic is fine so long as it works. But now he feels he's lost the magic. He's been betrayed, not by Bernard Brown, but by some mysterious something or other that's never failed him, until now. You know, he's still a kid who believes in the triumph of right. We all do to some extent, but he believes more strongly than most men because it's always worked for him.

" — And now he doesn't know what to believe. Behind the calm face and fixed smile his brain is whirling away hysterically. Really, Harry, sometimes I swear I can almost hear his brain working. It's imperative he find some kind of answer, but his brain's overloaded and the more desperate he is for an answer, the more incapable his brain is of finding one."

"So he's really lost his confidence?"

I had to smile. "Yes, you could put it that way — maybe that's the best way to put it. He's had extraordinary confidence in something, which always brought him success, which in turn gave him more confidence, and so on, ever upward. But now it's the opposite and a downward spiral. We don't like heroes like this; it's too messy. We like things neat so we can say yes it's a tough world and you have to be tough to survive."

"What do you want me to do?"

The waiters decided two drinks were our limit. Without a word we were presented with the menus.

"Come to Consente. He used to say to me dozens of times that we must get you to spend some time on Rimara. We haven't had visitors for too long now. We'll invite some people, plan some things, just like the old days. All he needs is to feel a bit of his old confidence and that might do the trick."

A month later Harry came to Rimara with his son Jeffrey. Harry's wife had been killed in a car accident when Jeffrey was quite young and the boy, who was a year older than Alexander, spent most of the year in a school in Geneva. Harry had completed the shooting of *Incidental Music* and thought a break of a couple weeks was in order before he began the final editing.

Jeffrey and Alexander became inseparable, exploring the island and going on expeditions with their fathers. I spent the weekends at Consente and Helen and Paulina often invited guests and planned entertainments. There were evenings when some villagers came up to do *raspe* and *tarantelle* (the slow, deliberate Sicilian version). There were nights when we all went for drinks and dinner to the village or had a moonlight swim and picnic supper on the beach. There were day excursions to Taormina and Mt. Etna. We went to Messina for the *teatro dei burattini* and in a small dark room filled with *contadini* watched the marionettes relive Roland's defeat of the Saracens amid the endless clanking of swords. And Paulina insisted that Harry should sample several *feste* of Saints Peter and Paul.

It was like the old days with Antonio taking pleasure in having a visitor discover the quaint and unique beauties of our Rimara, and Helen blossoming as the charming hostess who could not fail to win the affections of her husband's guest. I felt all would be well.

One afternoon Harry, Antonio, the boys and I walked the length of the southern shore to the salt flats. Two special *carabiniere* from the mainland stopped us (salt, like tobacco and matches, is a state monopoly and all flats are carefully guarded). The carabiniere knew Antonio's name and we talked a while. The flats were flooded, but when the water evaporated, the salt would be raked into piles for shipment to the mainland refineries. Later we puttered around the other side of the cove, joining in games with Alexander and Jeffrey, then swimming and eating the feast Jozef had packed for our lunch. I enjoyed the long, leisurely day and thought Antonio calmer than he'd been for some time.

Harry's presence did have a salutary effect on Antonio; of course he was nowhere near his old self, but progress certainly had been made. That evening he pulled me aside and asked if he should bring up the subject of Rosalind's death. During the visit Harry never mentioned his wife who had been a childhood friend of both of them.

"Well," I shrugged, "I think he would talk about her if he wanted to. But he's having such a good time with you, and he's quite taken with Helen, and you can see how pleased he is to see the boys get on so well — maybe he doesn't feel it would be appropriate. Or maybe he just doesn't have anything to say. I may be wrong, but I'd wait for his cue."

At the beginning of the last week of Harry's stay, Jeffrey was due back at school and Paulina accompanied him, stopping in Paris on her way back as she hadn't seen "her city" in years. She returned near the end of the week just when Antonio decided we would all go to Syracuse. Paulina said she was too exhausted by Paris and Joachim loved the sea but hated boats. Helen declined and thought the journey too long for Alexander. I also declined, thinking it would be appropriate for Antonio to spend the last day alone with his friend, but he insisted I come.

Three young men from America went to Syracuse on a boat.

We were silent on the way down, except for Antonio pointing out Catania as we passed. We had all been there the week before to hear Callas sing *Norma* at the Teatro Massimo Bellini.

The Ionian mist lifted as we entered the harbor; it was only eleven, but already scalding and bright, a perfect day for Syracuse, my favorite city. I'd been there half a dozen times before, usually with Paulina, who taught me how to see it.

Modern Syracuse clutters the long flat peninsula where the city begins and runs up the hills, more and more threatening to hide the treasures, much in the same way as hordes of tourists in June clutter a room in the Louvre. But when I go to the Louvre, I don't see the masses of tourists; I peek over their shoulders. So too do I ignore the buildings of modern Syracuse. They are mere transients, visitors whose existence must be acknowledged only because one must peek round them to see the real treasures.

We were all saturated with sweat by the time we walked the short distance to the Piazza Duomo — to me the best square in Sicily. I pointed out the Cathedral and Temple of Pallas Athene, which had been the model for Consente, but Harry found the resemblance slight and said he liked Consente better.

I led them to every part of the city and they followed silently, never complaining about the heat or the unending flow of sweat. A religious ceremony of purification? Pilgrims? I was not so much the tour guide as some sort of priest. Everything I knew and loved about Syracuse I was able to say, at times almost as if I were reciting poetry. I'd never attempted such a role before and Harry's enthusiasm made me feel I wasn't being tedious. Also, I felt I was using Paulina's words as if her spirit had taken over.

After a time, however, Antonio became moody, and worse than his sullen and long-suffering expression was his pathetic attempt at cheerfulness whenever I asked him if he'd had enough. He insisted we go on and finally I decided to ignore him and not ruin my day in the golden city, once the center of the world. (Cicero said it was more beautiful than Rome.)

From the time the Greeks drove out the Sicels in 733 B.C. until the end of the ninth century, there are sixteen-hundred years of unbelievable history. Everyone came to conquer Syracusa: the Carthaginians, the Romans, the Franks, the Vandals, the Ostrogoths. Belisarius had it for a time. Then it was the main base of the Byzantine Empire. Then the Arabs, the Normans, and the Spanish had it for two hundred years. Even nature tried to conquer it with an earthquake in the seventeenth or eighteenth century, when half the population was killed. And of course the Allies bombed it in 1943.

Everyone came there: Plato, Theocritus, Pindar, St. Paul, Archimedes, Simonides, Timolean, Aeschylus . . .

A couple dozen tourists were scattered around the huge semicircle of the Greek theater which once sat fifteen thousand, but no one was talking. Like the three of us, they were all sitting, just looking down at the city and the sea. Aeschylus produced his *Prometheus Bound* in the theater. And the Greek Syracusans had once filled the theater to watch their army destroy the Athenian fleet.

After lunch I led the way to the quarry, the Latomia dei Cappucini. We looked down at the lush paradise of flowers and trees, just as the Syracusans had once looked down at the thousands of their own countrymen they held prisoner after the Athenian fleet had been defeated. But then the quarry was bare and the prisoners had no protection from the sun. Each day the citizens of Syracuse came to watch them die.

"And I thought the Greeks were so civilized," Harry said.

"Well, they were, in a way. They freed any prisoner who could recite lines from Euripides. Ropes were lowered so these soldiers could come up and then they were sent back to Athens. Can you imagine any nation today releasing prisoners because of poetry?"

From the Anapo (the last place in the world where papyrus still grows wild) we walked to the huge funnel of rock with its echo chamber, the Ear of Dionysius.

"Except it was Caravaggio who first called it that, in the sixteenth century, and Dionysius was born before Plato. Supposedly Dionysius used the chamber to spy on friends and enemies by listening at the top end of the grotto, but Paulina says that's improbable. But Dionysius was a nervous Tyrant. His bedroom was built like a small castle, complete with moat and drawbridge so he could sleep without fear of being assassinated. And one day when a courtier said Dionysius must be the

happiest of men because he had everything, Dionysius invited
the courtier to live as he did and gave instructions for everyone
to obey the courtier's slightest whim as if it were a command
from the Tyrant himself. Anything he asked for was to be given
to him without question. But on the first morning of the
experiment the courtier noticed that above his head the servants had placed a sharp sword, held only by a horsehair, and
everywhere he went the sword was carried above his head."

Harry's face brightened. "The courtier was Damocles!"

"Right, and Damocles called off the experiment halfway
through the first day."

"Was Dionysius ever assassinated?"

"By his own poetry. He fancied himself a great poet and of
course everyone always applauded his works out of fear. All but
one man named Philoxenus, who was promptly sent to the
quarries. Later he was brought again before Dionysius to give
an opinion on the Tyrant's latest work. Philoxenus listened to
the poem, then turned to the guards saying 'Back to the
quarries.' Dionysius was a tyrannical Tyrant, but for once he
just laughed and let Philoxenus go free.

"Anyway, to your question. Dionysius was forever entering
his poems in the Athenian festivals, but could never do better
than a second or third prize. At last, however, when he was an
old man, he entered a minor festival and won a first. Immediately he ordered a sumptuous feast to celebrate his triumph
and everyone ate and drank all night long, but most of all
Dionysius, who was still feasting away at dawn. When the sun
came up he had a stroke and died."

On the Street of Tombs I decided we should head back. Both
Harry and I could have gone on for another hour, but Antonio
was too much a burden. Harry seemed fed up with him and I
didn't want to push things too far. Besides, it was a long journey
back to Rimara and Ionian storms were unpredictable.

We did run into a storm on the way back, but it was manmade
and at first I welcomed it. I was in the cabin, heading us back for
Rimara and not paying much attention to their conversation,
my thoughts still with my golden city.

Harry had been talking about Alexander and how lucky Antonio was that he could see him all the time. "You take him fishing; both of you go to the cliffs and paint pictures of the sea. He asks about elephants and you both fly off to see some. I'm lucky if I see Jeffrey three months a year." Harry almost seemed to be provoking an argument. Then he went on to say how lucky Antonio was to have someone like me, and Paulina and Joachim.

I heard nothing for a while and then turned round to see that Harry had drawn his deck chair directly in front of Antonio, who leaned back in his chair, looking uncomfortable. Antonio said something I couldn't hear, just a word or two.

Then Harry began speaking quietly and I couldn't hear, though I knew he hadn't lowered his voice on my account. It was to be the quiet before his outburst and then I realized he was talking about the night he received the news of Rosalind's death.

"I was too much in shock to feel the pain, but then the shock ended and the chaos was over and finally even the pain was gone. Time does heal things. It didn't hurt anymore, but something was peculiar, like I had only half a heart left. Like someone had come into my room that night I heard the news and cut out half my heart. The wound healed and scar tissue grew, but I had only half a heart left and time would never do anything about that. I'd be working and something would happen and I'd make a mental note to tell Rosalind . . ."

"Harry — "

"Wait. Antonio, the empty bed is painful. The empty rooms are painful. The empty place across the table. And the silence. Nothing is worse than that. Do you know what being alone means?

" — When you're young, being alone means sitting in a room and nobody else is there. That's what being alone means when you're young. Nobody *else* is there. But when you're a man, being alone means sitting in a room and *no one* is there, not even yourself.

" — All those years when I'd be away from Rosalind working on location, I'd sit in a room by myself at night, but I wasn't

alone then. I was everywhere. Because in another part of the
world there was Rosalind.

" — When you're young you ache for something to complete
you. If you're lucky and find someone good, the yearning and
aching stop and you find peace. Maybe not constant happiness
or even a lot of happiness, but deep down a sense of wholeness
and you do breathe easier and somehow there's a kind of logic
and sense, no matter how rotten or chaotic the world seems.

" — But if you've had it, and then lose it, then there's nothing
— at least for me. I go on living and working and loving Jeffrey,
but the Harry you knew as a boy and the Harry that was once a
man doesn't exist anymore.

" — I watch the world, I watch Jeffrey, I watch you, but all I
do is watch. As if there's only a mirror where my soul should be.
Just a mirror reflecting the outside world, and behind that
mirror there's black paint and nothing else.

" — Do you know Antonio what it means to have black paint
on the back of a mirror instead of a soul? It means there's no
longer any emotion to distort the truth. I reflect what I see on
the outside world and I don't distort it because I can no longer
care.

" — I no longer love my work; I just don't care anymore.
What's curious is that people are saying I'm doing my best work
now, and maybe that's true. Maybe by being free from emotions
I can see things more clearly now. But there's no joy in it. It
keeps me busy, but I just don't care. Only when I think of
Jeffrey is there some semblance of life still in me. There's still a
little joy and I do care where he's concerned.

" — That, my friend, is what it means to have black paint
instead of a soul."

Although a late-afternoon mist was blowing from the north,
Rimara had been in view for some time and I was able to head
directly for our end of the island.

"Maybe now," Harry continued, "you see I haven't been
saying this just to release my feelings since I don't have many
feelings left. I was just saying this for old times' sake, a gesture
toward a friend who's become a shit. Which is what you are
Contiorli — Antonio Miserable Whining Shit.

" — No. Just wait a minute. I was cataloguing your treasures, remember? Except I never got to the last one. I may not be capable of love anymore, but I can still feel contempt. Tony, if I'd never had my Rosalind and there was still life in me, I wouldn't think twice about solving your problem. People drown all the time, and if I know Craft, he'd back me up. Do you know what I'm saying? In your Greek temple or whatever, you have a marvelous woman like Helen, a real live goddess. She's beautiful and good and you waste all that love and say life is bitter!"

In the rearview mirror I saw Harry standing and pouring himself some wine. Rimara was looming before us and I could head directly for the boathouse. Above the beach rose the yellow sandstone cliffs. Above them the terraces began and then Consente itself. All yellow sandstone.

I turned round to see Harry and Antonio with their arms round each other. "You know, I meant it," Harry said, laughing. "Dump you and give Helen a man who'd appreciate her; wouldn't that solve your problems? After all, what are friends for? So just let me know when you feel life is bitter."

Antonio was smiling sheepishly. "Do you really feel like that inside? I mean about not feeling anything?" Antonio asked when we were gathering up our gear.

Harry laughed. "Just the Slav in me. No, it ain't really that bad. But I think there may be some truth in it." Despite his cheerful tone, I suspected Harry had been telling something very near the truth when he'd spoken about having only half a heart.

During drinks that evening they began reminiscing about their boyhood in Wersend, Ohio, and the more sentimental Antonio got, the more I was confident the crisis was over. During dinner he drank more than a bottle of wine himself and then called for champagne for the cheese, though he was the only one who drank it. He began talking about me and saying how lucky he was to have me. "Absolutely trustworthy," he kept repeating. We went in for our brandies and Antonio began planning a trip to Samos. "There's nothing like the Aegean. Everything's always bright and clear. An edge to everything. Joachim, can you get the boat all set?"

"Wait a minute buddy," Harry said, sounding as drunk and cheerful as Antonio, though I think it was partly an act. "I leave tomorrow."

"*Non possible!* Just the two of us, like when we were boys. A week in the Aegean and you'll be a new man."

Harry protested he had to get back to his film; he'd never put off editing for so long. "I'll lose my feel. I've got to leave tomorrow. Which reminds me — shouldn't I confirm?"

They argued back and forth and Harry no longer seemed so drunk. Helen sat there, a nervous smile periodically coming to her lips. And then Harry played his trump card. "How well do you know Reggio di Calabria? Do you know the big blue villa north of the port?"

Antonio looked mystified and suspicious that he was being put off. Then Harry announced that when I'd first picked him up at the airport in Regg', he hadn't just come off the flight from Rome, but he and Jeffrey had arrived two days earlier and put a deposit on the villa.

"It belonged to a friend of a friend. We're going to be neighbors. But it was a surprise I was saving for tomorrow."

I poured another round and we all drank to Harry's new home. We were all pleased and excited at the prospect of having him so close by, even if only for a few months each year. But after the excitement Antonio once again began talking about going to Samos.

"Aw, come on," Harry said. "I'll be back here in a couple of months."

"But I need you now."

"Look Tony, I'd do anything for you, but — "

"Then stay."

"I can't. Really I just can't. There are so many other people involved."

"That's your final word."

"Yes, Antonio, I'm afraid it is."

"But darling," Helen said, trying to hide her nervousness at seeing her husband so drunk, "Harry will be back soon."

"You ask him to stay," Antonio commanded.

Helen looked surprised, as if to say "me?"

Then she turned to Harry and asked, "Could you stay a little longer?" The piteousness of her plea could not be refused and Harry quickly acquiesced, though it was a compromise. The next morning Harry, Antonio and I would go up through the Straits to Stromboli. We'd spend the night there, then head back, dropping off Harry at Regg' to catch his flight to Rome. We'd also have time for a quick tour through his new house. I said good night and planned to pack some things for the overnight stay in Stromboli, but then I felt too tired and went directly to bed.

How clever he was. I thought of Harry's badgering Antonio and how it had brought him round. Then my thoughts drifted to my golden city and I fell asleep.

Antonio was sitting on the edge of my bed. "Your business days are over, Craft."

I sat up and then Antonio made his way through the darkness toward the door which was open. "What's up?" I asked.

He stood in the doorway. "Oh, you're not Mr. Rambulcek's pimp? Or are you my wife's pimp? Either way your business days are over."

I got out of bed as he disappeared into the hallway. When I was in the hall I saw him in the darkness down the other end, waiting for me.

"What the hell are you talking about?" I asked when I caught up with him, but he turned and headed downstairs and then onto the terrace.

He stopped at the low wall which surrounded the terrace and leaned on it, looking down toward the sea. "Notice anything Craft? Or is it business as usual?" He spoke quietly, in a perfectly level tone, very matter-of-fact.

I looked down to the beach. "There's a man and a woman down there," I answered like a child being quizzed.

"A man and a woman. Come Craft, what man is that down there?"

"I can't tell for sure. Antonio — "

"Are they standing too close together? Are they holding each other too closely for you to distinguish the whore from the pig?"

"Antonio! Maybe it isn't them."

"Maybe it isn't who? Who isn't it Craft? What are the names of the people it isn't?"

"Jesus, calm down!"

"I am calm Craft. But are you? Why do you look so frightened? Was she your whore too?"

"Jesus Christ Antonio! You're mad!"

"Am I mad Craft? Is that an illusion down there? You mean you don't see it? You look as if you see it Craft."

"Antonio, if that is Helen and — "

"If? Come now, my colleague, my friend, my partner. Do we have to go back and look to see if my bed's empty? I've just come from my bed; I assure you it's quite empty. And do we have to look in our honorable guest's room and find it's empty? Do we Craft?"

"Antonio, Helen has been worried about you. I've been worried about you. You haven't been yourself lately. And Harry's worried about you."

"Ah. The whore worries about me so you and Harry soothe her. No, don't worry Craft, I know you haven't betrayed me in that way. You're just the pimp who's sat by while my best friend fucked my wife. Did they let you watch them? Is that your line?"

"Antonio, cut out this shit! You're turning crazy!" He stared at me and I realized it was true that he was very calm and I was the one acting hysterical. His eyes were perfectly calm, almost bored, but deep in them was something strange. I'd never seen an insane person before, but that strangeness was frightening. "Please Antonio, will you listen to me?"

"I am listening Craft."

"What you're thinking isn't possible. And I know what we see down there is innocent. Both of them love you and they aren't doing anything but talking because they're worried about you."

"You're a boy, Craft. Only a boy could look down there and see what you see. Only a boy would have seen them holding hands after dinner and think it was innocent. Only a boy could ascribe innocence to the looks they give each other. And only a boy would realize why my lovely and pure wife was able to make him stay after he refused me. I suppose you didn't know this has been going on for weeks, ever since he came. And I suppose you didn't hear him on the boat when he said he'd kill me — and then take Helen."

"You're wrong, Antonio. You're all wrong."

But he was looking back down toward the beach and there was no mistaking that they were kissing. It was a dark night, and even with the great distance separating us, it was undeniable that the two were kissing.

"Tomorrow morning Craft, you and Harry take the boat. When you return, you'll return alone. Otherwise don't return."

"All right." I said too eagerly.

"You don't understand me Craft? Are you really as dumb as you act and you've just been pretending to be so smart all these years? You return alone. You take Harry in the boat but you return alone. Do you understand me Craft?"

"You're fucking out of your mind."

"Don't think words, Craft, just think what must be done. Show me how clever you really are beneath that mask of innocence. Remember that only *you* return, or else there'll be much to regret."

Whatever I said came out sounding pretty hysterical. But he was the cool Antonio from the old days of the meeting rooms, except for his eyes. As out of control as I was, I did realize that reasoning with him was useless; he was beyond the realm of rationality.

He was watching them make their way across the sands toward the lowest terrace. "You have one minute Craft. Either you do as I say or I'll kill her now."

Whatever I said was barely a whisper.

"Look at me Craft and then tell yourself that when they reach the middle terrace I won't be down there and that I won't kill her. And tell yourself that you and that pig will be able to stop me. Look closely at me Craft and tell yourself she won't be dead before she reaches the house."

"But she's innocent! I know she is."

"Answer me Craft, shall she live? Do you want her to live? I know you love her. Does she live? Yes or no."

"For God's sake Antonio! Yes!"

"That means you'll do as I say. There are no other possibilities, Craft, believe it. Time is going by. They'll soon be through the olive trees. Who is to live Craft? It's your decision. Her life is in your hands."

Clever me stepped back from the wall. "Okay, I'll do it but you've got to promise me something." Then clever me stepped to the middle of the terrace.

Antonio smiled, knowing I wanted him to follow me away from the terrace wall. Then he walked calmly toward me. "You will return alone? You will get off the boat alone?"

"Yes, I promise." I moved toward the house and then my hand was on the knob of the door.

"You wanted me to promise something?"

"That you'll never hurt Helen in any way. That you won't even tell her you saw her tonight. That you'll never even hint to her that you suspected there was anything between her and Harry."

"Is that it?"

"Yes, you must never harm her in any way. Do you promise?"

"Of course Craft. I promise."

I went to my room and began filling all the suitcases with clothes and my most important personal papers. When I went into the hall I heard no sound and then made the first of three trips down to the boat. When I'd finished, I lay on my bed, exhausted, and then must have fallen back to sleep.

I found them all in the breakfast room, chatting away brightly. Helen spoke enthusiastically about the prospect of Harry living in Regg' and offered to help him decorate his villa. He accepted her offer and said he couldn't wait to come back so they could begin. Joachim offered to look over the garden and make suggestions — provided Harry took him up there by plane. It was a bright and happy scene.

Antonio apologized to Harry for having been so drunk and so unreasonable. Not only was he feeling the hangover, but was feverish and probably coming down with something. He apologized for having imposed so much on Harry's time. He had already confirmed Harry's flight from Regg' to Rome and through to Lisbon. Since Harry was already packed, it was best that I take him directly to Regg' as had been his original plan. "You won't mind Craft, will you?" Antonio asked.

Only then did I give up the hope that the scene on the terrace last night had been a dream. "No, of course not."

They all came down to the boat to see us off. Alexander kissed Harry, who promised that Jeffrey would return soon and they could play together as often as they liked and perhaps even go to school together.

I started the boat and watched them wave good-by. The beautiful Helen in a soft tan morning robe, her long hair blown by the wakening sirocco; the only woman I ever truly loved. The golden-haired Alexander jumping up and down in the morning sun. Joachim as indomitable and honorable as an ancient olive tree. Paulina, the voluptuous prophetess in her inevitable blue and white. And Antonio, my partner and friend.

As we approached the western tip of Rimara, I poked my head out to take one last look at Consente, but only Paulina's huge house at the extreme tip of the island was visible.

Harry pointed questioningly to all my suitcases and gear half-hidden under a tarp.

"Anyone living up at your house now?" I asked.

"No."

"I'll be needing a place to stay until I decide what to do."

"You're leaving so Antonio will be forced to get back to work?"

"My leaving will have that effect, but my reason is that it's time for me to move on. I can't be of any more help and I've done enough damage."

"Jesus, you guys are nuts. First Tony begs me to stay; then when I agree, he packs me off. I think you've all been under this sun too long."

A little action is a dangerous thing.

But what could I have done?

For a few years afterward I cursed myself when I thought of a dozen things I might have done. (But I was to see Helen once more

and still was unable to help her.) Not until a full ten years later did
I learn the best course of action would have been none at all.

It had not been Helen with Harry that night on the beach. I
had cleverly led Antonio away from the terrace wall and into
the house. Had I not been so clever, in a few minutes we would
have seen Harry emerge from the olive grove with Paulina.
Probably even Joachim would have laughed at the "indiscre-
tion" of his wife.

But even though I didn't know that, I should have been smart
enough to realize why Antonio had got me out of bed and
brought me down to witness the scene: so that he himself could
avoid action. He was already half-crazy and in his rage he just
might have killed Harry. He hated Harry then and wanted him
away from Consente, but Antonio was no killer. What better
way to get Harry safely away than to ask *me* to kill him?
Antonio was even incapable of saying the words directly, of
saying, "I want you to kill him."

But most of all Antonio knew he must not confront a guilty
Helen. His self-preservation instincts must have warned him of
the consequences of such a confrontation. He could never do
anything to harm Helen, but to come face to face with her
betrayal would have made him go all the way and he would
have become completely and truly insane.

And yet the innocent did perish: Helen, Alexander, Joachim,
and Antonia, the infant daughter of Helen and Antonio. Only
Paulina survived. And of course Antonio.

Nineteen years have passed since Harry and I sailed away
from Rimara, and now on this childish morning we both return.

Harry had been silent most of the way down until he asked,
"What the hell do you say to a murderer?"

"Well," I said, "it depends on when we arrive. If it's before
noon, you begin by saying 'Good morning.' "

"Craft, what the hell's on your mind? What are you up to?"

I smile. I really don't know what I'm up to. I told Harry's son
Jeffrey I had a plan, but I really don't. God knows what's going
to happen, but my heart is light and I'm as happy as a kid.

HELEN'S LETTER

The Accomplices

FATHER:

I WAS LOOKING across the room at the carved chest you gave me for my twenty-first and suddenly I remembered the names you had for the three dragons perched on top: Christmas, Isthmus and Peninsula. Mother had looked at the chest nervously and under her breath asked, "A hope chest?"

The same question I ask now. More than half-filled with poems, even the earliest which I would sign with a great flourish followed by "age ten" or "age twelve."

Do you remember my Trash Poem? About how mother worked so intently on her crossword puzzles, often long into the night. Sometimes she could not complete a puzzle or sometimes not even begin. But completed, unfinished or unstarted, they all ended in neat bundles of newspapers which the handyman

(Andrew?) tied and left out for the trash truck. At the end of the poem I asked what difference it made if all the puzzles in those papers had been worked perfectly. (Again I look at my dragon chest full of poems and ask the same question.) You said it was my first real poem, but mother didn't understand and thought I was making fun of her.

Do you remember the parade of young men she produced for my benefit? And the only result of all her efforts was a short poem I wrote about young men with tanned bodies and hairy limbs in tennis clothes looking so ridiculous. I thought then they should either cover themselves completely or else wear nothing — either way they would have been more natural. Mother was shocked. That's when I took up gardening and stopped showing her my poems.

Do you remember the garden in winter — barren and frozen, with a soft tan crust, or covered with ice or snow? We talked of the things of the earth asleep, waiting for spring. Confident and waiting. And the foxgloves and hollyhocks which always kept a few leaves of green above their corms.

Mother did worry about me, but I thought I was happy. Was I mostly happy or mostly brave? I knew you understood. But after my twenty-first birthday I began to know a strange sadness.

I was in the garden, pinching back the chrysanthemum for the final time. I wanted an abundance of small flowers on short stems so they need not be staked. The plants would tolerate the second pinching back but not a third. It would soon be their time to bloom and nature could be altered only to a certain extent. Then you came into the garden and asked why I was so thoughtful.

"I think it's because the time has come for me to fall in love, but I can't find anyone I like. I would much prefer to write, really, but this strange feeling occurs more frequently. I suppose I am quite normal after all."

"You going to search for someone?"

"Certainly not. If it's nature's plan, then nature must do the work."

"And in the interim?"

"I shall write throbbing stuff, à la Millay. Won't be a bit good, I suppose, but it will be fun."

You put your arm round me and said you never worried about me and you never would.

"Shall I be a famous poet, do you think?"

"Yes, you shall, someday, though it may take a long time."

I continued to plan my epic poem about the city of Arthesia, though I knew it would be many years before I could set it down properly. Someday it shall be complete; life has ways of telling us the future.

I was never unkind to anyone. I was a good listener. I was thoughtful, solicitous, but people still were aware of the distance I kept from them. I didn't know I was being condescending, but people sensed it, I'm sure. I wanted only to write and had no interest in anything else. Everything else was ordinary. What I was incapable of realizing was that "everything else" was life and, my God, I was afraid of life. Giacometti said if he were in a burning building and could save either a Rembrandt or a cat, he'd choose to save the cat — and then let it go. Finally I can now understand that. Life above art.

The strange sadness intensified and even my poetry turned sour. I began to resent the whole business of "love" and wished I were sixty and finished with it all so I could concentrate on my work.

And then, after all that time, within the space of two days I was to fall in love with two men.

He introduced himself with such confidence I had to believe we'd met at a party the previous week as he said, though I truly couldn't remember. We walked along the beach and in answer to my question he said he'd never had a garden or thought much about flowers. Poetry? No, not really.

And yet I felt such ease with him. I could see things through his eyes and the experience startled me. For the first time I was "out of myself" and seeing the world as someone else did.

I looked at the thick but soft blond hair on the back of Craft's hands and wondered if his whole body was covered with such hair. I wanted to touch him.

We had dinner together. His hair was cut short and in the light it was more white than blond. There was a desire to place my arms around his head and bring it to rest on my breasts. I couldn't believe what was happening.

When he took me to my room that night and left me at the door, my only desire was to lie down and have him on top of me.

The next morning I came down to the dining room for breakfast, the sweetness of my desire unchanged. With some repulsion I stared at a man sitting alone some tables away. He was covered with black curly hair which reminded me of those young men on our lawn in their tennis whites. He was older and heavier, but the unnaturalness of that body hair seemed similar. My mind was made up and I was determined to pursue Craft until I had him on top of me. That's just about the way I said it to myself. I did not care what would happen afterward — nothing else was of importance.

"You're Foster Corey's daughter, aren't you? We haven't met properly but I've seen you at a party with your father. My name's Antonio Contiorli."

He didn't speak as I would have guessed he should. Another surprise was his very large grey eyes. I couldn't believe this childlike creature was the same man I had just been staring at.

Antonio Contiorli became my friend, my lover, my husband. But more than these, he was my accomplice.

I had been a stranger to myself and now I was with another stranger, but our isolation from the world made us accomplices. And I was satisfied: it was enough that we go down to death together. We would walk, hand in hand, and the dust of the world which covered us would not matter. I had my accomplice, my Antonio.

But I had not dreamed enough. I had seen clearly to his heart. I knew his strength and the light of his intellect. But I had not dreamed enough and did not know my Antonio could be more than these.

He was a hurricane at sea and no force of man or nature could challenge his power. He was not one to walk meekly into nothingness. His hurricane winds were wings that carried me from the world and brought me safely to the quiet eye of his storm where none could touch me.

I had not understood the world.

Perhaps I had understood it all too well and used my ignorance of words and details to pretend otherwise. Now it did not matter. I was carried to a place where words and meanings could no longer blot out the sun.

And still he was my accomplice, but not now in death. As if I were a specimen that could blossom only in the air of a secret garden, he took me away from a world which had been a sour mystery.

He was a hurricane at sea and in the calm center of his storm he gave me the strength to see that what we create and make exist becomes the new reality. If a flower were to grow and bloom in our new garden, no one could deny its reality.

All the words, the paragraphs, the details, were swept away and not a particle of ash remained. A new day and the sun filled the garden.

"What's the matter?" He may have been concerned, but my laughter made him smile.

"Don't you see, Antonio? The garden is finished. There's not a thing to be done to it. It's just perfect. Was that old man the gardener?"

"Yes, that's Joachim; his wife is the housekeeper. Look, we don't have to live here; we can find someplace else. Your father will understand."

"Oh, no. It's fate. I want to live here."

"We could dig this out and put in new gardens."

"No. They're just perfect. That man is a genius. There are so many new plants I don't know."

He wasn't a gardener at all, but a great artist, using shrubs and bushes instead of oils. There weren't many flowers in bloom then, but that meant his overall composition would hold year round. Everything was in intersecting circles all about the house and terraces, with great streaks of green unifying the pattern. Inch-high silver evergreens would be mixed with dark-green laurels, and from this small point would arise an ingenious arrangement of larger and larger silvers and dark greens. Then the silvers would be replaced by yellowish greens working in and out among bushes so dark they seemed black in the bright sun.

He was not deferential and I thought he took this prerogative because of his advanced years. But, no, it was because he understood me at once and I too felt it would be an affectation to be coy about our pleasure in meeting.

In the words of the world the garden was mine, but I knew this was not so in reality. "Will you let me help you tend it?" It was a bold question because he understood I was truly asking permission and acknowledging the garden as his property. Antonio gave a quiet laugh when Joachim took my hand, patted it, and said, "*Insieme.*"

And my boldness did not stop with Joachim. Secure in the protection of Antonio's love, I now approached people in search of their affection. I saw that most people also suffered from the pressure of words and meanings, but under this was that universal desire to exchange — no word is right for it. Even if only for a few minutes, most people wanted to feel the sudden warmth, to acknowledge that they too were accomplices. I was not so different from people as I had once thought.

I began to see things and sometimes what I saw made me ashamed.

I saw that compared to most women I was indeed beautiful, as you'd always said. And some of these women were quite plain and had to make great efforts to extend themselves to others.

As I came to understand these things, I looked at Antonio and wondered how he could have loved me when I had been so foolish and selfish. Whether he was aware of the realization that was coming to me, I could not tell. He seemed at times incomprehensible; yet when we were alone all I could see was a good man who enjoyed simple things. Never, life had never brought me such happiness as when we watched the twilight together.

He understood the world's foolishness, and also that he could not change it. He kept his affections simple and knew that was all that could be done. And yet he hoped — did he dream of shaming the world, thereby changing it?

You and Mother visited. Your last visit.

Antonio brought the phonograph onto the terrace and played nothing but Strauss waltzes. It wasn't sunset music, but it seemed right. You sat with your arm around me, holding my hand or placing yours on my belly, the nearest you ever were to get to your grandson. The sun was setting south of Etna; you never saw it set in the center of the volcano.

There is one thing for which I am grateful. Books are filled with sons and daughters regretting their failure to inform their parents of their love, but at least this was not the case with us. I am certain you did know. That evening in the twilight, with Strauss sounding more brave than wistful, I felt you understood completely my love for you. You couldn't have understood it better if I could find the words. I felt you did know how fully I loved you and for that I am grateful.

Mother was fascinated by Paulina and followed her about as Paulina swept through the house ordering servants like a goddess quietly giving instructions for changing the world. "And it's not embarrassing to look in her eyes, even if we're not speaking," Mother had said. "Isn't that remarkable? And her figure — like a schoolgirl!"

Can you remember the last dinner, when Paulina cried? "She is happy about the child," Joachim said. I believed him. I thought those few tears in her eyes were a sort of blessing as she looked round the table at each of us, then reached for her wine.

"We couldn't tell you," Antonio said. "It was my decision, but I also asked your mother and she agreed. And Paulina agreed and so did Dr. Tun and Craft."

They received the news you were dying when I was in labor. By the time Alexander was born, you were dead. Antonio didn't tell me until a week later.

A life for a life.

I felt as if the heavens had deserted us. Not maliciously or not with any vengeance, but as if their business had called them elsewhere, and casually, without a thought, they had turned away from us.

New life replaces the old. But I found no comfort in nature.

After a time, however, I began to believe you were with us, watching. Especially later when Antonio played with Alexander. I knew you must be pleased at how much time they spent together. "You're not giving Craft too much to do?" I asked.

"No, Craft would let me know. And the more he takes over, the happier he is. He's making me redundant."

Alexander, toddling up and down the beach, wore out Antonio. There were hundreds of castles they built, or rather, which Antonio built and which Alexander promptly sat on. Then Antonio began turning out rather clever sand structures connected by systems of highways and arches — I called him a frustrated architect — and his big problem was to keep Alexander at bay long enough so he could finish a project.

"Darling," I said to Alexander, "let's take a very, very, very, very long walk to the cove so Daddy can finish his city."

"A grown man building sand castles by himself?"

"There's no one to see you."

"Still, I don't think it would be as much fun," he laughed, at which point Alexander came charging from behind and flung himself on Antonio's superstructure. Father and son wrestled till they fell on me and the three of us lay on the sands with our arms around each other, laughing and panting, and Antonio kissing me on one cheek and then Alexander kissing me on the other.

There was a game Craft and Antonio played with Alexander, tossing him back and forth like a ball. I was nervous watching your grandson flying back and forth, but thought you must be enjoying it.

And you were always here for Christmas, amused, I was certain, at how Italian we'd become, with our *presèpio*, while Alexander received presents from *Babbo Natale*, the *Gesu Bambino*, and from the witch *Befana* on *Epifania*.

"*Natale con i tuoi, Pasqua con chi voui*," Paulina said, and I made certain you weré always here for both.

And you were here, in spirit. Your spirit in me which will last as long as I work at it. And then it would be gone, except for Alexander.

He's so athletic, climbing everything and jumping, and he has an exceptional arm and eye for sports. He gets it from Antonio. Even now in his still delicate bones and muscles you can see the man he will be: a golden hero, taller than Antonio and probably stronger, the muscles not so big but longer and smoother. Alexander will be a joy to see. He's innately happy, and a tease — definitely he gets that from Antonio.

But he's also creative and spends hours collecting special stones or odd bits of everything and then pastes them inside boxes which become small worlds of forests and gardens and beaches connected by complicated paths drawn with yellow crayon. Occasionally insects are dropped into these worlds and are cheered heartily if they manage to stay on the paths.

When I work on my poems he also fills pages which he staples together and in this way turns out several books each week.

And there's more. He understands so much. There are special moments when we'll look at each other and communicate something. I think in a way even now he can perceive more than I. I think a child, even though he doesn't have the words, can perceive the qualities of reality — possibly just because he doesn't have the words. Adults take in things only in context, only in terms of the labels available, the words. Do you know at times I am almost jealous of the poet Alexander will become.

We all went to Paris when Alexander could walk and Antonio was a bit shocked at how I joked with the salesgirls (and even salesmen) in the shops. He didn't understand I did it because you had done it the first time you took me to Paris. I walked down the Rue St. Honoré, but there was no trace of you and that was when I knew you didn't exist anymore. People walked by, oblivious of the fact that you had once walked there joking about things in the shop windows. There was no trace of you in Paris or of the easy way you had of striking up conversations with everyone. Nothing. And that's why I joked with the salesgirls. They were startled at first, but I was confident because I had seen you do it and I made it work.

Was I coming out of my old selfishness? Or was it you coming out in me?

Antonio often said our visitors at Consente found excuses for lingering a day or two longer because they were reluctant to part from me. Maybe this was true. You would have been pleased to see how I enjoyed playing La Grande Signora di Consente.

I think you knew Josh Henderson. Antonio told me he was an "implacable grouch" whom everyone found fierce and forbidding. But Antonio hadn't told me that until he'd gone (after staying two days longer than he'd planned).

"He was putty in your hands," Antonio said.

"He's just a very shy man, and really nice underneath it all."

"Well, my dear, let's just say you're able to make him behave like a nice man."

You would have been pleased at the hostess I'd become.

"Dark sons in the shadow of the day recollect
  When good times and bad were fixed in the echo of youth
  Remembered as this or that.
  Time times time gives pleasure of tomorrow

And remorse of yesterday.

Or is it the other way, better before and never again?"

"I keep seeing scenes from Wersend. Things that happened with friends. I can't remember their names, but I see their faces clearly."

"Are they happy scenes?" I asked.

"They're not traumatic. Just innocent things that happened, sometimes happy, but usually just quiet scenes. They're so real, as if those streets and alleys and woods still existed somewhere. I see myself and other boys playing, but I'm always seeing them from the other side of the street, as if I were a passer-by who just happened to turn and look."

"Would you want to be that young again?" He could not see my smile and in the dark my voice sounded more serious than I intended.

"No, I don't think it's that. What I get is the feeling that I'm watching something important. And what's important about it is that it was all once a definite reality. Does that make sense?"

As clearly as if it were the yellow sandstone of Rimara, I saw a wall arising around my Antonio. Apparently men must hold fast to some things if they are to think of themselves as men. It is weakness for them to let go of the world, of logic, and of reason. My Antonio held fast, unwittingly, not to these things, but only to the wall which separated him from them. The wall which each week increased the barrier between him and the world (and me).

"Antonio, just try to let yourself go, just for a while. I know no one can understand how it must feel to be ruined by that Elesco and Bernard, and then have to give up the fight, but just let yourself relax a while." I knew it was within my power to help him. It was simple. Imaginary things have power only so long as we believe in them. Stick out your tongue at them and at the habit they've engendered and they vanish.

"I'm sick of your trying to dominate me!" Darkness increases the sound of violence in a human voice.

*

"Wind on the road, ice on the wind;
A mood felt now and known before.
Urgency and calm together in the season
When a man felt most himself and least a part of the rest.
A part, a rest. Arrest this part
Known to be apart from parts unused to separation.
We wish that death, being a part of life,
Did not have so bad a reputation."

"How wonderful to meet you at last," I said to Harry Rambulcek, Antonio's boyhood friend. Jeffrey, his son, examined the scraps of colored paper Alexander had glued together as a present. Jeffrey, a year older and much more a man of the world, found the present curious at best, but then smiled and said, "Thank you." It was important that he should not immediately discard these presents on which Alexander had worked so many hours. He smiled again at Alexander and stuffed the papers in his pocket. They ran off together toward the beach.

"All these years," Harry said. Except for appendicitis, he would have been our best man. I had spoken to him many times by phone, and from *Diminishing Returns* and *Love Scenes* and his other films, I felt I knew him well, though this was our first meeting. "What incredible gardens!"

"You must tell that to Joachim. He's been working nonstop since we learned you were coming. It's been so long since we've had visitors — since the scandal — and I'm afraid we've all taken advantage of your coming to 'pull out all the stops,' as Craft says. I know you probably would wish for a quiet holiday, but we got carried away planning things; so you must forgive us if we've overdone things. Antonio's become somewhat retired lately and we thought a few parties and festivities would cheer him up."

We were having a picnic lunch at the foot of San Domenico, once part of a Saracen fortress, then later taken over by monks, but now only a scattering of crumbled stairways and walls. Jozef himself came to see that his cold buffet was properly served and I had such faith in him, I didn't hesitate when I saw the chilled

squid over which he poured a sauce the color and texture of
béarnaise, though of course it was cold. He had done some
potato pancakes, flaky puffs seasoned with truffles. I was at first
surprised at the huge container of them, but Jozef hadn't
overestimated. Alexander and Jeffrey kept running back and
forth from the water for yet another handful and I found myself
eating them as if they were potato chips.

Then the men and boys went off to explore the ruins as
Paulina and I lounged in the shade of the cliffs. I certainly had
eaten too much and looked with envy at Paulina's perfect
figure.

"Why do you think Harry doesn't like me?" I asked lazily.

I was accustomed at times to waiting for an answer from her,
but then I began to wonder if she'd heard my question or if she
was already fast asleep. I turned and saw her looking at me, her
eyebrows arched wearily. It seemed she wasn't going to speak
and I was about to repeat my question when she asked, "What
do you want for an answer?"

"The truth, Paulina, if you please."

"Harry loves you."

"That's absurd, Paulina. He seems almost to resent me!"

"Very well, but you should have told me you wanted that for
an answer."

"You can't mean it. What do you mean he loves me?"

"It is only my guess, my lady." Paulina called me that only
when she was weary and thought I was acting like a child.

"But Paulina, he acts so peculiar when we're alone. He's
charming when others are present, but he backs off when we're
alone."

"I'm certain my lady would not think it seemly if he openly
displayed his affections."

"Oh Paulina, don't scold now. I really thought he didn't like
me and I was afraid I was letting Antonio down."

She smiled. "Of course I cannot be certain he loves you, but I
think he does — and very much, I expect. The fact that he acts
awkward when you are alone seems to prove this is so. It
certainly shows he is a gentleman and a true friend. To me it
seems he has come to love you against his will, the way many of

our guests do. It is no reason for concern. His affection is proper, but he cannot help himself if his heart — how do you say in your country? — runs away on him."

"Paulina! The poor man. And I was going to ask your advice on how I could get him to like me!"

After that I found it difficult to look directly in his eyes and — it was silly of me — I even avoided seeing him alone. The poor man must have thought I disliked him.

Then one night near the end of his visit I almost literally bumped into him when the others were asleep. It had been an especially joyful evening with Antonio and Harry reminiscing about their childhood and Harry surprising us all with the news of his buying a villa in Reggio. I had had too much to drink and woke in the middle of the night. I took Alka Seltzer and decided to walk a bit on the terrace. Although I had not yet called Dr. Tun, I was certain I was pregnant and was planning a special way to tell Antonio. I was about to step out onto the terrace when I saw a figure cross before me. It was Harry and he hadn't seen me. He walked down the terrace and then took the stairs toward the beach. I decided my stroll had better take place in the garden.

There were swirls of mist among the plants and flowers and it was so beautiful I was tempted to wake Antonio, bring him into the garden, and tell him his daughter was on the way. I knew such news would make him forget my foolishness in waking him at that hour, but I relented, remembering the men were to set off early the next morning for Stromboli.

For a short while the moon broke through the clouds, making the garden even more fantastical. "Extravagant!" I said aloud as I raised both hands up to the moon. I was still feeling the effect of too much wine.

I had a sudden inspiration. "We'll call her Antonia!" I thought of you then, but there was no one to hear me except the garden and that brief moon. The last time I was to speak joyful words, and no one heard.

*

I could understand Antonio not feeling well after the last night's drinking, but it was a surprise when he canceled Stromboli and asked Craft to take Harry to Reggio to catch the flight to Rome. After we waved them off, Antonio turned to me and asked how I was feeling. I said I was fine, but that wasn't so.

"Will you be going back to bed?"

"No, Antonio, I feel fine."

"I think I'll go back a while."

I was feeling nauseous and considered calling Dr. Tun. I lay down on the sofa in the drawing room and planned the luncheon menu, though I wasn't hungry. Poached shrimp, that would be it. Poached perfectly in water and white wine with a bit of butter, a pinch of salt and crushed lemon. Perfectly delicate for delicate stomachs. Afterward I would tell Antonio my news.

When he did not appear by one, I went to our room and found the blinds down and Antonio asleep. Taking care not to disturb him, I lay down beside him — at which point he suddenly sat up.

"Are you going to sleep?" he asked, seeming wide awake.

"No, I didn't want to wake you. I made some lunch. Are you hungry?"

"No, I think I'll go for a walk down to the village." He dressed quickly and left the room.

I walked down the drive to meet him. "Antonio, something rather peculiar has happened."

He did not quicken his pace and seemed unaffected by my words. "What is it?" he asked almost without interest.

"You didn't see Tommas? He left here only a while ago."

"No, what was he doing here?" It was very curious that Antonio acted unusually calm, yet I had the feeling his heart was beating very quickly.

"He brought the boat back . . . the one Craft and Harry took."

"Calm yourself, Helen; that isn't possible."

I thought I was calm. "But Antonio, it's all very peculiar. A man from the mainland brought the boat to the harbor. He said he was paid by Craft to return it here, to Tommas. Tommas drove the boat round the island and put it in our boathouse. The message from Craft was that you would understand."

"Where's Tommas now?"

"I thought you might have met him on the way up. He just
left. He was going to find Domingo to take the man back to
Reggio. Craft gave the man money to pay for a ride back."

Antonio went inside and I heard him speaking on the library
phone, but when I tried the door, it was locked. Then Antonio
came out and took the car into the village.

"Goodness," Paulina laughed when I told her everything,
"what a fuss. Craft's a grown man."

I was alone on the front terrace when Antonio returned. I ran
to meet him, but he hurried past me into the house and into
Craft's quarters. In a distracted way I began looking round the
rooms to see what Antonio was searching for, but everything
seemed normal. Only Antonio's agitation and fierce look pre-
vented me from repeating Paulina's words about Craft being a
grown man. On a chair I found an envelope addressed to
Antonio, written in pencil; then Antonio grabbed it from my
hand. "Antonio, what's wrong?"

"Perhaps I'd better open this first and find out. Or maybe you
can save me the bother. You do know what's in here, don't you?"

I cannot remember much of what happened afterward or how
I felt until early evening when I was staring at my dresses,
gowns and shoes all in disarray outside the door of our bedroom.
Paulina was pounding on the door and saying she would not go
away if she had to pound all night. "Break down the door!" she
ordered Joachim, but he stood there, looking as puzzled as I felt.

"Break down the door! Must I do it myself?"

Then the door opened. Antonio was in his pajamas. "What do
you want?"

I was about to speak when Paulina cried, "What does this
mean?" Paulina's ferocity was as incomprehensible as Antonio's hostility. Paulina was always somewhat forbidding, even
when she was silent with only a calm smile, but now her fury
seemed indomitable — and yet Antonio looked at her with the
patience of a parent confronting an obstreperous child.

"I'll be sleeping here alone," he said. I heard Paulina's gasp
and knew she was about to break into a tirade again, but

Antonio slowly closed the door and then we heard it lock.

"Just when he was getting better," Paulina said weakly. We stood there a long time in silence until Paulina told Joachim to help her take my things. We picked up the clothing and in a silent procession made our way outside, along the terraces, across the fountain garden and through the wall into Sontern.

Half a dozen times Paulina had me repeat each detail, but she came to no conclusion. Perhaps it was because she was so agitated and raging that I remained calm — stunned as a child at events it cannot comprehend. At last she led me down passageways to a large bedroom, helped me undress and put me in bed with assurances that everything would be resolved the next day. Joachim had gone to check on Alexander, who fortunately had slept through the scenes of that evening.

The bad dream persisted. The sun had long been up and Paulina put a breakfast tray for me on her terrace. She had already spoken to Antonio but was evasive when I questioned her. I could not eat, but took some coffee, then arose; I worried about Alexander.

Paulina held my arm and would not let go. "Paulina!" It was the first ever I spoke as mistress to servant, but still she would not let me go.

"My lady, you must not go." Only her strangely tragic look stopped me from trying to force myself free. I sat down and then she told me what Antonio had said. "He gave us *terms*," she said vehemently, though her voice was no more than a whisper. "These are the tyrant's *terms*." I could stay with Paulina and Joachim at Sontern, but should not approach Consente. I was to have "no *access* to the child" and should take care that he never see me. If I wished to leave — which Antonio advised — he would make all arrangements and undertake all expenses. Of course I could not take Alexander with me. Paulina and Joachim could stay or leave as they pleased, but if they stayed Paulina was to conduct herself "in a dignified manner" and run the house as she had always done. She was to speak to Antonio only about matters of the house. She was relieved of her duties as Alexander's governess; she could speak to the boy only in the presence of Antonio, and if she did speak, it must be "with dignity" and "remembering her place." If she behaved in an unseemly manner, she and Joachim would be dismissed.

I stood up and made my way toward Consente. I think Paulina was trying to stop me but enough nonsense had been going on for too long.

As I rounded the main terrace, I saw Antonio before the door. He grabbed my arm as I attempted to get by him. He didn't hurt me, but I could never have broken free of his grip. I looked at him but my resolution began fading as I stared at the boundless contempt in his eyes. I don't know what "pure hatred" is, but I saw vicious hatred. It was vicious. It glared at me and had a life of its own as if it were some wild and hideous monster from the underworld.

Paulina had followed me and then she led me back to Sontern. Not a word had been spoken.

"But why Paulina?"

"A thousand times I asked him. I finally said we would all do as he wished, but he must give us to understand why. I said I would bring you to him and that he must explain. Then he became agitated and said I would bear the responsibility for what happened if I brought you to him. At last I told him I would get *on my knees* before him and beg so he might tell us. He became embarrassed and milder. 'It's not your fault,' he said. Not our fault!" She banged the table with both hands. " 'But you must not interfere in business you don't understand.' 'Then, please,' I said, 'make us to understand.' "

"Paulina, please. What is his reason? Tell me."

"You are to look into your heart, that's what the villain said! He said that was the answer and the *discussion was closed!* He said he had answered my question and if I asked again he would dismiss me 'on the spot!' "

"To look into my heart? What does it mean Paulina?"

"What does it mean? You look for meaning from a madman? He is mad; that's what it means. Helen, something has upset him, but his madness cannot last. We must be patient now. We must just wait a while now and do as he says until he calms down."

"Joachim, help me," Paulina ordered as she tried to restrain me. "Helen, you must not go out there now. Please wait!" We watched as Antonio and Alexander walked down the beach. I knew Paulina was right, but I had to see Alexander. "Helen, for your son's sake! Joachim, bring some brandy."

"No, Paulina, I'll be all right. I'll be calm."

Joachim asked so little of anyone I could not refuse the glass he held out to me. "It will help you," he said.

After I had sipped half the brandy, Paulina decided I had sufficiently calmed down. "You must forgive me, Helen, but there is a question I must ask, even though I know the answer. May I ask it?"

"Of course Paulina."

"Now I know that it is impossible there should be anything improper between you and Craft — "

"Paulina! Between me and Craft! You don't think — "

"No, I don't think, but is it possible that *Antonio* might think? It is too mysterious — this disappearance of Craft. Antonio was surprised by it; yet the message was that Antonio would understand. And what had Craft written in that note? Maybe he was in love with you — a young man like that living alone — but I know Craft. He is no villain and no fool. He would not leave such a note and run off. There is no one so discreet as Craft. Look, they are far up the beach. We must find Craft. Where could we find Mr. Rambulcek's phone number?"

Like two schoolgirls, Paulina and I ran across to Consente and in Antonio's office found three numbers for Harry: London, New York and Connecticut. With London we left word that he should call. There were several separate phones for Antonio's business, but these were in his and Craft's offices. The rest of the villa, including Sontern, was served by only one number, except for the kitchen at Consente. We left instructions he must call only on that number. Anna would take the call and fetch Paulina.

The next step would be for Paulina and Joachim to act "in a suitable manner" — Paulina's eyes were wild as she said the words. They would conduct the business of the house as if nothing had happened. And Paulina would see to it that Alexander was all right and not too much disturbed by the sudden disappearance of his mother.

At last Craft called, on the kitchen phone, wanting to speak to me. Paulina led the way to the house, making certain Antonio would not see me. I wanted so much to hear Craft's voice; I felt the moment I talked to him all would be well, that he would have all the answers.

But he would tell me nothing until I first told him the exact situation at Consente. I told him everything. "But why is this happening, Craft?"

"I'm afraid he thinks you and Harry were lovers."

"How could he think that? Are you sure?"

"He woke me up in the middle of the night, the night before we left. He was a desperate man. You must take my word for it Helen. I know that's the reason. What has he said about me?"

"Nothing. He won't let me speak to him. Or see Alexander!"

"Do you want to leave Consente for a while? It might be best."

"No, I won't leave Alexander here. Antonio wants me to leave, but he won't let me take Alexander."

Paulina rushed into the kitchen. "He's coming!"

Craft gave me his number. He was staying at Harry's house in Reggio and would wait for my call.

One week later the situation was not much altered. Antonio had told Alexander I was in a hospital for a contagious disease and allowed no visitors. Paulina saw Alexander every day, but all she could do was assure him I would be well soon and that we must be brave and pray for my health.

"He is mad, but he is clever," Paulina had said. "He knows we will not upset the boy by letting him know you're here and so you won't dare reveal yourself. And you mustn't. We cannot upset him by letting him see you. That tyrant is clever!"

Antonio asked Paulina where Craft's things should be sent.

When she pretended ignorance, Antonio said he was having all Craft's possessions put in crates. If the men did not have an address by that afternoon, the crates would be dumped into the sea. "I phoned Craft and he said he would call Antonio and give him the address himself." But Antonio would not speak to him and told Anna to take the address.

Mother phoned and Anna came running to tell me. Mother's bronchitis sounded much worse, so I told her nothing and tried to sound cheerful.

By the end of the second week nothing further had happened. Antonio refused to accept the calls from Craft and Harry, but I spoke to Craft each day, taking care to call only when I saw Antonio was away from the house.

Paulina saw Antonio each day. He said good morning if she spoke first, but apparently he was barely civil. In very businesslike tones he would discuss any matter concerning the house, but would allow no further conversation. Several times she attempted to talk about me, but he cut her off. Once she did go further, but he said, "Not one more word! Not one more word!" He raised his finger in warning. "Not one syllable or you're fired! Believe me, Paulina, I mean it. Don't ever try it again. And once you're fired neither you nor Joachim will ever come back here. Believe my words."

"Oh, the tyrant! Believe his words!" Paulina was puce as she reported the story.

But one thing had changed: Anna said that Antonio, when he was not with Alexander, was working busily in his office each day.

I was now convinced I was pregnant and Paulina called Dr. Tun. "I'm not certain what we should do," she said. "I do not know how Antonio will take the news if he learns it from Dr. Tun. You should tell him. Write a note. I'll take it to him myself. I think he'll read it. It is a girl you are carrying."

My Beloved Antonio:

I once lived in a large and beautiful garden. My father was rich, we had several cars, I could travel where I pleased, no one held me — and yet I was a prisoner because I feared what lay beyond my flowers and my poems.

Then my Antonio found me and freed me from the prison which was myself. Your warmth and strength made my fears vanish. I joined at last with the people of this earth and through you I found my happiness.

And now I sit in Paulina's house. There is a telephone with which I might contact all the new friends I made with your help. There are many men — and women too — who would come to my rescue. In all the world I think I have no enemies; I think all who know me would be my allies. I have money and my health is sufficient that I could walk from this place and find my way to anywhere in the world I wished. But once again I am prisoner, but now by the man who first set me free.

Must I tell you I am guiltless of what you accuse me? No man or woman is without fault and it is possible I have been guilty of things which displeased you. But though you might accuse me of being negligent in many ways, you cannot accuse me of being unfaithful to you. I have never been unfaithful to you in any way, my dear. How could I be? Would it be possible for me to desert even for one minute the man who freed me from my first prison?

And see what has happened. My whole life I was a prisoner until you came. Now you have withdrawn your support and what has happened to me again? I can live free only by your grace.

No, my Antonio, I have never been unfaithful with Harry. If for some reason you loathe me and wish to be rid of me, you must find some other excuse. Better you should give no excuse and simply say you despise me.

It is six years since we sat on the terrace for breakfast and you had your arm around me. I was timid and several times I had to try before I could tell you your seed was growing inside me. Can you remember that time, Antonio? And the times that followed? Was your joy feigned?

Again I carry your seed in me, but this time I feel not timidity but fear. I cannot reach to touch your hand — you will not allow it. I can't say the words — you refuse to hear. Each hour your seed grows, but what nourishment shall it have when its mother is a prisoner?

Paulina says it shall be a daughter. Let us call her Antonia. Paulina says one day you will knock on the door of my prison and everything will be as before. I ask one favor of you. If you no longer wish for the happiness we once shared — one favor:

I sleep in the room with the arched windows that look into the garden. I have lived too many years as prisoner and am now too weary. Free me from this world and free this prisoner within me, your daughter Antonia. Free me either with my death or with your love.

Ever faithful — ever,

Helen

Paulina delivered my letter and Dr. Tun came and then Dr. Tun went to speak to Antonio. We waited all night, but Antonio never came. The next day he left Rimara with Alexander, saying they were going on a holiday and would return in several weeks.

I asked Craft to visit me, but he suggested instead that I come to Reggio. He'd been in communication with Tommas (who was beginning to understand what had happened); Antonio had expressly forbidden Craft to come to Consente and ordered Tommas to have him arrested if he should approach the house. Tommas was our accomplice and would have disobeyed Antonio, but Craft didn't wish to come to Consente under the circumstances and thought the short sea voyage would do me good.

Tommas took me over and we met Craft at the Lido, where we had lunch and spent the afternoon trying to decide what should be done. None of us thought there was a chance of Antonio accepting professional help, and Craft and Tommas felt it couldn't be forced on him. "Three times he has called me at Consente. The one time," Tommas smiled, the only smile of the afternoon, "to tell me Craft was forbidden in his house. He did not tell me I was the chief there and must do my duty — not like that. He said it with politeness, without saying the words. I know the Signor is not now the man he was, but a stranger's eyes will see a strong businessman. A smart businessman who

speaks softly and politely but has much command. People would
think we are the crazy ones, not the Signor."

Craft felt that at the moment any legal recourse was untena-
ble; Antonio's influence on the mainland was still considerable.
"And," he added sardonically, "he's the man. You're only the
wife."

For the third time I spoke of the baby, confident that a new
child would do what the lawyers or psychiatrists couldn't, that
Antonio had gone away to think things out. "How can he think
clearly in that place? All the muddle of the scandal — he
needed to get away to sort things out."

But Craft was not convinced. (One moment Craft was the
staunchest ally, the next some arbitrator trying to be impecca-
bly *objective!*) "Helen, it's worse than you think. I hoped you
would never have to learn this. I don't want to tell you — forgive
me if I'm doing the wrong thing." He looked at Tommas for
support, but Tommas only looked pained.

"What could be worse? Could anything be worse?"

"Before he left Antonio asked Tommas about certain laws of
Rimara."

"Laws? Does he want a divorce?"

"Helen, prepare yourself for news far worse than you can
imagine." He took both my hands and looked at me with such
pity I felt whatever the tragedy was, it must be his and not
mine. "Antonio thinks it's Harry's child."

But that was not the worst. Craft had more to tell me, but he
could not speak. And at that moment I didn't have the courage
to learn more.

"Villain!" Paulina shrieked, her cry like lightning and
thunder. "And there is worse than this! What could be worse?
Black, black, black villain!"

"Whatever more there is, Paulina, and if you find out, don't
tell me until I ask you. I can bear to learn no more now."

Dr. Tun came one day when Tommas was there and both
joined in a plea that I should return to America.

"And leave Alexander?"

"Is Alexander here now? Antonio has taken him away and

there was nothing you could do. You must think of yourself and your new child."

"And by leaving acknowledge that what Antonio suspects is true?"

"Antonio doesn't matter anymore. As your doctor I must insist you think only of yourself and your child."

I could postpone it no longer. I had to learn the worst. *"E la cronaca nera?"*

"If a woman gives birth to a child that is not her husband's, the husband has three choices." Dr. Tun expected me to interrupt or say something, but my heart was steeled to hear what was to come.

"After the child is born, the husband may choose to carry it to every house in the village and introduce it as his child, even though everyone knows it is not his. He calls at every house and the man of the house must come to the door — it is a point of honor — but he can refuse to let the husband and child enter. But if he chooses to let them enter, it is a point of honor that the household accepts the child as legitimate and may never slander the child as a bastard.

"There are stories that almost all families admit the child, but the Catinis on the north shore to this day do not speak to the Licatas because — the story goes — several generations back the Licatas scorned a Catini bastard.

"The husband also has the right to send the child to some relative on the mainland or to an orphanage."

"And the third choice?" I felt like a patient who at long last would be told the name of some incurable disease.

"It has happened in Tommas's lifetime. Pietro Farsa threw his illegitimate son into the sea."

"I was only a young man then," Tommas said quickly, as if his voice could erase Dr. Tun's words from the room. "But it did happen and no one stopped him. Off the walls of San Domenico."

"Helen," Dr. Tun cut in, "this of course will not happen, but the point is that Antonio has spoken to Tommas about the tradition. No one is going to let Antonio throw your child into the sea, but Antonio is very sick. Do not look on this as a tragedy, but do not be so foolish to ignore the dangers of Antonio's illness. All may still be well, but you must be sensible."

I asked Tommas if he would stay a while when Dr. Tun left. How like my Antonio is Tommas, I thought — my old Antonio. A simple man, but clever and strong and dependable and faithful. "Tommas, what can happen to me if I stay at Consente?"

He was embarassed, as if he should not acknowledge in my presence that what was happening was a reality. And to me it was not a reality. Each morning I awoke with the hope that Paulina would lead me down the terrace for breakfast with my husband and son. That Alexander would be on Antonio's lap, listening to him singing "Cielo e Mar." And Craft would say something in a very solemn voice and suddenly we would all realize he was making a joke.

"For Sicilian or Italian," Tommas said, "nothing is so sacred as a mother carrying a child. It is unthinkable that anything could happen to you."

"So until Antonia is born I shall be safe here."

"That is the law and the tradition; one cannot think otherwise. But I no longer know your Antonio. Why should Signor Contiorli be so blind?"

"Would you think me foolish if I stayed for a while — till Antonio returns?"

"You do not wish to leave. You wish to stay here near your son. Maybe Antonio will change. Women know things men do not. I do not know that I can give you advice; it is a great responsibility. But if you believe you should stay here, then that is what you should do."

A week later a letter postmarked Rome arrived from Antonio:

My Wife:

I've been a fool. For thirty-eight years I've been living and I still haven't learned. But now I must no longer be a child. I grew up hoping I believed in the right things. My brother Philip had a big heart and he didn't let ugly things bother him. He knew what love was, and loyalty, friendship, kindness, and gentleness were important things to him. He was a big man who could stand up to anybody, but he always got trampled on somehow. So I knew you had to have more than strength and I thought the answer was being smart.

I know Harry isn't really a bad man. But he's just an ordinary man and I thought he was more than that. When I was a boy I opened up my heart to him and I trusted him, but he didn't understand these things. I used to think if the two of us stuck together we could change the world and make it possible for people to be faithful and loyal and kind without being stepped on. That's the kind of thing a child believes.

So the fault was mine for hanging on to such beliefs for too long.

I knew that as your husband I could never be unfaithful and I thought this was virtue, but maybe it's only the way I was brought up, the way I was trained. That's why I say I've been believing in things like a kid for too long.

But the world's different from what I want it to be, from the way I was trained to believe in it. And yet, even though I've got to start looking at the world as a man should, there are some things about me that I'll never change.

I could never marry again. I still love you. I can't see myself living with anyone else. Again I know it's not virtue; just the way I was brought up.

The boy is sick and keeps asking for you. I want to come home next week. I will come home next week with Alexander because I know he's homesick. I must learn to live with the way things are in the world and I know I'll need your help. It won't be easy for me, but if we forgive each other, for the sake of the boy, and for my sake —

I would prefer you had an abortion, but again I've got to realize that probably you were brought up not believing in abortions. I must accept that too. If you don't want an abortion, then we'll have it adopted.

It's going to be hard for me to face life with my new eyes, but I know I must change now, that life has to go on. Please let us be patient with each other. You are still my only love and I know we can find a way.

Faithfully yours,
Antonio

"Do you have in your country the saying 'Protect me from my friends, my enemies I can conquer'?" Paulina raised the letter above her head. "Protect us from the good, the evil we can conquer!"

"Just when I think the worst has come . . ."

"Oh, the villain! But Helen, it is not so bad; he sounds — rational? He sounds milder, not so violent. At least now we can speak to him. He will let you speak to him. This is not so bad now."

As the helicopter settled down I saw Alexander waving. The propeller eased and began to wind round more slowly. We stood back and watched the door open and Antonio lifted Alexander down, followed by a great grayish-white furry dog, a puppy, though it was already enormous.

"Mommy! Mommy!" Alexander cried and I could not stop my own tears as he ran to me and I lifted him in my arms. He was so thin. I lowered him to the ground and knelt before him, holding him tightly as our tears continued. I didn't want anything else to happen. I wanted time to stop just as it was. He looked too pale and his eyes were large and pitiful. Only the bouncing of the puppy —

"Is he your dog?"

"Yes," he said shyly; then enthusiastically, "And do you know what? He's only a puppy! Did you think he was a dog?"

"Yes, I did. He's so big. He's the biggest puppy I've ever seen. Does he have a name?"

"Friendly. I named him Friendly because he's friendly. I named him myself." He smiled but also we were looking at each other in that special way we had and I knew that in some way he knew so much and then I began to cry again, and I knew it was wrong to cry and even Friendly stopped bouncing.

Antonio and Joachim eased the helicopter into the shed. Joachim came back, but Antonio stood there, writing something, logging the flight. Then he was standing at the entrance of the shed, half in shadow, his face strained and the mixture of sun and shadow made it seem distorted.

Paulina took Alexander's hand. "Come, my darling, into the house." Then she whispered to me, "Go to him."

I got up and as if by magic I was coming closer and closer to Antonio.

He spoke my name and then I was crying in his arms. But time did not stop and he suddenly was apart from me and smiling a piteous smile. We walked side by side toward the house — I knew he did not want to touch me.

We were sitting in the library, Antonio and I, watching each other across the expanse of brown rugs. I felt we were in some men's club and were slight acquaintances attempting conversation across too great a space. I had put Alexander to bed and Paulina brought a tray for Antonio, but the food remained untouched. He was drinking a martini when I entered. I asked about the trip.

He placed the empty cocktail glass on the floor. "What have you decided?"

I searched for something to say.

"I thought you wouldn't want an abortion. We'll have it put up for adoption; there'll be no problem about that. There is an orphanage in Nancy which will handle everything."

"Antonio, she is *your* daughter! Why can't you believe me?"

He was calm, almost emotionless, as if negotiating some business transaction. "Helen," he said very slowly, "the world is not the way we would like it to be. I've faced that reality and you must face it too. If I hadn't had Harry here, we might still be in our dream world. I share in some of the blame. I acknowledge it. I must learn to live with it. We have a lot of work to do together if we're going to make anything come out right, but we've got to start with the truth."

*

"There, there, darling, you mustn't cry. Uncle Craft will come back soon."

He shook his head. "Daddy says you're sick and have to stay with Paulina until you get better. Why can't we eat together?"

"We will soon, don't worry. I'll be better soon. You and Friendly must help Daddy and Paulina take care of everything."

"I hate Daddy."

"Alexander, that's not true." I would speak words, lies, but I knew there was more truth in Alexander's look . . . "Daddy has so much to take care of. He has so much work to do. You must try to help him."

He continued looking at me, then called Friendly, and the two headed back for Consente.

For the first week I was allowed to see Alexander for an hour in the morning and an hour after lunch. He was permitted in the fountain garden but couldn't enter Sontern. Antonio himself timed the visits and complained to Paulina when Alexander stayed beyond the hour. (Antonio would speak to me only if I agreed to the adoption.) Then Alexander's visits were stopped and I could hear him crying at times during the day and he cried each night until at last he slept.

"Paulina, I can have one child, but not two. I can leave here and live somewhere with my daughter, or I can *renounce* her, call her bastard — and then I can live with my son and husband. When Alexander was born I lost my father. And if Antonia is to be born, I must give up my son."

By my fourth month Alexander became so ill Antonio had to relent and allow the garden visits, but only once each day. I told Alexander he would have a sister and when she was born we would all live together.

"Is she the disease you have?"

"No, my darling, she is not a disease. She is a fine girl and someday you'll play together on the beach, but you must be kind to her because she'll be so small and you'll be her big brother and look after her."

And I wrote the same to Mother, all the while thankful she was too ill to travel to Rimara. I said she mustn't worry, that all would be well and after the baby was born we would all come to Boston.

Antonio had most of the phones in Consente disconnected, even in the kitchen. Only in his office, the library and main hall did the phones remain. Craft wrote in care of Tommas who passed the letters to Paulina.

In my seventh month Antonio again stopped the daily visits and again Alexander fell ill. He could not eat and cried each night. But now Paulina would no longer be silent. I heard her shrieking at Antonio, and though he fired her, she dared him to have her removed from Consente. One day Tommas appeared and Antonio ordered him to remove Paulina from the house.

"Poor Tommas," Paulina reported. "I told him I regarded him as a brother, but I would be forced to tear his eyes out if he listened to the villain."

After half an hour, despite Antonio's threats, Tommas merely shrugged his shoulders and left. "I tell you," Paulina said hoarsely, "I can't keep it up. I'll lose my voice over that villain. And what power do I have without my voice? But he won't try that again. He knows he's wrong; I know he knows he's wrong. Tomorrow I'll bring Alexander into the garden."

"But if Antonio makes a scene — we mustn't upset Alexander."

"Helen, Alexander is very sick. He won't get better until he sees you again. We don't have anything to lose. Oh, that villain!"

The next morning I heard Paulina's shrieks, but couldn't distinguish her words except when she repeated again and again, "The boy will die!"

Then silence and after a while Paulina carried Alexander into the garden. He was too weak to cry and gave only faint moans. His little heart beat weakly and his chest moved up and down too quickly. I held him in my arms the entire morning. When the sun moved onto us, Paulina brought out an umbrella and held it to shield us.

*

That evening I resolved we would act. Craft believed that as long as I remained in Italy, there was no chance of my taking custody of Alexander. Antonio's influence was still considerable. "He'd go right to the top. We wouldn't stand a chance."

Craft would pick up me and Alexander by helicopter and go to Reggio where a small plane would take us to Athens. There was only a small chance that Antonio would have time to stop us if we flew to Rome, but Craft didn't even want to risk that. From Athens we would fly to London where Harry would put us on a plane to Boston. I would immediately file for a divorce and initially there would be some publicity. "You'll have to tell the press everything and by the time there's a hearing, everything will be in your favor. We mustn't give Antonio any time. And you'll have to make a firm resolution not to accept any offer from him — unless it's the right one and he makes it on paper. I know him and the first thing he'll do will be to promise you anything to delay you from acting — anything to give him time. The only thing we'll settle for short of divorce is a legal document from him acknowledging your innocence and guaranteeing, in the event of any legal separation or divorce in the future, your custody of Alexander and your daughter. And he must legally acknowledge the baby is his. Once you decide to do this, you must be firm and not change your mind or he'll have time to act and there's no telling what he can do, even in Massachusetts. But if you act quickly, I think he'll see he hasn't got a chance."

Paulina, Joachim, Alexander and I would go for a morning picnic to the San Domenico ruins where Craft would take me and Alexander and a few clothes we would conceal in the picnic baskets. Paulina scoffed at the possibility of any reprisals against her and Joachim. Antonio could only order them from Consente at which time they would both join us in Boston.

The only problem was getting Antonio's consent for the picnic, but by the time the appointed day arrived, Paulina had shrieked and hollered so much that he did agree. Craft would come by at eleven.

We were at the ruins at ten-fifteen and spread a large white tablecloth on the grassy slope. Our picnic baskets also contained a red tablecloth which we would put out if for some reason the plan had to be called off. As soon as Craft sighted the red, he was to fly away and wait until we phoned him that evening. If we put out the third cloth, a blue one, he was to leave the area immediately, but return in exactly half an hour. And he was to keep returning each half hour as long as the blue was showing.

Alexander was still frail, but he recovered his appetite and began eating as soon as we spread out the white tablecloth. He was excited returning to the spot where we had spent so many happy hours.

"It is too early. Why don't you eat something?" Paulina admonished, but she could not keep her own eyes from the sky. I held a sandwich in my hand and once or twice put it to my lips, but I could eat nothing. And after a long while it was only ten thirty-five. After another long while it was only ten-forty.

It was ten forty-five when I became aware that Paulina had stopped looking at the sky and was looking at me. "What is it?" I asked.

"Nothing. Please eat something."

But the hand of the clock refused to move and Friendly began a timid growl.

"Joachim, take the jeep and drive up to those rocks." Joachim was as puzzled by this as I was. "Go do as I say. He's watching us. I know he is. I can feel his eyes. He must be behind those rocks. We must not watch the sky anymore. Go up there and begin talking to him. Talk to him about anything." Then she spoke in French so quickly I could understand nothing. Paulina reached for the blue tablecloth as Joachim hurried to the jeep — the only time I saw him move so quickly.

He drove to the ridge and stopped, looking toward the outcropping of rocks. He did see Antonio, but Antonio quickly disappeared.

Craft never came.

The helicopter he hired at Reggio became erratic the moment it lifted from the ground and the pilot refused to take it or let Craft try. Something was wrong with the stabilizing system, though it had been fine the day before when Craft tried it out.

Craft and the pilot and a mechanic worked on it till two before they gave up. A bolt or something had snapped and was ground up in the mechanism and without new parts it was hopeless.

"My first thought," Craft told Paulina when she phoned him that night, "was that somehow he had found out about it and had the copter sabotaged. But I don't think so. I'm sure it was just an accident. Those men couldn't have put up such an act for so long. And if the pilot knew about it in the first place, he wouldn't even have tried to take it up. We'd have been killed."

The huge walls that separate Sontern from Consente run in both directions to the tip of the island, cutting us off from the rest of Rimara. Behind these cloistered walls I took my walks. From the tip of Rimara my only views were of the sea and Sicily. I thought often of our gardens in Englewood. I thought of my twenty-first birthday and smile on your face as you turned to me.

At eight months and a week my labor began.

THE LADY PAULINA

Mourners All

I REARRANGED THE LETTERS on my rack: L-E-V-E-N-T-H. There was an open E on the board and by spelling ELEVENTH I would hit a double-word score in addition to the fifty bonus points for using all seven letters. I smiled to myself. I saw that other word, but it was over a year now since I had put the word HELEN on the board. There was a temptation to do it again, but Antonio was already too upset.

Certainly it is not allowed to use names of people, but when Antonio and I began passing time with the game, I sometimes put down H-E-L-E-N or A-L-E-X and even once J-O-A-C-H-I-M. Antonio would look up at me, again the tears beginning, but without a protest he counted the score and wrote it down. To make him cry was no feat; with only a look I could do it sometimes. Eighteen years and no sign the tears would dry up.

I made the word E-L-E-V-E-N-T-H.

"Ah, very clever!" but he was relieved. My score was so much it was not necessary to continue the game.

"If you will admit that I win, we can stop and go to bed. They will certainly not come tonight now."

"Yes, you're right. I concede. The game is yours." He went to the chart on the wall and placed a mark. "I think that's about 351 to 360. If I'm not careful, you'll overtake me someday."

"That I will certainly do, my friend." I bade him good night and began the walk toward my house.

What sins can eighteen years of tears erase? "You have done more penance than any man has done sin," I used to tell him. "Do as the heavens have done — forget your crimes and forgive yourself."

But would I have him cease to mourn? It is a balmy night and the crickets sing of many things. I pause at Joachim's grave. No, I am reluctant to have Antonio cease his mourning. I confessed that I too was a murderer, but my burden has not eased much.

I try to be very quiet as I tidy up, as if the crickets must not be disturbed. It will be difficult to sleep tonight. I turn on the television softly. The French have walked out of the oil meeting. Solzhenitsyn has been kicked out. But no important person died today, so there is nothing for my diary. Jeffrey will be here tomorrow.

I will go for a walk. Is Jeffrey coming to look for his playmate of eighteen years ago? I walk toward the bergamot grove, but Antonio is there, standing before the marble cherub that marks Alexander's grave. It is the same white marble without flaw as the statue of Helen in front of Rimara's new hospital. I will walk down to the sea.

I rehearse the tale of Alexander's death, but I will not tell it to Jeffrey tomorrow. He will be a young man, as young as Craft was when he first came to Consente. He will be full of life and have no care about the graves on this island. And he is bringing a young girl with him, his wife.

There is a strange cry, but it does not silence the crickets.

*

Alexander cried. During the first days of Helen's labor he cried all the time. I could not comfort him and Antonio stayed with him every night, but Antonio could not comfort him. Antonio could have comforted Helen, and I pleaded with him to visit her, but he refused. We were approaching a flaw in the universe. (There are such things, flaws in the universe, like small clumps of dry flour discovered in a rising dough.) I should have shrieked at Antonio until he was driven to go to Helen, but my voice for scolding was gone and I could only plead.

Dr. Tun could not understand Helen's labor. A night had passed and a full day and still the pains were thirty or forty minutes apart. The second night came and passed and with the new dawn I awoke with a great dread. Helen said the pains were sharper, but they passed quickly and she fell back to sleep. I left her and crossed the garden to Consente, pausing, I pretended, to watch the morning sky, but the howling of Alexander's dog left no doubt.

Alexander was on the floor near his bed, looking peaceful for the first time since his father had gone mad. Antonio was still asleep in a chair near the bed.

Worse than the scene of death was the dread that it was a prelude; it was only the beginning of the flaw. More would follow. All my voices were gone and as Antonio awoke I could only point to the angel at my feet.

Behind me there was a cry and then Anna was beside me, picking up Alexander. I watched Antonio take the body from Anna and press it to his heart; I knew the thought that would soon form in his mind. He would stay as he was for several minutes and then begin to cry. After the tears a thought would find its place in his mind: he would take Alexander's body to Helen: "You have taken my child from me," he would accuse her. "You shall not have yours."

I ran to the phone and Serafina told me Tommasdo was already on his way to Consente with Dr. Tun. I ran to the servants' quarters and shook Salvatore and Rusko till they were awake and sitting on the sides of their beds. My voices were back. "Get dressed and come to my house." They caught up with me as I reached my garden.

"Alexander is dead. You must wait here and see that Signor Contiorli does not come near my house. He must not see the Signora! Joachim will come to help you. Tommas and the doctor are on the way now and they will help you." I raised my hands like claws. "You will go to bed tonight blind if you allow him to pass. Believe it, you will! Do you understand? He must not enter this garden or get near the Signora!"

*"Secret du monde, va devant! Et l'heure vienne où la barre
Nous soit enfin prisé des mains! . . . J'ai vu glisser dans l'huile
sainte les grandes oboles ruisselantes de l'horlogerie céleste."*

I had not overestimated Antonio. Only the presence of the five men and Tommasdo's threats made him give up his madness. But he would not let go of the boy and Dr. Tun had to do an examination in the library where Antonio held his son on his lap.

The speck of imperfection in the universe was coming into bloom, not as an evil flower on the jungle floor destroying what comes near it, but like a star gone berserk, slipping from its orbit, chaotically drawn one moment toward this system, then pulled the next toward another.

What elegy is yours, Alexander?

Certainly I mourned your loss. A sun just coming up, it makes people hope. But then dark clouds that do not go away, and the sun is lost. That was our loss.

But you were not prepared, and that was the horror. Adults learn from each tragedy to bear the next, but you did not know about things like that. You could not understand the terrible things that were happening to you. Fish and flowers and castles and all the time the waves splashing in the sun; you could not be prepared for all the sorrow. More than your loss to us I have sorrow for your suffering, for which you could not be prepared.

Your soul must have flown to the edge of the universe, where only the most delicate light can penetrate the black of nothingness.

That night I held Helen's hand and prayed to Alexander — that he, now dead, should help his sister — but I knew he could not hear me. That is not the way things are. He is only energy while we are the mosaic trying to make God.

"*Et l'étoile apartride chemine dans les hauteurs du Siècle vert,*
Et ma prérogative sur les mers est de rêver pour vous ce rêve
du réel . . . Ils m'ont appelé l'Obscur et j'habitais l'éclat."

I cannot have children of my own, but through the years I have watched fifteen times as children were born. Once in Padua I knew the boy would be born dead, but nothing could be done except hold the woman's hand and wish the child would never come out, but it came out quickly.

But Antonia did not wish to come into the world. I had never known labor to be so long. With each hour Helen grew more pale and exhausted. Near the end Dr. Tun injected into her some painkiller and when some minutes passed she called for Antonio.

"Paulina, Paulina! Why don't you call him? Can't you hear me? Call Antonio!"

Once Antonia knew she must enter the world, she did so quickly.

She was a lovely peach color, not red like most babies, and not too pale. There was a little brown hair, but I knew she would lose that and then have blonde hair or else black hair, but her blue eyes would always be blue.

Time.

All we have now is time, we have nothing but time. Time to waste with the television, time that must be used up. Eighteen years of time and who knows how many more? But when we had need of time, where was it? Now it is our enemy besieging us with its abundance. Then, when it could have been our friend, we did not have it.

Three men and two women arrived at Consente — a man and a woman doctor and a nurse from the orphanage and two lawyers. The papers were all prepared, and more. Antonio had left nothing to chance. Everywhere Craft sought help, Antonio had been there before him, buying whom he needed in the Italian and American governments. The Italians passed the word to the Americans that it was purely a family matter which the Italians could handle.

And more. Antonio told Tommas a squad of security carabinieri from the mainland would come if Antonio should call and say Tommas was failing to uphold the laws of Rimara. Antonio was mad, but he left nothing to chance so he might be rid of his daughter.

He needed Helen's signature, and had believed at the crucial moment he could get it because of her guilt and her fear of losing Alexander. However, there were more sets of papers, neatly typewritten. These papers had no signatures at all, but certainly the vile creatures who invaded Consente would not hesitate to declare Helen incompetent and unfit. Our Antonio had left nothing to chance.

"There's no law of any country that will allow a child to be taken from its mother," Craft repeated each time I called.

"Craft, I do not know about laws, but I know what is happening. He showed me the papers! And those fiends will sign them; I know it!"

"But they can't get away with something like that."

"So you say, Craft, but they are getting away with it."

"But Tommas — "

"Craft, he can do nothing. Antonio is a man of desperation. He blames Helen for Alexander's death. He could kill the baby with his own hands. You tell me he can't do what he is doing, but I am here and I tell you he is doing it. Craft, we do not have *time.*"

"How is Helen?"

"She does not know Alexander is dead. The funeral is to be tomorrow and she does not even know her child is dead."

"Harry's sending some American lawyers from London; they're on their way now. Shall I come over?"

"Harry can send the American President, but it will be too late. It's *time,* Craft. He's given me until seven tomorrow morning for Helen to sign or . . ."

"Or what? What can he do?"

"Craft, he can do anything. He will sign for her. He'll bring

Alexander's body to her. He'll have them say she is insane. He says he'll kill the baby with his own hands! And you ask me what he can do!"

"Okay, I'm coming over tonight."

"*È troppo tard'!* He is a man of great desperation. Those *sbirri* will be here before you and if Tommas doesn't stop you, they will. Craft, Tommas and Dr. Tun are without power. We've been holding off those vultures for three days . . ."

"Paulina? Paulina, are you there?"

"Craft, they are taking Antonia with them tomorrow morning. Antonio says it will be. Or else Antonia will be dead. Craft, you say we can get her back. That we can go to the courts and someday get her back. That it is only a matter of time. Shall we let them take her?"

"I'm afraid you're going to have to tell Helen everything and let her decide. I know it's a terrible thing to do, but it can be only her decision. And tell her it is definite we will get the baby back. There's no court in the world that would rule against her, I don't care how much money Antonio has or how clever he is. Right now all he wants is revenge for Alexander, but once Helen leaves Rimara, he won't put up a fight."

"And I must tell her Alexander is dead, and then tell her to sign a paper saying it is all right to take her baby away?"

He was silent a long time. "Paulina, we failed once before. We won't fail this time. Do you know what I mean?"

"I think it is the only way."

"Look, it may be too late for me to get a big-enough boat. Can you and Joachim bring them to Pellaro?"

"But what if he discovers we're gone and follows us?"

"Paulina, I think once Helen and the baby are off the island, he won't care. I think all he wants is revenge now for Alexander because he won't admit that he himself is responsible. How about Taormina? Can you see Etna tonight? It's closer and Joachim won't have any trouble heading straight for Etna. Antonio would never expect that. I can still get a ferry tonight to Messina and drive down to meet you. Look, I'll call the Grand and book us rooms in my name. And I'll leave word that Harry's lawyers are to join us down there when they get in. Paulina! Can he be listening on another phone?"

"No, I am watching the other doors and halls. He's in the Blue Parlor with those vultures. Craft?"

"Yes?"

"Don't fail us this time. Come to Taormina."

I saw Etna as I crossed the garden to my house. There were a few stars and no moon; it was perfect — clear enough for us to see Etna and cross straight to Taormina, but dark enough for us to leave without being seen. I prayed the night would stay as it was. I paused a few minutes in the garden, not far from where Joachim would soon be buried. Why did I pause? Certainly I did not understand then, but I was saving my life.

"Don't worry, Paulina, it's just to make her sleep well tonight," Dr. Tun said as I entered Helen's room. If I had not paused in the garden, I could have stopped him from giving Helen the injection. He frowned at my look, as if I did not trust him. "Anyway, I don't want her to nurse anymore. She's too weak. You'll have to feed Antonia from the bottle from now on."

Helen looked at me weakly, as if she had not heard Dr. Tun's words.

"And how long will she sleep?"

"Paulina, she'll be all right. She'll probably sleep until morning. There's nothing to worry about."

"Nothing to worry about?"

He led me to the hall and tried to assure me that they could not take the child. "Over my dead body." But Dr. Tun knew there was nothing he or Tommas could do tomorrow. The *sbirri* were on their way and all Tommas would be able to do would be to fight a little before his power was taken from him. It was senseless, but Tommas would do it because he was a good man, even though it would mean prison and his family without a father. Five, ten years in prison for a one-minute fight, but Tommas would do it because he was a good man.

Dr. Tun would not leave and at last I told him I had a plan but

would not tell him what it was. "There is no need for you to
know. It will not help us and it will not help you. But you must
leave now. Give me whatever medicine we will need, as if you
wouldn't be coming for several days — but come tomorrow, just
as you planned."

Joachim had much difficulty starting the boat and I wished it
were not such a still night. The noise was fierce and must be
heard up at the house. I saw lights coming on, but then the boat
was running well. Joachim had driven it several times before,
but he did not like driving boats. I saw another light go on, in
the main hallway. The boat was out of the shed and I urged
Joachim to hurry. Then the boat headed west, along the south
shore of the island. From the house it might be seen, but it was
the same route as if the boat were to go round the western tip
and up north to Pellaro on the mainland. But Joachim was to
keep his lights off for a while from the western tip and then
continue due west to Taormina. I hurried up the long flight of
steps toward Consente.

I crossed the long narrow terrace after the second flight and
was to start the next stairs when I saw a figure down at the
other end of the terrace. I stopped, with one foot on the first
step, and slowly turned. Every minute I could keep him from
moving would mean one minute more the boat had gone down
the coast.

"Why do you stay behind?" His voice was even, almost
sarcastic.

"Oh, you know me, Antonio. It was a temptation I could not
resist, to meet the devil face to face."

He paused for a long time. I could not tell what he was
thinking. Then at last he asked, "I am the devil?"

"Who else could you be?"

"I suppose they're taking the bastard to its father."

I began to walk down the terrace toward him. "No, that precious baby is being taken away from her father because he is a
coward and a villain. Oh, if only Antonia had a man for a father!"

"Antonia? The bastard will really be called Antonia?"

I could see his face clearly; we were only a dozen feet apart. "Antonio, may I ask a question?"

"Paulina, as many as you like."

"No, just one, but will you think before you answer and speak what is really in your heart?"

"As far as I know I always speak what's in my heart."

"Do you really believe the child is not yours?"

"Paulina look at me. What do I have left in the world? Alexander is dead. Craft has left to go with the man who was once my friend. I have no more Helen. Even you and Joachim are no longer my friends. What do I have left? Money. Don't you think I would jump at any possibility that the child is mine? Don't you think I know I lost everything because of that child and if there were the slightest hope it was mine — Can I be that much a fool?

"Do I have one friend left on this island? Any friend anywhere? And what about the name Antonio Contiorli? I'm a fool because I let my best friend get my wife pregnant and I'm a villain, as you call me, because I persecute an innocent wife and drive away my friends and . . ."

"And you've murdered your son."

He was past me and walking up the terrace.

"Antonio! She is innocent! There's still time."

And then it was he poised with his one foot on the first step. "No, you lousy bitch. There is no more time for anything. You've done all there is to do. Or do you still have more surprises? I want you off this island tomorrow morning. You stay for the funeral, but then you leave."

That was why he was not surprised at my staying behind. He did not suspect Helen was still in my house. He had not seen just Joachim and me quietly make our way to the boathouse with Antonia.

I did not like the ultimatum that I must leave the next morning. Again time would be our enemy.

But he had seemed mild. Craft was perhaps right, that he wanted only revenge, and once the symbol of his imagined betrayal was off the island — but I could not trust him. His revenge was only to pretend he was not the murderer of his son.

He wanted Helen separated from "her" child because he had lost "his." I could not trust him.

But at least Antonia was now beyond his reach.

Helen slept late and awoke looking better. She even smiled, but then began looking for Antonia.

"It is not what you think. Antonia is taken away, but not by the villain. She is with Joachim and Craft in Taormina."

"Is that the truth, Paulina?"

"It is. The truth is all we have time for now. But everything will soon be well. All we need do is go ourselves. The villain doesn't know you're here. He thinks you went with Joachim and the baby last night. Dr. Tun gave you something to make you sleep and we could not carry you down to the boat. It was too much of a risk."

"But how shall we get away? He won't let Alexander go."

"Helen, he has let Alexander go."

But she had known, suspected, that Alexander was dead. I was frightened by her calmness. "I am accustomed to childbirth" was all she said.

I put Helen in the back bedroom and when Dr. Tun appeared — expecting to find no one, he was not even carrying his bag — he was surprised when I answered his faint knock on the door. "There is someone who is sick and needs help, but he lives at the main house. I will be leaving soon, after the funeral."

The security *carabiniere* did not come. It was a bluff, Antonio told me later, though he could have had them if he wished. The vultures from the orphanage did not stay for the funeral. And they did not seem upset that they had not done their mischief. They were being well paid, no matter what happened.

My heart was not with the dead but with the living and I could not cry as Alexander was laid in the bergamot grove. Tommas heard the news that Joachim had taken Helen and the child away and he offered to help me leave.

"Yes, I shall need your help. Come at two this afternoon."

"Shall I hire a boat for Regg'?"

Perhaps we could. I would call Craft, tell him it seemed Antonio had given up his revenge; he could go back with

Joachim and the child and meet us at Reggio. "Yes, please. He
wants me to leave immediately, but I will not be rushed."

We were standing on the main terrace and Antonio had just
passed a moment before and went into the house. Now we heard
the phone ring. "Perhaps that is Craft. I must speak to him," I
said quietly to Tommas.

Antonio was at the phone and when he saw me he held up his
finger as if I should wait. "Is Tommas still here?"

"He's outside."

"Would you ask him to çome in please."

I was prepared to give a sarcastic reply, but Antonio seemed
strange, extraordinarily calm, but strange. Just the way Helen
was when she heard about Alexander.

"Tommas I've just had a call from the inspector at Ali. He has
asked me to come and I thought you should come too; if you will.
We'll take the helicopter."

"Ali!" I screamed. Ali was just up the Sicilian coast from
Taormina. So Antonio had not given up his revenge! He had
known what was happening all along. "So it *was* the devil I met
last night! And all the while you had your lackeys lying in wait!
That's why you didn't care. *Diabòlique!*" I went toward him, I
might have torn out his eyes!

But he regarded me without emotion or fear. "Paulina, maybe
you should come with us. We have to identify Joachim's body.
They haven't found Helen or the baby yet. The boat was
smashed on the rocks."

Joachim was buried in his garden. Everyone on the island
came to file past his grave and place a flower or olive branch. It
was cloudy and there was a wet wind. "A day for a grave," I
thought. Joachim and I had always lived in the sun; it was right
the sun should not appear.

The long procession left the garden and was winding slowly
down the hill. Tommas and Dr. Tun asked to be the ones to
cover the grave. Very carefully they were placing dirt over the
plain cedar coffin which Ilario had built. Then Antonio came
into the garden carrying large orange daisies — Helen had

brought them from America and Joachim had liked them. They are like the sun, he had said. The grave was half filled as Antonio walked up to it, bent over, and placed the flowers. Tommas and Dr. Tun continued to fill the grave, trying not to cover the daisies, but at last the dirt ran down from the sides, gradually covering the flowers. And then the flowers were covered and then all the dirt had been replaced, mounded high and looking like a swollen wound in the earth.

I did not mourn my Joachim. I mourned, but perhaps only for the rest of us. All the living, so weak and so ignorant. We shift from one foot to the other, our martini glasses held like chalices by priests and priestesses who fear belief as much as doubt.

The night came without a sunset sky. Antonio reappeared and asked if he could get me anything or do something for me.
"Can you raise the dead?"
I could not tell in the darkness if he smiled. And then he said, "Now I must visit my dead."
I thought I was having a vision and seeing myself as a young girl come into the moonless garden, but it was Helen, wearing my shawl and carrying a flower. She placed it on the mound of earth that somehow seemed sacred, though only our minds in weakness make such things sacred. Joachim was not there. That which had been his body was there, that which belonged to the earth and had returned to it. But that wasn't Joachim.
I did not think as she led me into the house. I rose when she took my hand and I followed her as she guided me toward the door through which my Joachim would never again enter, his body filling it and moving slowly like some peaceful god.
"Mourners all."

It is a human law that someone will fill the vacant role, no matter how inappropriate it may be.
The next day I found myself at the window, looking west toward Sicily. Helen was still very weak, but she became busy, clearing up the clothes we had packed, preparing breakfast and lunch for me, and urging me to eat.

I resented the bright sun, but after it set I saw my selfishness. We were all mourners, but I acted as if I were the only one. And there was Helen, solicitous to my every move, sitting or standing in wait, and her newborn daughter buried in the sea.

The next morning I took hold of my grief and dismissed it. I made Helen breakfast and lunch and sat with her, and only then did she begin her mourning. Must it always be that only one is a mourner and the other a comforter? If I had kept my grief, Helen would have stood by me as comforter.

Anna came several times to my door when Craft or Harry phoned. They both hoped I would understand their not coming to the island for Joachim's funeral. "It was best you didn't," I said to Craft.

The search extended in both directions along the coast from Riposto to Messina and on the Italian mainland from Melito to Reggio. "If they're anywhere here, we'll find them."

"Craft, Helen is alive."

"I hope so, Paulina. The fact that we didn't find either body gives me hope. It might be possible to miss the baby, but not both of them. If they're anywhere here we'll find them. Is there anything I can do for you? Do you want to leave Rimara?"

"Leave Rimara? No, Craft, I'm fine."

"Is it because of Joachim? You don't have to stay there. Harry and I will take care of you. I get sick thinking of you over there with that madman."

"Antonio? He is not to blame."

"Not to blame?"

"Yes, he is to blame, but he is only a man. I have no hatred for him."

"I'll come over and get you. Just say the word."

"No, Craft. I don't want to leave here. Not now. Give our regards to Harry."

He was silent.

"The regards of the living and the dead. How long do you think they will continue the search?"

"Everyone's joined in. We'll search until we find them. It's impossible both could disappear without a trace. We'll search until we find them — or at least until there's some evidence . . ."

"I must go now Craft. Call anytime you wish. Anna will fetch me. Antonio will not interfere."

It was a week later when the thought occurred to both of us at almost the same time, that perhaps, truly, Antonia might still be alive.

"That is why we must not let them give up the search."

"But Paulina, how long can we live with such hope?"

"Helen, they must either find her or else we must still hope. There is not much left for any of us."

"And if they find her, and she's dead?"

"Then we can no longer hope."

I saw Antonio at least once each day, but sometimes several times.

"Good morning Paulina."

"Good morning Antonio."

We spoke as two former enemies might, or two soldiers from opposing sides after both armies are destroyed and only these two remain to wander the battlefield, greeting each other with neither hatred nor enthusiasm, both overwhelmed by the scene of death over which they walk.

On most days Antonio would give me a brief report. "They're searching Rimara now, but only because there's almost nowhere else to search." One day he asked me to dine with him, but I only shook my head.

"I spoke to Helen Corey's doctor," he then said, as if he had had no hope of my accepting his invitation. "She's become worse and can't speak. They think she probably can't understand anything anymore. It's probably just as well. It was her third stroke."

I told Helen of each report from Craft or Antonio, but after a time she seemed not to hear. Why should she want to hear over and over bad news? By July she seemed in a trance, eating too little and spending the day at the window. "Your mother is dying, Helen," I said one day in desperation, fearing she was becoming too remote.

"Does she know what has happened here?"

"No, she does not. She had another stroke. The doctor believes she can no longer understand anything that happens around her."

"Then I could not help her, could I."

"I think you should go to America. I will take you there. You could show me the garden you made when you were a girl."

She turned to me. Her speech was distinct, her manner very ordinary. "My father is dead. Alexander is dead. My mother is dying, but she is already dead — you said she could not speak or understand. I am alive, but that seems just an accident, almost a technicality. And my Antonia? Her grandmother lives, but only barely. Her mother lives, but no one knows it. Is Antonia also in some limbo? We're all three dead. Three generations of women, barely alive."

"You should leave here Helen. Things will seem much different once you're out of here."

She smiled. "I know that. I know that things will seem different if I leave here." She smiled again and turned to the window.

"You can't sit here each day staring at the sea."

"No, I can't. But by your leave I can. Will you give me permission to stay here? If I am a trouble to you I will leave and find somewhere else to look at the sea, but I will look at the sea. Each day, as you say. But only by your leave. Do I have your permission Paulina?"

Antonio let Rushko go, but kept Salvatore to look after the gardens and house. "We must let Jozef go. His talent's being wasted here. I can find him a good job somewhere."

"Will you keep Anna?"

"Yes. She says she can get help again from the village if she'd ever need it. I think Anna and Salvatore should be able to keep things in order. But you, Paulina — what is to become of you?"

"What is to become of you, Antonio?"

It had become our manner to speak to each other only when both of us were standing — perhaps it was a formality of our truce. He was about to sit down, then stopped himself. "I don't know, Paulina. It seems there is no place else for me, except here. I'll continue working as long as I can." I knew he worked a full morning and part of each afternoon in his office. "But you — will you stay here? There are many places you could go. Would you like to go back to France? We could find you a small house in the country, or a nice apartment in Paris."

"No, I'll stay here — if that is suitable. I will help Anna run the house. Do you object?"

"No, Paulina, of course not. It only seemed . . ."

And there was nothing more we could find to say to each other.

The sirroco began blowing each morning at sunrise and I expected some change. Helen was completely withdrawn, but she was also at peace. She prepared breakfast and lunch for me (for both of us, though she continued to eat very little). I cooked dinner and only after weeks of nagging did she eat most of what I'd put on her plate without constant prompting.

Craft told me the search had been called off, though Antonio never mentioned it. I told Helen, but she did not react. Perhaps I should have given another speech about burying herself, but my heart would not have been in it. For the moment Helen seemed content in her strange way.

The sirroco did not bring change. The winds only made me realize how fixed our lives had become in so few months. We all carried out our simple daily routines without enthusiasm, as if we had been living that way for years.

Craft had become Harry's financial manager and he now phoned me only once a week to ask after me and try to persuade me to join him in Harry's villa. Harry was away most of the year, working on his films, but there was the boy Jeffrey during the holidays and also frequent guests whom Craft said were "quite interesting."

I saw Antonio usually once each day on the main terrace, but we spoke little; there was little to say.

Occasionally Tommas would come to my door and we would
sit in the garden. He was solicitous and always brought some
guiggiulena or *fellette* from Serafina. He spoke of events in the
village and asked me to come for dinner, but I refused. Tommas
and Antonio never spoke to each other.

Helen had begun sewing and when she asked me to obtain
materials it was Serafina who brought them to my door. I was
tempted for once to ask her in. Helen always went to her room if
there was a knock on the door, but she never closed the door of
her room. I was tempted to have Serafina discover Helen. But I
asked myself what could come of such an encounter — what
would happen if the world should discover Helen was alive? As I
could not find any answers to these questions, I had coffee with
Serafina in the garden. I had meddled too much in too many
things.

It was the Eve of Christmas when Antonio realized the truth.
I found him face down on the sand, his arms stretched out and
his legs twisted. There was sand in his eyes and all around his
lips. His breathing was convulsive, but he did not speak until I
had helped him up to the house and took him to his bedroom.

"I killed her! I killed them all. I killed Alexander. I killed
Joachim. I killed Helen. I killed my daughter."

Perhaps it was near midnight when he was calm enough. He
wanted to talk and I asked him how he at last realized the truth.

"Maybe I knew from the start. I think I did know, you know.
Somehow I did, though I couldn't recognize it. I was a kid
throwing up sand walls all around me to keep out the sea.
Tonight the sea broke through.

"I was crazy, I know, but that doesn't — it doesn't help to
know that now. Do you know one night I even thought I saw
Helen and Harry making love on the beach — that's how crazy I
was. I know now it wasn't true.

"In all my life I've never wanted to go back to anything, to do
anything over. Now it seems so simple if I could just be back in
last year, back to when Harry and Jeffrey just arrived. Now I
would know what to do. Everything could be so simple again if
only we could all go back. I've never asked for a miracle or

anything in my life. Why, just this once, can't I wake up and find it was a dream and that we're waiting for Harry to arrive tomorrow? And Craft's getting the schedules, and Helen's preparing . . ."

For almost a week I kept this knowledge to myself and at last, in a weak moment, because I didn't know what else to do, I told Helen. I told her that across the garden her husband had finally realized the truth. "Every time I look at him he begins crying."

She spoke his name as if he'd been someone she had met casually years ago and had not pronounced his name since then — as if she were seeing if she could still pronounce it properly.

"Maybe I was wrong to tell you. Forgive me."

"It doesn't matter that you told me," she said. "I mean, it wasn't wrong for you to tell me. But it doesn't matter." Then she went back to her notebooks. Shortly before Christmas she asked me to find her some papers. In Craft's old study there were boxes of notebooks. I felt foolish as I placed before her six large notebooks; certainly she had wished only a few sheets to write a letter or some notes. But a bright smile came to her face and she gave an enthusiastic thank you.

At first I doubted Antonio: about the truth coming to him so gradually until its certainty overwhelmed him. But by the time of spring I believed him very well; the truth had come to me in just that way. More than a season it had required for the meaning of his words to become clear — that in his craziness he had a vision of Helen and Harry making love on the beach. (We will not see what we wish not to see; we won't understand that which we think can destroy us.)

I joined Antonio for dinner twice each week, on Tuesdays and Saturdays. He was grateful for my company, not because I was a distraction, but because I was not. I did not force him to act cheerful — sometimes we spent the dinner hour in silence. I allowed him to bring out his regret and despair and show them. At times we made jokes, but they were always bitter, with no humor and no relief.

"I fear only one thing now," he said one evening. "That I will

begin to feel at home with my despair and hatred of myself. I
think I'm beginning to enjoy my sorrow. Is it because we must
attach ourselves to something and if we have nothing else, we'll
make a friend even of our misery?"

He believed there could be no forgiveness and only an
unending diet of self-torture was suitable. And when he became
numb at last even to his own torture, he would seek new ways to
keep the pain fresh. But that spring evening I would not help
him with his penance.

"Antonio, I was with Harry on the beach."

He had for so long accepted the scene as only his imagination,
he seemed to understand not even the reference.

"In these novels we read," I went on, "the people are unfaithful many times and still they can go back to their ordinary
worlds. Maybe they do not even repent, and yet nothing comes
to an end. Do you believe the novels? You see, my friend, it was
only two kisses I gave Harry. Did you see us kissing? And I
kissed him perhaps only because that night I should have
refused the last glass of champagne but I did not. You see, one
extra glass of champagne and two kisses and now how many are
dead? How many are dead?"

I think he did not wish to hear me further.

"I have never — what is that wonderful expression? — *known*
any man except Joachim. Never. But that night I flirted with
your friend. He held my hand. I kissed him twice. I put my arms
around him. I should have done more, don't you think? I should
have tempted him to bed and spent a month with him. Why
not? The punishment could not be worse. For my two kisses my
Joachim is in his grave. A month in bed with Harry would not
have brought worse punishment, *n'est-ce pas?*

" — You cannot believe it? Is what horrifies you that I am an
old woman? I am ten years older than Harry. Is that too much?

" — I had an old husband . . . In years, yes, but until he died he
loved me as when we were first married.

" — And I liked Craft too. Does that shock you? In the
mornings he would swim naked in the cove and I enjoyed
watching him."

He came round the table and put his hands on my shoulders.

"No more, Paulina. We have enough misery for many years."

In the twilight when Craft played his recording of the Pachelbel Canon perhaps my eyes would become wet *(pleurer de grâce, non de peine)*, but until the night of my confession I could not remember ever crying in regret.

The relief from my confession was good, but I could not confess to Helen (though years later I did tell Craft), not because I lacked the courage, but because I thought it would be cowardly. Helen was lost in her notebooks — an epic poem I would be allowed to read when it was completed. She had lived through agonies and now found a world of peace for herself. To bring back all the memories — to what purpose? We must be careful with confessions; they relieve us of guilt but sometimes at the expense of pain to others.

Helen had made her way into a new world, each day filling the pages of the notebooks with her poem and soon the six big notebooks were not enough. I brought her six more and assured her the supply would last for years. Also, and this caused me to cry at first, she began tidying and trimming the plants and flowers along the path to the sea. Then each day it became her routine to spend some hours in the midmorning and again at evening, bringing back to shape even Joachim's trees. (Now I think there is not one weed on all the hectares.) And sometimes I still cry when rows of flowers come to bloom, but it is a pleasant cry because I know how Joachim would be pleased to see his work carried on. That is very important.

The blooms are all on our side of the wall, and though no one sees them but Helen and me, that does not matter; they thrive.

Then Helen even began taking the brick from the crumbling walls around the original terraces and began making patios and these are delightful places to sit and watch the sea.

I learned of the death of Helen's mother only months afterward. The family fortune passed to Helen and then to Antonio. He accepted the money, all of which he would use for charities, and his first plan was a hospital and a new school for the island.

They would be dedicated in honor of Helen and he sought a sculptor to do a large statue of Helen for the front of the hospital.

He asked me to be present when Tommas and Dr. Tun came to Consente at his request. He needed their advice on what was best for the island and began by asking both men to put aside their contempt for him and think only of the welfare of Rimara and the memory of Helen. His speech was short, but neither Tommas nor Dr. Tun was unmoved, though each acted businesslike when they promised their full cooperation.

"I could almost forgive him," Tommas said to me later. "Almost."

Antonio bought an enormous television aerial for the island and from it ran cables to the hospital, school, village hall, Consente, and Sontern. Helen and I were sitting at lunch when the man came to install the set in Sontern. He was from the mainland and probably would not know about Helen, but afterward he might make some comment about the *two* women in the cliff house . . . especially the beautiful one (he kept watching her). All the dresses she made for herself were plain, and her hair was pulled back simply, but these peasant touches only set off her beauty. The sun and sea mist and her hard work in the garden made her skin fresh and glowing, and her posture was still that of a young woman. She was more radiant than when she first came to Consente as a bride.

She was so absorbed in her poem it seemed she saw no significance in the stranger's visit, though he was the first person to enter Sontern in years. I sat eating my lunch, trying to be ordinary. I wondered what would happen. Whatever would happen would happen without my interference. If it was to mean the world should discover Helen, I would do nothing to prevent that, though my true feeling was that it would be cruel to have anything disrupt the world of work and contentment Helen had created for herself. The man pulled a cable through the window and attached it to the television set. Then he was gone.

Helen's poem at first was about an imaginary city, but later she abandoned those notebooks and began writing another poem of three people who played tennis each day! Beyond that she would tell me only the title, "What To Do." "But then again I might call it 'Engaging Lies,' " she said. I looked at the stack of notebooks filled with only one poem and thought what nice madness it must be to be a poet.

After the television arrived, I too began using Craft's notebooks. I recorded interesting things from the news and things I remembered from my childhood, but mostly I put down the names of those who died whom I had admired.

In 1957 Humphrey Bogart died and the next day Toscanini. Then Josef Hoffman, Sibelius, Ronald Colman, Nagy, (Americans cross *under* the North Pole), Tyrone Power, DeMille, Maxwell Anderson, Ethel Barrymore, Camus, Pasternak, (the North Pole moved thirty feet toward Greenland), Bjoerling, Emily Post, Hemingway, Eleanor Roosevelt, Flagstad, Marilyn Monroe, Bruno Walter (my favorite), Faulkner, Frost, Huxley, Braque, Hindemith, Pope John, the American President, Nehru, MacArthur, King Paul, Harpo Marx, Edith Sitwell (Helen loves her), Eddie Cantor, Cole Porter, Monteux, Churchill, Baruch, Buber, T.S. Eliot, Le Corbusier, Edward Murrow (a man of great courage), Schweitzer, Francis X. Bushman, Walt Disney, Buster Keaton, Giacometti, Adenauer, Sandburg, Vivien Leigh, Oppenheimer, Maurois, Kodály, Spencer Tracy, (the tower of Pisa stayed still during 1967), Robert Kennedy, Martin Luther King, Munch, Tallulah, Duchamp, Helen Keller, Thomas Merton, Ramon Novarro, Steinbeck, Eisenhower, Jaspers, Judy Garland, Gropius, Robert Taylor, Miës van der Rohe, Jan Palach, (in July men walk on the moon), de Gaulle, Gypsy Rose Lee, Russell, Remarque, Mauriac, Reik, Barbirolli, John Dos Passos, (the Italians pass the divorce bill), Stravinsky, Fernandel, Pier Angeli, Bobby Jones, Coco, Chevalier (it is not possible), Nijinsky's sister, Grofé, Jean Casadesus, Ezra Pound, George Sanders, Jackie Robinson, Eric Korosy, Harry Truman . . .

Helen said it was morbid to keep a "diary of death." "My lady, to me these were great people. We know the times by the people that lived then. Diary of Death indeed! It is a book of great lives. Can you expect me to record their names as they are born? Perhaps my lady is afraid I will use all her precious notebooks."

"Speaking of which, how is the supply?"

"Oh, we can last a few more years. Will your poem ever end?"

"Yes, Paulina, you will not believe it, but it will. It's coming along rather nicely at the moment."

Craft had not phoned since Christmas, when he asked if the notebooks had arrived. We had run out of his supply years before and the only presents I would let him send were more notebooks.

"You're writing a history of the world?"

"In poetry, of course."

But then he phoned again yesterday, very excited and asking if Jeffrey could visit me and Antonio. He'll be bringing his young wife with him."

"What is her name?"

"Sandra."

"What color eyes does she have?"

". . . Brown, I think. Yes, they're very dark. Why?"

"Why? Brown eyes are not good, Craft. Only blue eyes or grey eyes will do. What do you say in your country — think about that?"

"Now they say 'Check it out.' No, Paulina, she's not Antonia."

"Craft, would you think me a madwoman if I told you Helen is alive and I have a feeling that Antonia is also?"

"Well, let's just say I would think you — poetic? Are you really writing poems?"

"No, but Craft I think sometimes it is possible for a person to live twenty years in the same room with another person and neither will know the other is alive."

"Well, I guess that's true in a poetic way."

"And poetry is not true? Do you think Joachim is dead? Someday, Craft, perhaps you will come to Sontern and see a great garden with many little patios, *les petits patios,* and paths

to the sea and always flowers blooming. Then I will ask you if
Joachim is dead. Don't think so quickly what your answer will
be. Who is Antonia? She is the child of Helen and Antonio. We
fix in our minds what the world should be, but love ignores such
conditions."

"You should write that all down."

"Ah yes Craft, you think me a crazy old woman."

"By the way, crazy old woman, there may be another surprise
for you, but I can't promise."

"And maybe someday Craft there may be a surprise for you.
And that I can promise."

The birds begin. A new day. I have not told Helen that Jeffrey
is coming.

Rêve, ô rêve tout haut ton rêve d'homme et d'immortel! . . .
"Ah! qu'un Scribe s'approche et je lui dicterai . . ."

And that there was in us such a desire to live at that height —
is it not that, O gods! which qualified us?

"Qu'un Scribe s'approche et je lui dicterai."

Book Two

ANTONIA

JEFFREY'S STORY:

Circumlegentes Devenimus Rhegium

THE STORM'S OVER and I guess everyone's exhausted. The earth's quiet, not chirpy.

It looked calm in the usual way from up at the house, but now down here at its edge, I find the sea just tired, not really calm, sort of like the morning after the proverbial.

I'm in front of Veringetorix's cottage as he emerges. "What wisdom?" I ask perfunctorily.

He looks past me, the lids of his eyes halfway down. He sighs and makes the effort. "I'm older than you, Jeffrey, and remember, I will always be." Without a hint that I should join him, he starts down the beach.

In terms of damage it wasn't a bad storm: just a few trees down and the odd limbs scattered about; shutters askew. Things seemed worse during the storm, probably because of its duration

— almost two complete days of winds and rains pounding the coast without a letup.

The best thing to do would be to haul myself back up the hill to the house, get undressed, get into bed and pull the covers over my head and wait for tomorrow. This is just what I do. The exhaustion of the earth is saddening, but tomorrow there'll be a strong sun and everything'll be chirpy again.

"Jeff, your friend's here," Dad says, trying to keep his voice even. As I predicted, it is a chirpy morning. Even Dad, despite his voice, seems somewhat chirpy. "How are you feeling?" he asks, bringing his body into my room to join his head.

Well, still a bit sleepy, but I'll be fine soon. Meantime, however, I must answer my father's question. His question isn't perfunctory; he's trying to be nice to me.

"Oh, I'm feeling pretty good, Pa," I say, making the effort to acknowledge his attention. We had a fight during the storm and now we're both anxious to make up.

I'd been on the couch in the bay window of the parlor just as the storm was starting. The Moody Blues were doing "Melancholy Man." The wind had picked up and was blowing the first traces of the rain into the room. I was enjoying it. I needed the storm.

He came in, gave a funny sort of smile and began closing the shutters. I was quite comfortable as I was and didn't think a little rain would hurt things. But when he'd closed three shutters I forced myself to get up and help him close the rest. What choice did I have? Can you imagine me lying there, stretched out on the couch with my feet up and smoking a cigarette and drinking cocoa and my father going round the room with a grim smile, closing shutters?

But as soon as I'd helped him — after all, I didn't want the fucking shutters closed — then I could relax, maybe act a little sullen. By the time the first thunder thundered, we were into it, following the classic pattern.

"Jeff, it isn't easy being a father. Don't you think it would be a hell of a lot easier for me if I were twenty-one or if you were my age and we could just be pals? But that's a condition contrary to fact and — "

"Twenty-four, Dad, not twenty-one. Must be one of your bastards, which is to say illegitimate children somewhere you're confusing me with." A cheap shot. He doesn't have any illegitimate children.

He went and sat on the sofa on the other side of the room. Unfair. It was okay for me to be stretched out on my couch as long as he was pacing back and forth, but once he sat down on the edge of the other sofa facing me, I couldn't remain in my comfortable position. It would have been disrespectful. Isn't that funny?

I got up and sat facing him. His arms were on his knees and his hands were folded in front of him. He was slumped over, but then he raised his head and looked at me. "Go ahead, Jeff." Completely defenseless. He might as well have said, "Hit me again my son." A good strategist.

After half an hour of our traditional, predictable sparring, I came up with something new: "Why don't you marry her?"

"Because I don't love her," he said immediately, placing great stress on the last word. "Her" was a constant parade of them, always new ones and always pottering about the kitchen the morning after. Their nationalities and hair colors varied, but there were two things they all had in common: gross minds and foxy bodies — real good lays in the classic tradition. "Jeff," he suddenly was stern but not unkind, "you're a young man now, not a baby."

"Yes pal, I understand. But you don't think you'll marry them — one of them?"

"Look, I know that growing up without a mother —"

"Dad, at this point I don't think I'm really looking for a mother. Theophilia provides most of the benefits of a pampering mother with none of the disadvantages, meaning she doesn't nag." (Theophilia's our cook.)

"You're losing me. So what's this all about?"

"Just a new ploy I guess. Look, Pa, it comes down to what it usually comes down to. I'm messed up and unhappy and so I take it out on you because you've got it made. Once I get myself straightened out everything'll be fine. That's the truth."

And it was and for a couple minutes we talked calmly until he started trying to help me as usual by taking things "step by step." That's when we really got into it.

Dad's behind me as I go downstairs. Veringetorix is in the main hall, looking out the open French doors, his back to us. "Thank you, Mr. Rambulcek," he says without turning.

It's not only that he speaks with his back to us — that alone couldn't account for it. It's his voice. Even without looking behind me I can sense Dad's hurt and anger. And yet, to a stranger, Ring's voice would seem perfectly natural. It's pleasant, cheerful, but somehow he manages an almost imperceptible tone of contempt.

After we're out of the house I ask him, perhaps for the tenth time, why he takes pleasure in irritating my father.

"*Do* I take pleasure in it?"

"Why else would you do it? You know it hurts him."

"Thanking him for waking you up? That irritates him?"

There's no talking to him. You can't ever pin him down.

"Got a surprise for you Jeffs."

"I'm broke." I know he'll be after more money.

Ring is remarkable. He assumes a posture of utter dejection. Of course only a fool wouldn't know he's faking it, but he does it with style. Then he begins talking of something else, the self-pity in his voice is pretty bad stuff. Sooner or later I'll give in of course, but I have to make it tough for him. A pretense of pride I guess.

He steals from me and from any one with anything worth stealing. In town he's called Veringetorix *il bandito*. And my God, does he lie! I really don't mind his never paying back what I "lend" him; it's his blatant phoniness that's so gross. He likes to see people squirm. He really does.

We're walking up the beach toward San Giovanni. We go round the small promontory where the cliffs begin and see figures on the next *punta*. They disappear from sight as we climb to the top of the plateau and then suddenly we're near

some picnickers: three young men and two girls. One of the girls
is some hundred meters down the peninsula, sitting on the tip
and facing the Strait. I know it is she for whom Ring has come.

We exchange greetings with the three men and other girl.
They look quite ordinary, but their picnic is not: whole lobsters,
French champagne, linen cloths on the ground, and the silver
looks real.

"Angela," Ring calls to the girl on the cliff's edge. She turns
her blonde head slowly, obviously not surprised to see Ring.
Despite her light eyes and hair she doesn't seem Nordic, but
there's nothing Italian about her. Some of the picnickers were
light, but all were definitely Italian.

"You're Jeffrey," she puts out her hand. Ring sits at her side
and dangles his legs over the edge. Angela motions for me to sit
on the other side of her. "You're Ring's best friend," she says
brightly. "He says you're inseparable."

She's dazzling. I bend forward, in front of her, so I can look at
Ring. She puts her hand on my arm as if to stop me from
toppling over the edge, but she must be used to men toppling
over cliffs for her. (It would almost be worth it to feel her hand
on my arm again.)

Ring is bright and smiling, as eager and enthusiastic as a
sixteen-year-old and looking just as innocent. He'll be nice to
me now and it won't be just an act. He behaves cordially, even
charmingly, toward everyone when he's with a woman he likes.
And not just so's he can make a good impression on the woman
to get something — he's nice to me or anyone even when he's
with his regular woman.

It's because Ring believes it would be *disrespectful* to the girl
for him to behave badly in front of her. Ring has only one virtue
so far as I can discover, and it's that virtue which makes me
forgive him for the way he aggravates Dad and steals and lies
and cheats — and generally betrays any friend, especially me,
just for the purpose of hurting people. Ring treats women with
kindness and respect. And it's no act. His present regular, who's
been living with him for a year now, is treated with just as much
consideration and attention as he's showing Angela. It's not
fake. It's as if there were two of him, one rotten and the other

an angel and when there's a woman around the angel completely obliterates his other self.

Speaking of which: I wonder how much he'll hit me for so he
can entertain this Angela. Top-drawer stuff. Even my heart's
going thump, thump, thump.

"Your father isn't *the* Rambulcek? Ring, you didn't tell me
that!" She's enraptured. "And the big blue villa is yours?"

She's English, that's what she is. Her Italian is impeccable,
absolutely impeccable, the English can never manage such good
Italian — yet I know she's English.

"Did you grow up in Italy?" I ask.

"Mostly Rome and Florence." She misses the compliment.
"Have you met my friends? I think we'd better not be rude."

Why should we go to meet her friends? We were perfectly
content as we were. At least I was. But she is a girl of good
manners. She's wearing a light pink dress and her ass is
beautiful. I'll bet there's not a blemish on it. I've never seen such
an ass. We're standing by her friends and I have a decent
erection which the other girl stares at. I can't remember the
picnickers' names, but I take their champagne. Maybe it'll
sober me up.

"Won't you have some lobster, please," she asks, holding out a
plate with several claws and tails. I take a claw. They're all
talking about Northern Ireland, Italian inflation and legalized
pot as if they were the same subject.

"Why don't the Catholics go to Catholic Ireland?" someone
asks.

"Because it's not their country, truly. They've lived where
they are for several generations." Angela says. "But mostly it's
economics. There are jobs in Northern Ireland and there aren't
any in the Free State."

I have sympathy for both Irish, but the talk wearies me. Our
talking won't help anyone and I want to be alone with Angela.
Her fingers are really delicate, real fine. "Why don't you come
for dinner tonight?"

Everyone's a bit startled and Ring looks as innocently startled
as everyone else. But Angela isn't startled at all. "Will your
father be there?"

"Yeah, sure. He'd love to meet you."

"I don't think he knows me."

"We have drinks about eight-thirty, but come earlier if you can."

"Fine. I shall."

On the way back Ring curses me, but not too much; I haven't promised him any money yet. When we get to the bottom of the stairs that lead to my house he pauses. "Say Jeffs, how about a loan of twenty-five thou. I'll pay you back next week." He won't try to barge in for dinner tonight — or will he? Am I going along with everything just as he's planned? Quite possibly. And now I'm being blackmailed like the proverbial. But I'm excited about Angela.

"I'll bring something down this afternoon."

"Make it twenty-five."

"I'll see what I can do."

"Christ, man, I need twenty-five. I really need fifty, to tell the truth."

"What the fuck is this? I've got to scrounge around and — "

But he's walking toward his cottage. "Twenty-five, Jeffs," he calls without turning around.

Sandy says she doesn't know where he is and asks me in for coffee. I've dug up a little over twenty-three thousand. I've never given her the money before and she handles it as if it were extremely fragile or else horribly germ-laden. She knows it won't be spent on her, but I don't feel sorry for her since Ring always gives his women a fair shake. Sandy's not a fool and she knows he plays around with a lot of women, but she'd be an idiot to make an issue of it. I've never seen him act anything but extremely considerate toward any of his women, whether full- or part-time. The women know they can do a lot worse than Veringetorix.

We used to have the cottage before Ring came and we "rented" it to him. Sandy's fixed it up. It's kind of pretty in a way, I guess — bright colors everywhere, Peace and Pot posters. Cheerful, but too distracting and hard on the eyes. My eyes can't stay put or linger on anything. Everything calls for attention; everything distracts from everything else.

"But you will be going back to your pictures?" Angela asks.

"I certainly plan to, Angela, as soon as I can get my friend over there settled." He means me. I groan; I see it coming.

"Jeff's mother died when he was three and I'm afraid it's my fault he hasn't had the attention he should" . . . "His mother was a good pianist, but Jeff can be a great one if he'd apply himself" . . . "I don't blame him too much, I know it's been my fault." Etcetera. Etcetera.

Uncle Craft reaches over and offers me a cigarette and a look of sympathy.

"But Uncle Craft," I say as if we had been in the midst of a conversation of our own, "he misses the point that she's spaced out on him, not me."

That stops Dad for a second. Angela looks as if she didn't understand.

"But then again," I say, "she also hasn't understood that Dad is trying to get her married to me so I can settle down and be happy and all that."

Uncle Craft gives me a quiet laugh, indulging me; he's a good guy.

"Is that what I'm trying to do, Jeff?" Dad asks sternly.

Angela really and truly hasn't taken any of this in. "What was your wife's professional name?"

"Rosalind Rambulcek, but it's not likely you ever heard of her. She gave recitals in Europe and America, but, well — she was a great wife and she would have been a great mother to Jeffrey, but she was only a good pianist. I'm afraid I have to say that."

"Only room for one great in this family," I say, immediately regretting it. Dad brings out the worst in me. "I'm sorry."

"Jeff says you're a linguist," Uncle Craft rescues us. "I know that doesn't mean you simply go around speaking languages. What *do* you do?"

"I'm a phonomecist, really — a branch of phonology." Now

she's into explaining about phonetics and phonemics. Remark-able. Either she's pretty dumb or exceptionally cool, probably the latter. She's wearing a low-cut light-green dress which shows the tops of her small but perfect tits.

Something bothers me about Angela being a phonologist or whatever. I don't dislike all academics, only middle-of-the-road academics, which is to say the vast majority. (What's a *vast* majority?)

I play the first two movements of my Babi Yar suite for Angela. "Very haunting," she says. "You don't give concerts, do you?" There is a reprimand in her voice, but it's a sort of complimentary reprimand.

"You give concerts only under one of two circumstances. Either you're a first-rate pianist with at least a substantial repertoire, or else you're a composer with a substantial body of work. Pigeons on the grass, I'm only somewhere between the two and time is running out."

"How do you mean, about time running out?" She's getting aggressive.

"I'm twenty-four and I'm far behind for my age."

"But so many men have blossomed late in —"

"Writers, poets, some painters, yes, but not musicians, Ferrier being the incredible exception." And so saying I come to the sofa and sit next to her. Good Uncle Craft gets up to leave and I know I can count on him to drag my father away — or at least have a good try at it.

But Dad rises and comes over to the sofa, offering his hand. "Thank you for coming tonight Angela. I've enjoyed meeting you very much and I hope I'll see you again." Perfectly fine words, but Dad fills them with intimacy, warmth, desperation, sounding so much like the very loving father-in-law he is, sans daughter-in-law.

Most fathers want their sons to take up where they them-selves left off. Usually it's a family business or some kind of profession, but Dad's been so successful in his own work, he has no understanding that I too must be very successful in my life's work. All he thinks necessary for me is a wife as good as Mom —

the one area where his success was short-lived because Mom got killed in a car crash when I was three. Mom and Dad were really happy together and he thinks I'd solve all my problems by . . .

Of course I'd like to find a woman like Mom and discover that kind of ecstacy, but a man first needs a life's work. Four years ago I saw myself as both a virtuoso and a composer who would bring some fine music into the twentieth century — music that's first-rate but also appreciated by the masses. Something irresistible to most people and yet with depth to make it live a hundred years. That's all I want — just one hundred years at the top of the charts.

Four years ago I had the confidence, the certainty, but maybe my mistake was trying to do both things, both play and compose. Unfortunately I'm not Liszt, but I won't settle for anything less than Chopin. And when I hit my twenty-fourth birthday I started to panic. This is supposed to happen to most men in their late thirties or forties, but I guess musicians are really different.

"Good night, Dad. Thanks, Uncle Craft. Good night." Angela seems unaware of my hand on her shoulder. "On the other hand I'm plagued by a desire to be a construction worker."

She laughs. Maybe she isn't so literal; maybe there's hope.

"Really, Angela, I mean it. And don't think I don't know that part of it is being scared of the competition. I mean the competition of the past six hundred years. After what's been done, what can I hope to do? But it's not only that. What good would a late-twentieth-century Chopin — and I mean a really new music, not a rehash — what good would it do?"

"Everyone has to try to do the best he can. That's all there is to it." Deep down I get the feeling she is *not* trying to put me on.

"I like doing construction work. It makes me feel good."

She turns with a look of disapproval. "You really wouldn't like it, I shouldn't think."

"But I do. I've built the new *ufficio postale,* among other things." I get up and take off my jacket. "Here, let me show you." I push my sleeve up and sit down close to her again. "Feel my muscle." I'm getting too much like Ring, about absurdities I mean.

"Have you really been a laborer?" she asks pityingly with only a nervous glance at my quite good though not utterly remarkable bicep. My hand slips up on her knee. Small bones and delicious melon flesh.

She takes my hand and holds it in her lap. "You say you're worried about time running out, and yet you entertain frivolous thoughts." What's unbelievable is that she's not referring to sex, but to my being a "laborer." "Jeffrey, have you ever thought seriously, but I mean very seriously, that you might not be as determined or as serious as you might?"

I put on some Pink Floyd. She even dances like an academic. "You're not at all like your father."

Getting her undressed is almost too easy; then I discover why. She lets me do anything — except the important thing. Is it that she realizes the best resistance is no resistance? Or maybe none of this means anything to her. I try not to hear the inanities she insists on muttering. Whenever I haven't had a woman for a long time (when isn't it a long time?) there's an aching in my arms, I guess the aching of emptiness. At least the soft, juicy body of Angela, the soft, juicy, unrequiting body of Angela, eases the aching a bit, though from time to time I have to take her arms and place them round me. Does this only feed the hunger?

Even if I were the kind of man who could rape a woman (I'm not, and proud of it), I somehow suspect this anomaly named Angela could defend herself with ease.

I drive out of my way up the Via Crocefisso to wave at St. Paul outside the cathedral. "*Circumlegentes Devenimus Rhegium.*" That inscription on the outer wall is the only part of the original cathedral that the earthquake didn't destroy. I think it's beautiful. As if St. Paul were still there, saying it now: "And from thence [meaning Syracuse] we fetched a compass and came to Rhegium." Right on.

It's part of my ritual. I always pass Paul before heading for my casino, though sometimes I pass after I've been. Now I'm through the town and am ostentatiously parking the Fiat in front of the Gladstone, a wonderful name for Regg's best whorehouse. There's a small restaurant and bar in front, and though I've dimly been able to make out people in there, I've never been inside and don't know anyone who has. I open the side gate and walk up the *gradini* and down the *vicolo* to the wooden door which is distinguished for having neither a window nor a knob. I push it in and walk down the dimly lit corridor toward the small room where a radio is playing.

It's too late. Uncle Craft has seen me. My wishing to retreat has nothing to do with Uncle Craft seeing me here, but with my seeing *him!* The puzzle is solved. Through all the years I'd wondered what he did for sex and now I know. He's almost fifty and yet it's *he* who blushes.

"Well, time for servicing, I see," I say cheerfully. In a small archway at the other end of the room, behind a rope which serves as a gate, are three girls (fat and forty), trying to coax the half-dozen men and me to try them out.

Uncle Craft tries a hearty laugh and almost succeeds. "I don't know that it's proper you should see me here. Or that I should see you." I stick out my hand and he shakes it; some sort of ritual by which I want to put him at ease. Well, for the past five years he's been trying to get me to drop the "uncle" and just call him Craft — he's not really my uncle anyway — maybe I'll be able to do that now. After all, as Dad says, I'm a big boy now.

I'm puzzled as I knock on the cottage door. Yesterday Ring invited me to a picnic down Sousse, just the two of us. He says it'll be our farewell. What puzzles me is he said he'd provide the picnic. Could mean he's serious — or more likely up to some outlandish trick.

"He is gone," Sandra says. "He asks you to follow him, please."

"Did he take anything to eat?" Sort of a dumb question I guess, but Sandra regards all questions equally.

"Oh, yes. There is a nice basket. He went to the *fiera vècchia* himself this morning. He said it was special."

Sousse is not a popular place. (It isn't Sousse at all, but Ring calls it that because it reminds him of the Sousse in Tunisia.) It's

an isolated peninsula down toward Pellaro without any real
beach and rather dreary. And yet at times it's poetic, maybe
only because so few people go there. It's a two-mile walk down
the coast and I consider going back up to the house for the Fiat,
but decide to walk instead. Ring can wait. He didn't wait for me.
What the fuck's on his rotten mind.

It was at Sousse Ring once gave me the only clue as to what
goes on in that rotten mind. "To find the limits of acceptable
behavior, of course." And why? "Because the limits tell us how
far we've gone as a civilization. It's my field of study. You are the
pianist, Veringetorix is the social observer." Feeble.

Now I'm in sight of the peninsula and what must be Ring
when the sun disappears. There are heavy clouds and it may
rain in the afternoon. Just the right sort of day for Sousse.

"Look at it this way," Ring says, "you'll only have to support
Sandra. You'll save half the money."

But I can't believe he's going to leave. And yet I know it's
true. He's acting awfully nice, just as if a woman were present.
And he's brought a nice basket: mussels, a melon, fresh bread, a
red tomato, *moscato*, and my favorite cheese from the *salsamenteria*.

He's going to Paris with Angela. "And what will you do for
money?"

"You don't think I can work?"

"No, Ring, I honestly don't think you're capable of work. You
don't love Angela that much, or do you?"

"It's time to move on. The time's right and that's all I know."

He's slicing a beautiful salami. "And you'll let Angela support
you?"

I can't make out what his look means, beyond showing
disappointment. "No, I don't think I'll do that Jeffrey." He's
acting kind of meek.

"But you said you never liked Paris."

"I was just a kid then. It's like Milton, something I've put off
until I'm old enough. Mind you, Milton'll have to wait."

"But what do you feel about Angela?"

He's silent a long time and I almost forget my question as I watch some birds fluttering down the end of the peninsula. There will be a storm. "I just want her to love me, that's all." There's a shyness I've never seen in him before, as if he's made the biggest confession of his life.

"But Angela's so damned organized — in her mind, I mean."

"Maybe that's the answer then. Maybe I want her to get me organized."

"In a funny way it makes sense," I say.

He just laughs. We don't talk until the rain begins. We throw the remnants of our picnic to the birds, who have formed a circle around us. Across the Strait Sicily is disappearing in the mist.

"So what happens to Sandra?" I shout as we walk back through the mildly churning surf. The rain's pouring and we're completely soaked.

"You've already answered that yourself. If you didn't feel she's your responsibility, you wouldn't have asked. That's your answer. Anyway, like I said, you'll be saving a lot of money. She doesn't eat much and makes her own clothes. Anyway, cost you less than the Gladstone."

When we come to the stairs leading up to my house, he sticks out his hand. "Any hard feelings?"

I take his hand. "Yeah, just a couple. But I guess I'll forgive you as soon as you're gone. And when shall we three meet?"

"Bad luck to quote Macbeth."

"Old witches' tale."

"I've really liked you Jeffs, you know that."

We shake hands again. I'm suspicious of his last remark, thinking it's meant to keep his foot in the proverbial, like when he runs out of money in Paris, which is likely to be within a week. But as I walk up the steps I let myself enjoy the sentiment. I'm at the top and turn and see he's been standing at the bottom all the time. He waves and then heads for his cottage. I don't think I'll ever see Ring again.

It's Theophilia's day off and I'm fixing my own breakfast.

Sausages, scrambles, fried tomatoes, fake refried beans and pickles.

"Mmmmmmmmmmmm. That smells yummy."

I've never seen this one before. American. Probably about twenty-seven or older, long hair like a teenybopper, but through her averagely provocative nightdress I can see she's kind of dumpy. Slim, but still dumpy. Almost no ass and yet it's a dumpy ass.

"Come join me." I'm sitting on a high stool and eating off the service counter. I pull another stool over. "Get yourself a dish from in there."

I'm feeling generous and give her more of my breakfast than I want to. "I'm my father's son."

"Show me the man who isn't," she says without looking up. She eats greedily. If I don't hurry she'll be after more from my plate.

"How's about boiling some water for coffee?" I ask. "We have only instant coffee." After all, it's only fair; I made the goddamned breakfast.

She looks resentful as she goes and puts the gas under the kettle.

"My father's the man you fucked last night." She gives me a cool look, but isn't troubled. "Is he any good? . . . The cups are up there on your right."

She takes down two cups and puts instant coffee in each. When she returns to her stool, I've spread my legs and am facing her. My cock's slipped out of my pajamas and it's standing like a cannon. She sees it, but acts indifferent and then settles on her stool.

"The son also rises," she says at last.

She takes another sausage from my plate while I'm laughing, but I don't care. Pretty high caliber compared to Dad's usual stuff.

After my shower I stand before the mirror. I'm starting to deteriorate again, so it's time for the road gang. All I have to do is stop working on the road for a couple months and the weight really comes on. It's in my genes or something. And yet Dad's very trim — and he doesn't exercise much and eats more than I do.

Dad took some movies of Mom giving a recital. They show a trim woman coming on stage and bowing. She probably was just average height for a woman, but looked taller. She doesn't smile at first, but then on her second bow a big smile comes to her face, almost against her will you'd think. It's wonderful the way that smile appears; you know it's real. I get a thrill each time I see it.

Then she's at the piano and the camera zooms in — her fingers, her hands, her arms. Her arms are long and thin, but there's a lovely roundness to them at the shoulders and elbows. Is that the origin of my propensity? That suggestive roundness? Probably I *think* fat. I know I do. I have a fat brain.

When I was writing my first Italian Rhapsody I looked one day to the side and in a mirror I saw this slob laboring away at the keyboard. I listen to the tapes I made when I was fat and there's little question but that they're better than my "thin tapes." Thy name is Jeffrey Rambulcek, oh, vanity! I have a fat brain is what the real problem is.

I remember I haven't given Sandra any money and go to the bank and withdraw 100,000 for her payoff. If she's smart she can live on it a couple months while she decides what to do. I haven't seen her since Ring left.

"*Avanti!*" The cottage seems neater. Sandra acts as if she's busy with some project, but there's no evidence of cooking or sewing and everything's neat and in its place. I glance toward the closed bedroom door and wonder if she's already set up shop. She catches my glance.

"I hope I am not disturbing you. I just came to see how you are doing. I won't be but a minute."

"As you see, Signor, I am fine." There's a nasty edge to her voice.

"I was sorry to hear Ring was leaving; I guess you were too."

"*Sisignor, mi dispiace.*" We both remain standing near the

table. I reach for my wallet and quickly take out the pile of lire, but she turns away and begins dusting the window which is already devoid of dust. I put the money on the table.

"Here's a little gift to tide you over until you decide what to do." She goes on dusting. "Well, got to be going now. Let me know if I can help you in any way."

Now her head is completely turned from me and it seems she will keep at her dusting until I leave.

"*Arrivederl'*."

"*Arrivederl'*," she says without turning.

She was a free-lancer when Ring picked her up and brought her to live with him. He offered her a roof over her head, her board and a weekly allowance (most of which I was to provide) in exchange for her keeping house for him and sharing his bed. I was sure Ring was going to use her — that he'd send her back into the streets and keep her money. But I didn't know Ring very well then and I was wrong. Seeing Ring and Sandra together in the cottage was like seeing a highly sophisticated and mature married couple in their home. Their behavior had a civilizing effect on me.

The thank you I didn't get from Sandra isn't so important, yet it would have been nice. Did she think I expected to sleep with her just because I gave her money? Then again, maybe she did, I mean from her point of view. Maybe she might have been happier about the money if I said it was payment for my pleasure, but I have no appetite for a hole that Ring's been reaming for a year and was reamed by all the cocks in Regg' before that.

Dad gave a party last night. Not a party party, but a let's-encourage-Jeff party. I knew it would be that when I saw Giovanni Ballegna from La Scala, but I didn't mind. It had been some time since I'd given a "recital" and I like Ballegna — he's kind of "impressed" with my music. And we've worked out our act pretty well.

Right after dinner Ballegna puts his arm round me and calls for everyone's attention. "Do you think it will be possible to

persuade our young friend here to entertain us with his latest
composition?"

My face shows both humility and surprise as I look each and
every guest in the eye. Most of the thirty people there didn't
have a clue, but Dad's claque around the room began a hearty
applause as Ballegna led me to the piano.

"And what may I say you'll grace us with tonight, Jeffrey?"

"How about Fellini film themes?"

He leaned over and said sternly, "If you don't believe in your
music, do you think anyone else can?"

"I've finished 'Babi Yar.' I'm going to play the whole fucking
thing." I did. And it went pretty well, though I dropped the
longish fourth part for fear of losing the audience. I felt good.

I think I could go through life very nicely if I didn't feel I *had*
to be happy. The obligation to be happy is depressing. Just do
what has to be done and don't worry about the happiness part.
Then I could be content.

The dinners began naturally enough: a couple of weeks after
Ring'd gone, I went down to the cottage to see how things were.
I'd been down to the beach many times and occasionally I'd see
Sandra puttering in the little patch of garden. I'd usually wave,
but we didn't speak.

She was wearing a yellow two-piece swimsuit when she
answered the door. Her hair was matted as if she'd been
swimming. She gave a big smile.

"Just wondered how you were getting on."

"Oh, it is very kind of you, Signor. I am fine."

"And everything's going all right?"

"Oh, yes! Please excuse me. I have been in the water for my
dinner." She pointed to a small stove, but I didn't understand.
Then she hurried to the stove and with a big fork turned over
some small fish.

"Hey, that smells good." I looked at the fish in a chunky red
sauce. "What's that smell?"

"You mean the garlic, Signor? Is it too much?"

"Is that garlic? I've never smelled garlic like that. I like
garlic, but that smells super."

"You make the garlic into a pâté — *una còlla* — then put it in the tomatoes and cook them together. The tomatoes change the smell." She gave me a taste of the fish and sauce.

"Super! You caught these fish yourself?"

She laughed. "Why should I pay all money for stale fish? With my hands I catch them. It is easy if you have patience." She was enjoying herself. "See, I take some pasta and hold it in my hand. And they will come. Did you never do this? Come have dinner with me."

"Ah, no thanks. It tastes great, but I've got to be going." I lied; I don't know why. "I just wanted to see how things were with you."

And then she suggested she could make dinner for me sometime.

I've been back with the construction crew for almost two months now, through the hottest part of summer. Dad's furious, of course, and what's ironic is that it's only through Dad that I work on the road. There's not enough work down here for the people who really need it, but I persuaded Dad to use the brother of the foreman and one Pietro Mandanelli as extras in a film when he was shooting down here. Mandanelli received more than a year's wages by his standards and now I split half my pay with him whenever I want to take his place with the gang. It's true, Americans can buy everything, even work on a road gang at half pay.

I'm up at six and with the crew by seven. We're building a road toward the Aspromonte. At the end of each week it seems like no progress has been made although the foremen work us hard. I like the punishment of sweating like a pig (do pigs really sweat?) under the hot sun. I'm darker than the Italians now.

We work till noon and then go down to the beach and eat and swim then sleep for an hour under the trees. At three o'clock it's like starting a new day, and we work until seven. Then I go home and shower and eat and collapse. There's almost never a thought in my head.

I can't do hard physical work and compose at the same time. The hard work refreshes my body and clears everything out of my head, especially serious music. Hard work makes everything simple. In the evening I meet my coworkers at a *birreria* or play billiards, drink wine, or sometimes go to dances. Screwing is as uncomplicated and satisfying as eating.

Sometimes I go down to see Sandra and eat my dinner there — once or twice a week. I give her money and tell her when I'm going to come by and she cooks elaborate meals. Yesterday she made lobster and mussels that filled the whole table. And yet I ate it all. She helped a bit, but not much. Just sat there looking happy as I shoveled everything into my mouth.

She's painted all the walls white and I notice that more and more the gaudy colors are disappearing. Those yucky orange curtains are gone and most of Ring's posters have disappeared from the walls.

Working on the road is punishment, but I love it. Even by 7:30 A.M. I'm soaked. I just plod on and on. Bertolucci our foreman is tough and mean and often makes fun of me, but the hot sun mellows him and I find him amusing and not threatening. The other men are fine and accept me as one of them. They've even stopped pestering me to fix it so they can go to America. We share extras in our lunches with whoever happens to be nearest. With the exception of Bertolucci, we're all interchangeable. I like that. It fits with the sun.

I am perverse. Dad'll be off to Scotland to start his new picture in a few days and I could have waited until he was gone, but I invite Sandy up to the house so I can play the piano for her. My motives are good, just a little dinner and music, a gesture of gratitude for her making all the dinners. But why don't I wait until Dad's gone? He knows Sandra by reputation as a local whore, but the fact that she shacked up with Ring for a year and gave up her profession won't seem all that redeeming to Dad. He'll say, "Well, at least I don't invite mine to the family dinner."

But it's too late. I'm waiting in the cottage as Sandra dresses in the bedroom. It seems the place gets starker and starker all the time. And that's good. More and more white things are replacing those disturbing colors and more and more of the junk has vanished. Right now, with the late afternoon sun coming through the window, the place looks like something Vermeer would have painted.

Sandra always hides her feelings, which is why she often seems cold and even mercenary, but now as she emerges from the bedroom I can see she's more nervous than I've ever seen her. She's trying to look calm and unconcerned, and she needs to have me say something. That's easy. She's wearing a plain white dress and almost no make-up. Her long black hair must have been brushed a thousand times. It falls down, perfectly in place — just like that picture of Anouk Aimee in the bedroom. "Hey, you look great!"

She carries her high-heeled shoes until we're across the sand and at the bottom of the steps. "How old is your father?" she asks as we begin walking up.

"Fifty-four or fifty-five, I think. Nervous?"

She gives me a bitchy look, but I see through it. "You really look very smart," and I take her hand to reassure her. She's surprised. It's the first time I've ever touched her. We continue up the stairs in silence. Near the top she pulls her hand free of mine and turns to face the sea.

"Nice view from here, isn't it?" I say pleasantly. Her head goes down and I look to see what the attraction is. Well, it's vomit — though it takes me half a minute to realize that. And she's shaking like the proverbial.

I lead her down the stairs, the only direction in which she'll move. Vomit is down the front of her dress and she starts to cry when we're near the bottom. I'm lost. I put my arm around her shoulder and I feel that this is just the point where a man should let a woman cry on his shoulder, but it just isn't done with vomit between you.

She won't let me in the cottage. I sit on the front steps and look at the timid surf. I examine my clothes and somehow I'm a little disappointed that I can't find any vomit. Makes me feel cheated, like I haven't participated.

I'm knocking on the door again, but there's no invitation to come in. It's not likely she's killed herself just 'cause she can't hear my piano tonight. Yet who knows?

I don't like Sandra because she's withdrawn — a nice way of saying she lies. Not lies like stating conditions contrary to fact, but just faking things. Saying what she thinks *should* be said. Talking like she's really not talking to you. I can't blame her, I guess, but I feel sorry that she has to lead her life that way.

Okay, the real truth is that I think I'm being taken. I'm not ungenerous with the money I give her, but those meals she makes for me have to cost something and the way she's fixed up the cottage means money; so where does the money come from that she salts away? Maybe she's learned her discretion from Ring. And why should I mind if she's practicing her trade again?

People are funny. People like me, I mean. If she were doing her whoring blatantly, I'd complain that she should be discreet. That I wouldn't mind her servicing the whole town as long as she did it discreetly so I wouldn't know about it. But since she is so discreet, I complain she's doing it behind my back.

Why the hell should I be paying for her support? No, that's not it. She gives me really fine meals and I do enjoy just coming down after work and sitting in the Vermeer setting.

"Signor," she calls after me as I'm heading toward the stairs. "You okay?"

She's wearing a robe and her hair is out of place. "I'm sorry I got sick. Please tell your father I'm sorry. Her eyes are hard and tight.

"No problem. Wanna try again? We have plenty of time. I mean do you want to put on another dress and come up? Plenty of time."

She smiles as if she knows something I don't. "No, I don't feel right. I am sorry. Will you excuse me, please?"

We're finally nearing the crest. For the past couple weeks, after we'd worked up over the last hill, it seemed we were stuck forever between the two crests. I made a special point of never walking up ahead to see what lay beyond the hill; determined

not to look ahead until I had to, when we'd brought the concrete
ribbon to the crest.

Of course it all looks the same. About a kilometer or two in
the distance I see another crest with a valley in between, just
like the one we've finished. With a hedge of wild geraniums
along one side of the road. Looking very Sicilian.

I don't even touch the piano anymore. There's no desire.

Sandra's made me a dish of shrimp and scallops in her tomato
sauce seasoned with plenty of garlic. She's grown the tomatoes
herself in the little patch between the cottage front and the
beach road.

"Maybe you should open a restaurant," I say cheerfully, but
she only smiles. "How old are you now, Sandra?"

"*Diciotto.*"

"Ring says you were brought up in an orphanage."

"*Sisignor.* For a little time."

"You didn't know your parents, your mother or father?"

"Oh yes, a little. My mother a little and then she died. My
father took care of us and then the *polizia* took him away. And
for a little time I lived with an old woman who took care of me."

"You have brothers and sisters?"

"Yes, many, but I do not know where they are. I went to
Filadelfia to see, but no one knew them."

"Sandra, do you mind if I ask you what you think you'll be
doing in the future? I mean do you have any idea what you
might be doing in five years? Or what you'd like to do?"

She is suddenly bright, but she tries to restrain her enthusiasm. "I would like to have a dress shop. A shop where I can
make dresses for women, not to be a *piccola sarta* only. I buy the
fashion magazines and I know I can make those dresses."

"Ah, very good. Do you have any money put away?"

That scared her. Now she's trying to find the answer she
thinks I want to hear. "A little."

"Do you mind if I ask how much a little is?"

"It is just a little. But if I save a little at every time, it becomes
a lot."

"*Conto corrènte postale?*"

"Oh, no! It is not that much." She seems relieved.

"Would you mind if I had a look at it?"

"You want to count it?" Absolute terror.

"Yes, would you mind?"

She gets up and fumbles with her hands. "But it is not all in one place. I keep some in the cupboard." For the first time ever she asks a favor of me with her eyes — that I drop the subject.

"I was just curious. Do you think we could count it after dinner?"

Another thing about me is that I'm a rotten son-of-a-bitch. After dinner we went to her hiding places, but found some odd notes only under her mattress and in the cupboard. A total of less than two thousand lire, enough for one fair meal in Regg'. She's scared to death and trembling because she thinks she let me down by not saving more. I put my hand lightly on her shoulder and then bend over and kiss her cheek.

"It's okay Sandra. I just wanted to see if you were getting enough money. Don't worry about the dress shop, we'll work it out. Don't worry about it."

I know she cries the minute I leave the cottage.

Dad calls once a week and talks mostly about the trouble he has reaching me. I tell him all's well. Uncle Craft calls once in a while and I tell him I'm not touching the piano. He tries to cheer me up. In his old age he's begun collecting bad jokes and he always tells me one or two. They're pitiful, but then they're supposed to be since that's the kind he's collecting. We laugh together.

"I'm sorry I'm late. We worked a little late today." It's a lie. I went to a bar and stayed longer than I planned.

"You are not late, Jeffrey." I'm glad I took the time to wash up properly. The cottage looks spotless and the table is carefully set, though none of the dishes match, but they all look good on the white tablecloth.

"It is hard work, I know," she says.

Just pasta? I glance at the stove and see that that's it. Not that I deserve better for being so late. But then there's a creamy sauce of tiny pieces of squid and scallions. Restrained elegance.

I tell her her cooking is *cordon bleu* and she knows what that means. She blushes beautifully.

Autumn has come, changing the earth and changing me.

I was born an old man, I think. The changes come so quickly. My legal age is now twenty-five, but I know I am in my fifties really.

I quit work in September and though I'm at the piano full-time, none of the old fat has started to come back. I think I get fat only when I have fat thoughts and I haven't had any lately. Also I haven't been to bed with any girl for over a month, but I've had two wet dreams, including last night.

Ring rang up day before yesterday, asking for money. "Very anti-climactic, Ring. I've gotten used to the idea that you're no longer part of my life. You became a good friend as long as I thought I'd never see you again. I won't give you any money."

"How's Sandy?"

"Fine. How's Angela?"

"Angela's fine. Look Jeffs, is this the end of us?"

"For the time being, anyway. I've got to find myself."

"But you can't stay here," Uncle Craft said in amazement. "Nobody comes to Edinburgh and just stays at the airport! You mean you plan on staying here and then leaving — without having left the airport?"

"I came to see you. Edinburgh I'm saving for my old age."

We're stretched out on the beds of my airport hotel room. It's near two in the morning and we've been talking since my plane arrived at ten. I'd brought two bottles of Scotch, but I've hardly touched mine. Uncle Craft has finished half of his, but he seems dead sober.

". . . And she's so good. She's never had a chance in her life; the world's been against her and she's been battling alone, but still her heart . . ."

"In my time," Craft interrupts, "we used to make jokes about the prostitute with a heart of gold."

I give him a dirty look, or is it a hurt look.

"Look, Jeffrey, I had the impression you didn't fly all the way here just for me to pat you on the back and hum 'Love Is Many Splendored.' You said I should say whatever I felt needed saying."

"Right, okay. But there's such virtue in her. She's kind and generous and wants to be loved — just like everyone else. But there's more. Deep down there's this intelligence and marvelous humor. Like the ruins of Pompeii or something. Dig down through seven civilizations and you discover this astonishing intelligence."

"She keeps it that well hidden?" he asks politely, but it's meant to be sarcastic. It's the same way he plays chess.

"To you she's a whore. To the whole world she's just a label and labels are so wonderful. They save us so much time. We don't have to give a thought to someone if there's a label handy, especially if the label is 'whore.' Oh, sure, we'll say, I know a whore has feelings and all that, only they really don't count. The label justifies our dismissing any further thought as unnecessary. But you see, Craft, Sandy doesn't believe the label. Deep down she knows none of that is real."

"Jeff, the only thing wrong with being devil's advocate is that I get all the clichés. Here's another: 'So you're going to save her.'"

I smile. "First, yes. Is there anything inherently wrong with saving people? Second, there's that cathedral in Washington — some president's daughter was married there. Well, when they first built the foundation they ran out of money and construction stopped and that tremendously strong foundation started to crumble, not because it was defective or anything, but only because there was no cathedral on top of it. Without that enormous weight on top that it was designed to support, it began to deteriorate. Only when it was repaired and the cathedral finally built was it really strong."

I can see he likes the analogy, but still he must speak his objection. "So your whole life is to be devoted to supporting the cathedral of Sandra?"

"Why not? If I don't use my strength, it will go to ruin.
Besides, I don't have fat thoughts anymore."

"Any other reasons why you must marry this girl?"

"Just one more. 'There comes one moment once, and God
help those who pass that moment by, when Beauty stands
staring into the soul with grave, sweet eyes that sicken at pretty
words.'"

"What astonishes me is the way everyone breaks into poetry
the moment love is mentioned. Jeff, do you mind if I ask if you
take drugs or anything like that? Or smoke pot or whatever?"

"Really, no, but maybe I drag someone's joint a couple times a
year just to be social."

"Good. My first point is that it appears you're not following
any kind of guru or taking drugs or doing the things most young
people are doing. You're full of belief as all young people are, but
to your credit you're finding your own way, not following the
crowd. It's very much to your credit. You will fail as the young
must always fail, but at least it will be your own failure."

"Jesus! And that's only point one?"

"Second, if you should decide to marry Sandy, then in half a
year or one year or five years, you'll eventually throw her past
life in her face — as they say in the films. Again a cliché, but
true nonetheless. And if you don't, that'll be worse. All the time,
even if you're not thinking about all the men she's had, she'll
think you're thinking it. One way or the other, you're doomed."

"Uncle Craft, you often said you'd like it if I dropped the
'uncle.'"

"That would make me very happy. As your father says all the
time, 'You're a big boy now.'"

"Craft, is it too late for me to change my mind? Maybe I
really came here for you to pat me on the back and hum 'Love Is
Many Splendored.'"

He tips up the bottle and empties it, and appears even more
sober than when he first came in this room. "Jeff, point three
begins with a question. How long have you been sleeping with
Sandy? Since Ring left?"

"I've never slept with her."

"Curious; it was contrary to the probabilities, but somehow I had the feeling you were going to say that. So now I'll ask why."

"I haven't slept with Sandy because we're not that far along yet. It's not natural for us yet. I'm courting her the way girls all over the world are courted."

"In short, you're afraid because you can't get out of your mind all the other men she's been with, and, worse, the circumstances."

"You know Craft, I don't think I'm afraid. Sandy doesn't think those things are important now and I don't either."

"Jeffrey, it's too late now to argue. Can we resume in the morning? I'm staying with some people in the city. How about if I come back here for breakfast and we can continue if you like?"

"Fine, but whatever's most convenient for you."

"No problem. But I want you to promise me one thing."

"No problem. What is it?"

"If you decide to marry Sandra, that you sleep with her first."

"No way. I won't promise that."

"Jeffrey, I've got to go now, but think about this: you wake up the morning after and you're disappointed, you realize you made a mistake; maybe you can't even stand to look at her. Please see that it's a possibility. Why risk hurting her in the worst possible way? Don't be selfish. I'll meet you in the dining room for breakfast about eight. Think about it."

I shake his hand. "Sure. See you at eight."

I'm still undressing and there's a knock on the door. It's Uncle Craft again. He has a funny expression.

"Maybe I'm making a big mistake, Jeff; please forgive me if I am. We all have to make decisions in life and sometimes we can make very bad ones — even with the best intentions. I sincerely believe I'm doing this out of love for you, but still it may be the wrong thing to do. If I am wrong . . ."

He looks like he's preparing a long speech. He turns toward the open door as if he's about to leave again. He stops. I can't think of anything to say except just nod my head.

"I'm saying this because I think you'll find out anyway. I've slept with Sandy — about two years ago."

*

I take a seat near the windows where I can see the planes taking off. I'm early and very hungry. I order a steak and scrambles. "But no salt on the eggs please." I usually have salt on my eggs, except if I'm having a breakfast steak, in which case I put the salt on the steak and leave the eggs plain. A highly recommended combination.

Uncle Craft arrives but can't see me despite my waving. It must be the glare from the morning sun. "Craft, over here!"

He looks wretched, as if he hadn't slept at all. He stands dejectedly by the table. "Please forgive me Jeff. I never should have told you that. I can't say how sorry I am. I couldn't sleep all night. I wanted to . . ."

"Easy on, Craft. The world's not at an end. Have some breakfast."

"Jeff, believe me, I'd do anything to take back what I said last night. But I thought someday you'd be faced with it anyway."

"Craft, I already knew you'd slept with her." The waitress is at Uncle Craft's side. "Why don't you try what I'm having? It's great, but ask them not to put salt on the eggs. Then you put the salt on your steak. You won't believe what a difference it makes."

"Uh, no. I'll just have coffee, please."

"Sandy told me. I already knew."

"But — how does she know me, I mean my name?"

"I was bringing her up to the house for dinner. You were on the balcony; I didn't see you, but she did. She remembered you. And got sick. But really sick. Vomit everywhere. We turned back, though I never knew why till about a month ago."

"Oh Jesus!"

"Look Uncle Craft, it doesn't matter." But he can't look me in the eye. "By the way, there are some important objections you forgot to raise last night. Like about her not being socially acceptable. I mean even if no one finds out about her past and I'm a famous composer, she won't know how to behave properly. What about that?"

"I thought you said she was unusually intelligent." He gives a small smile at my being devil's advocate, but still he can't look me in the eye.

"Craft, we have to forget this other thing. Life has to go on." I stand up and offer him my hand. I've shaken more hands in the past year . . .

"Okay Jeff. Then I'm going to forget it if you can."

"A deal."

"You seem awfully bright this morning. Does this mean you've come to a decision?"

"Yep. I came to one a long time ago, except I wasn't so sure till now."

"You're going to marry her?"

"Yep."

"Is it love or pity?"

"Sure I feel sorry for the life she's had. But I know what kind of person she is and that calls for admiration and not pity. Besides, I've always pitied almost everyone really, but not Sandy. Speaking of pity, how do you think Dad'll take the news?"

He signals the waitress. "I think I'll take that steak. And not to put salt on the eggs?"

"Not on the eggs."

In the end I did promise Craft one thing: that I'd wait ten days. They were just winding up the shooting and Dad was losing his mind as it was. I promised to return to Regg' and wait till Dad got there before telling him.

"What it comes down to," Dad says, "is that you feel sorry for her!"

"What it comes down to Dad is there's this great good in her and it seems I'm the only one who can see it and bring it out."

"You're going to *save* her!"

"I'm going to save myself."

"Throw away your whole life to save her — if she can be saved! Jeff, listen to the words! Don't you know what they mean? It's good you want to help someone, but you don't marry under these conditions — ever!"

"You know Dad, somehow I don't find it so appalling to 'throw away my whole life.' To tell the truth, seems the best thing to do."

"Okay, Jeffrey, okay. If that's what you think, then here's what I think. You and me are finished. No more father, no more son. I'm going to stop you from marrying her for your own sake. I'm going to do everything I can to stop you, but I know that in the end if I don't succeed, it'll end with us busting up."

"Oh Christ."

"Just think about it tonight. Just for this one night promise me you'll think about it. I know I'm going to lose you if I oppose you, and I *am* going to oppose you. Until it's all over and finished I'm going to oppose you. Will you promise me that just for tonight you'll think about that?"

"Dad, for Chrissakes!"

"Jeff, I'm resolved."

"Okay Dad, I'll make you an offer. I'll promise that if you'll promise me something."

"What?"

"That we ask Sandy for dinner tomorrow night."

"Just that white dress. No jewelry or anything. Just the dress and those black shoes."

She sits on the other side of the table and takes my hand. "Jeffrey, I am not going."

It's invisible, but I know it's there. It's creeping in under the door. It's coming in through the window. I know it. I know it.

"Jeffrey, I am not going to marry you."

Dear old déjà vu, it's now completely filled up the room. Everything is now completely predictable. Two thousand years' accumulation of déjà vu. "Do you realize, Sandy, that if we took an earthwide poll, for the first time everyone in the world would agree on one thing?"

"Jeffrey, I do not understand you."

"I am not surprised. Let me put it this way. There is no one in the whole world who wants me to marry you, including yourself, except me. Including yourself, except me. I think there's a title in that."

"Jeffrey, please, I do not understand you."

"Then how about this: you've got a pussy there that's been fucked by the whole town. Well, that's too bad. We can't change

history, but we can decide the future. Sandy, I'm going to marry
you. I'm going to marry you because I love you and there's not a
thing you can do about it, so get up and put on that white dress
and those black shoes and come to dinner."

I'm the only thing that's not predictable, or am I wrong?
She's crying and feeding the déjà vu.

"Sandy, this is all so fucking predictable! Please stop crying."

"I will go to your dinner, Jeffrey, but I will not marry you. It
will be very much pain for me to see your father and your uncle,
but I will do it for you. But I will not marry you."

"I'll tell you what. Let's skip the dinner and get married
instead."

"Jeffrey please, I want to be alone."

There comes a time in every man's life when certain things
must be done. I take a deep breath. "Okay, Sandy. Why won't
you marry me?"

"Because it is not right."

"I'm older than you and I think it is right, so it must be right.
Oh for Chrissakes Sandy, please stop crying."

"Go home Jeffrey, please."

"I am not, Sandy, a violent man. But I am going to take off all
your clothes and then I am going to dress you in that white dress
and those black shoes and then probably even comb your hair
and then carry you up the stairs and in through the back door to
the dining room and will sit you down at that table. Then I will
give my father a good belt in the mouth and maybe even Uncle
Craft if he gets out of line and then we'll get married. I hope to
Christ I don't have to add that we'll live happily ever after."

"Jeffrey, you are a fool. You are hurting me. Don't you know
that? Why do you want to marry me? Give me that answer."

"Didn't you once say you loved me? True or false? Oh sweet
Jesus. Please stop crying." Déjà vu is the one thing no one can
fight. But we must try, sweet Jesus we must try. And I do.
"Sandy, I've seen the error of my ways. We're not going to
dinner. Why should you be put through all that — that 'uncom-
fortableness' for my father who is just going to sit there and act
shitty? No, indeed no. If he wants to meet you, he comes down
here. Why should you have all the pain? That's settled then.

Why don't you have a rest. I'm going up and telling him, first, that you're not coming to dinner, and second, that we're getting married *tout de suite*. Now get some rest, love, and I'll be right back."

I'm getting annoyed. Truly annoyed. It's maddening to be the only one acting sensibly while the rest of the world's gone crazy. There's almost no describing Dad's unreasonableness. If I chose, I could sit down for two minutes and come to understand his attitude perfectly, but I'm not, as Richard the Third said, "in the vein."

My only ally now is Uncle Craft. He's got this perpetual smile of amusement; I've never seen him enjoying anything so much. There's never any overt encouragement from him, but all I have to do is look at that grin of his to get my necessary approbation.

Was it utterly predictable that Sandy should run away? The déjà vu was nauseating when I discovered this, and yet I think I'm right in believing that it wasn't absolutely in the rules, not completely proscribed.

"But this," I tell Uncle Craft, "is, of its kind, a classic. My hope is you'll agree." I hand him the letter that's come this morning.

My dear Jeffrey,

I wish to thank you for everything. You have been a good friend and I will always think of you. You will be blessed because you are a good man. I am always happy because you said your wish was to marry me. I know you are sincere and I thank you. Please if you will allow me I am coming to the cottage to get my other clothes. If I see you I will say good-by and tell you my thanks. If I do not see you it is my wish that you know I thank you and say good-by now. I know the Virgin Mary will bless you.

Sandra, your friend

"Do you need further proof?"

"It depends," Uncle Craft says. "Proof of what?"

"Oh do not fail me in my hour of need dear uncle. The sentence about coming back for her clothes! 'If I see you'! She wants me!"

"You mustn't force her Jeff. She's been hurt enough."

"I won't hurt her. These feelings cannot exist without a reason."

"Yes, Jeff, young people always believe that, until they get old."

"I'll pursue her either until I'm convinced she really doesn't want to marry me or until she does marry me."

"What will it take for you to realize she doesn't want to marry you?"

"There is no answer to your question. And may God have mercy on our souls."

And yet he gives me the smile. As long as people can smile like Craft, I think we need not worry about hydrogen bombs.

I've seen the tide come in and go out. And in and out. And yet again. I wait on her cottage step for her return. "I'll build me a willow cabin at your gate and sing sweet songs of love, even into the dead of night."

I look up and see Craft descending the steps. He's bringing me some sandwiches and milk. It seems to take a long time for him to come down.

All the world's become beautiful and Craft descending adds to it. I begin composing "Craft Descending," a slow understated triumphal march. As so often happens, I'm composing for orchestra which is annoying 'cause I don't know how to. It's just something I'll have to learn.

He's reached the bottom and now begins crossing the sand. This part will be for the flutes — just when you'd come to expect the thundering of the full orchestra. And yet none of the power is lost.

His smile has become a fixed grin and I know I'm right because he doesn't speak. Just hands me the sandwiches and gives me that grin. I believe for some reason Craft has never been so happy in his life.

He sits on the stoop and we both watch the greens and blues of the sea as I stuff the sandwiches into my mouth.

And now he astonishes me with this: " 'Make me a willow cabin at your gate,
And call upon my soul within the house;
Write loyal cantons of contemned love,
And sing them loud even in the dead of night.' "

"You know," I say after a respectable silence, "I just did that as you were coming down the stairs, but I didn't know the right words."

"And then Olivia says at the end of the scene: 'Fate, show thy force: ourselves we do not owe; what is decreed must be, and be this so!' Theophilia's making fried chicken for dinner. Do you want some ice cream for dessert?"

It must be the fried chicken coming, but not by Craft's hand. My father descends. I have already composed three fourths of a symphony while waiting for Sandra to return, but my father is no inspiration. Maybe Beethoven's father was bringing him fried chicken when he did the Rush of the Goblins in his Fifth. But I'm not up to that. There is a dried weed. I run my hand down its length and knock off all the dried leaves and with a flourish wave the stick in the air like a sword.

"Power of darkness," I shout at him as he starts across the sand toward me, "do you come to tempt me?"

But his silence is not the silence of a friend. He wears no grin. He is all sadness, but in my heart I know it is a purposeful sadness. I remain standing on the stoop, my sword ready for anything. He holds out the box which, please God, contains fried chicken. I will not take it from him. I judge him to be a practical man who will simply place the box on the stoop, which is what he does.

"Don't you know a man shall leave his mother and father and cleave to his wife?" I ask, meaning to make him smile.

"Cleave? or cling?" he says without a trace of humor.

Smart son-of-a-bitch. Just stands there, looking me right in the eye, then turns and heads back. "Displaced the mirth" as

Shakespeare would say. Taken the edge off the poignancy.

Against my will I turn from time to time to see him disappear up the steps. And now it's lonely when he's gone. The effect he'd calculated. I guess one of the reasons I love him so much is that he's so fucking smart.

"Jeffrey."

My vigil is over. Sandra stands at the corner of the house, pushing back a strand of hair. I've never seen her dressed in green before, a simple sort of dress like a robe that wraps around and ties in front. I've forgotten all my speeches. All I can do is offer her some chicken. She accepts. Now that's true love. Think about it. Check it out.

"Live with me and be my love and we will all the pleasures prove."

Her answer is a look that makes me hate all the world and the people in it, save one.

Neither of us cry. She has put her hand on my knee and I take her hand and hold it. My mind is vaguely forming the Cyrano speech about Give me giants to fight, but I let the thought go. Unnecessary.

Let us, Jeffrey, now be concerned with what must be done.

"Sandy, we should talk only about what we have to do. We should talk only about packing our suitcases and where we're going. Just practical matters, like as if we've been married thirty years and don't need to talk about anything except suitcases."

"Where do we go, Jeffrey?"

"We go somewhere; we don't stay here."

Craft does it beautifully. He suppresses the grin, but it's still in his eyes. He sticks out his hand and she takes it without hesitation. "I wish you all the best luck in the world," he says to Sandy. "You will be very happy. I know that." We are giants and no one may stand indifferent to our joy.

"But," he turns to me, "I'm full of news. How about the bad news first?"

I wait and now find myself grinning at him.

"I said *bad* news, Jeff. Don't bother going to the bank. He's taken out everything from your joint account and put it in an account in his name only. He's gone through all the house and picked up all the loose lire you always leave under the vases."

"But some of that money's mine! I worked all summer on the road for that money."

"Exactly what I told him, but he pointed out, and with some measure of truth, I would assume, that you've spent more of his than he's taken of yours. Anyway, I think he told you this was all-out war."

"Bastard."

"Worse news follows. Ready?"

"I don't need his money. Okay, ready."

"He's made me promise not to give you a solitary lira, whether in cash, money order, check, or anything."

"Craft, you're crazy! You're a grown man — let me go so far as to say you're a pretty old grown man." But even that doesn't take the grin off.his face. "People your age just don't go around making promises like that. I mean I hadn't given a thought to taking money from you, but the idea of such a promise! You're not serious."

"I am, alas, serious. And it's a real promise and one which I must honor. Our generation is different from yours."

"This is unbelievable. Even Shakespeare wouldn't have strained the concept of honor so much."

His grin won't stop. Sandy's even picked it up. "Well, that's the end of the bad news," he says. "Your father limited my promise to money. I see nothing wrong with my giving you a lift in the car."

"To where?"

"The airport."

"Beloved uncle —"

"A helicopter will fly you to Rimara. I know the people in a villa called Consente."

"Isn't that where I was once when I was a little kid?"

"Exactly."

"And Pa's old buddy! Who killed his wife and kids and a couple other people! My God Craft, I see what — I feel so inadequate. I never came near to giving you enough credit for you sense of humor."

"I'm glad you like my plan."

"Sandy, Craft here is our only ally and he's stark raving bonkers!"

"I'm sorry, Jeffrey, I don't understand that." But she and Craft are smiling like a couple of nuts.

"Jeff, I don't know if you can understand — if I have time to explain — but the man's reformed. He lives next door to an old woman — you'll love her and she'll love both of you; her name is Paulina. She says the man Antonio has been doing penance for nineteen years. She's been begging me to come back and see him — to forgive him."

"Forgive him? Did he think Dad was playing around with his wife? Hey! Was Dad playing around with his wife?"

"No, he wasn't."

"So this Antonio kills his wife and kids — "

"He didn't actually kill anyone. He wasn't directly responsible. They all died of accidents. Joachim, Paulina's husband, capsized in a boat as he was taking Antonio's wife and their baby to Taormina."

"But still he was responsible. I mean, it sounds like he forced them out of there. If he hadn't — wouldn't they still be alive?"

"Yes, I think they would."

"Look Craft, I've got problems of my own. I'm awfully sorry for all those people, but this isn't the right time. If you want to go to him, go to him. What does it have to do with us?"

"Jeffrey, someday, for your birthday or Christmas or something, I'll give you a notebook. The name of it will be 'Things to Remember.' Somewhere on page one you should write that the right time is always when people need us. He needs you Jeff. He needs you and Sandy."

"He doesn't even know us."

"People have to know us to need us? Trust me, Jeffrey. You can get married over there and Paulina and Antonio will take good care of you. It's a beautiful place for a honeymoon."

"Yeah, corpses all over. Man, you've gone bonkers."

For the first time in weeks his smile is gone. "Jeffrey, no love can live in isolation. For a time maybe, but not for long. If your love doesn't join up with others, it's doomed. You think Jeffrey and Sandra just appeared one day with nothing before, and you'll disappear another day and that will be all? In books maybe, but not in life. You're part of the continuity and that's the only reason you're here, the only reason any of us are here. I'll call the Lady Paulina. I can take you this evening or early tomorrow morning."

Go, the comedy is finished —
— And with thy spirit.

When Sandra was five or six, she and a boy named Robito played on the beach. But one morning he simply vanished. Without warning he and his family simply were gone. Then in her early teens she'd pretend they'd meet again. Always the fantasy had her turning a corner and finding him.

"When he saw me he would smile, but he would not move. He was a young man and very handsome. He was leaning against a building and smiling and his arms were crossed. He takes my hand and says we will go back to the sea at Filadelfia where we played as children. A big car comes around the corner and Robito opens the door for me and on the back seat is a picnic basket so big . . .

"*Affannari pani è duru, lu pani è duci.*"

Which is a Sicilian proverb meaning it's hard work to get bread, but bread is sweet. Then her fantasy could take either of two directions. Either Robito knew all about her and said nothing because it was not important, or else it came as a shock to him. He would feel shame for her, and pity. If she saw that Robito did not understand she was still the same friend of their early years, she would leave him. "I could say no words to him. With him I would be nothing. It is better to be alone. I know what sin is.

" — Sin is what happened on the feast of Sant' Agatha when I was walking down the Via Cavour. I came from the good *salsamenteria* with a nice cheese and bread. The shops were closing. I saw an old man begging and I saw he was hungry; it was not a mistake. That is the first thing I saw and my happiness became greater because I would give him a little of my cheese and bread. Then I saw a second thing; there were young men around him and they tormented him. I walked down the street on the other side because I was afraid the young men would also torment me. All that afternoon I was sad because I had done something bad. I think I know what sin is.

" — One thing I will tell you, Jeffrey, is this: if I could change history, for your sake I would wish I grew up in a palazzo like this with Signor Antonio for my father and the Signora Helen for my mother. I picked flowers in her garden and wore always beautiful dresses and I waited for you to come. I was a virgin and we became married in *cattedrale*. For you, Jeffrey, I would wish to change history that way. But for my sake I would not make such a wish; it is foolish to wish to change the things of a heart. I cannot believe I would be a better person if I could change history in that way."

I told her I understood. I told her I did not love her because she'd had a difficult life and missed the happiness and love she should have had. "I love you Sandra because you are good and generous — because in all ways you are a beautiful woman and will be a good wife and a good mother. All these things, yes. And I guess there're other women like this. But why I love you most is *il tuo orgoglio*. There's a pride people have about the past — about the things they've done. But your pride is of the future — what you believe you can do. It's that pride you have that makes me love you. Like the pride of an osprey or hawk. It *inspires* me, Sandy. It makes me believe in the future.

" — You know something Sandy? I wouldn't want your history changed, either. You're the woman I admire and respect — and mostly the woman who *inspires* me — because of *how* you lived your life, not *what* you did. A person doesn't deserve special credit because he has tuberculosis, just as you don't get special credit if you don't have it. It's how we behave if we have it or don't have it. Life's always *how*, not *what*."

*

She smiled, but only for a little while. Then her eyebrows raised — just slightly — but full of challenge.

"Then I will tell you the second thing Jeffrey. I ask for your forgiveness. I ask only this time. No, Jeffrey, wait. Listen to me. I want you to forgive me for the things I did. No, wait, please! It takes a humble person to say an apology, yes, but also a person must be humble to give forgiveness.

" — Wait Jeffrey, this is important. If you *do* forgive me, you will see that I will become another person. Maybe I will act like a virgin, maybe like their daughter Antonia. That is the forgiveness I want. I will act always as if I did not understand what *la puttana* means. Believe me, Jeffrey, this will be so. I will never put my head down with shame. I will look at you and talk to you with ignorance of these things, like I spoke to Robito on the beach when we were children.

" — But someday maybe you will forget you gave me this forgiveness and expect me to put my head down and be sorry again. Maybe you will forget the forgiveness, but I will not. Maybe you will call me *la puttana,* but I will not understand. Believe this Jeffrey, I will not understand."

Then she knelt down right in front of me. "Jesus, Sandy, get up."

"Get up? I did not ask your permission to get up. It is easy to say 'get up!' But can you say you forgive me the way I ask you?"

It is easy to say Get up, Forget it, We won't mention it again. After all, who am *I* to forgive? Isn't that presumptuous?

But Sandy was right. Forgiveness requires humility. I learned then that it's the acknowledgment that we too are human and so are capable of that which we are asked to forgive. A proud person can't forgive because he can't admit that under certain circumstances . . .

We can't lift a burden off somebody else without just for a little while holding it ourselves.

I found they were the most difficult words to say, but at last when I said them it was like a miracle. That strange burden suddenly was gone. Absolutely it had no existence.

Our vows exchanged, the marriage could proceed. And now it is consummated. If the omens are bad, I will ignore them. If the omens are good, I will believe them.

It's near dawn and Sandy's asleep. I'd love a cup of coffee and a cigarette (and maybe some *fellette* like Theophilia makes) and to go down to one of those terraces and decide the future as the sun comes up. (Is there an etymological relation between "happiness" and "happen"?)

It's taken a long time to find the kitchen in this great palazzo, but now I've got some water boiling for instant coffee. I'll take my coffee back to our room and have a cigarette and rehearse the future. I'll watch the glow from Etna and then the sun'll come up and I'll be suddenly tired and I'll go back to bed and be there when Sandy wakes up.

All that remains now is to tell the part before tonight. How we have come to be where we are now.

"You are Jeffrey." A handsome woman, though old, and dressed in blue and white. I felt I was in some painting, with the morning colors and dominating yellow stones of the terraces and house. But not Vermeer. It was maybe Tiepolo. Very definitely she was Tiepolo. "I am Paulina."

"I'm happy to meet you. This is Sandra. We're going to be married."

"Ah, to be married. It is wonderful!" She kissed Sandy on the cheek. "Craft was very mysterious, but he said you would explain everything. But later. Now we must get you some breakfast."

Then onto the terrace came a man, great head of curly gray hair, big shoulders — really a Tiepolo figure, except for his eyes. He was eating me up. My hand was still in his huge fist and he held me by the shoulder as if I might escape. "I am Antonio Contiorli. I was once your father's friend. Welcome to Rimara."

I was overpowered. Then the woman said, "This is Sandra. She and Jeffrey are to be married."

"Anna! Anna! Bring the breakfast. We'll eat out here."

There was melon and sausage and eggs, but it was really me he was having for breakfast. Paulina kept watching him watching me. Then she asked Sandy, "And when are you to be married?"

Sandy blushed and couldn't speak so I said, "At once, as soon as we can."

"Ah," Paulina said. "And where is the wedding to be?"

"Anywhere. Anywhere we can get married."

"But your father —" the Signor said, wiping his mouth with a napkin, "where is he?"

"Signor Contiorli, I believe he is at home."

"And you parents?" Paulina asked Sandy.

"Sandy's an orphan; she doesn't know who her parents are."

"You will get married without your father's blessing?" the Signor asked me. He seemed appalled.

"I should like to get married with his blessing, but I shall get married without it if that's what has to be."

"You see, Jeffrey, we understood that you were already married and were on your honeymoon."

"Did Craft say that?"

A strange look came into his eyes at the mention of Craft. Then Paulina said, "Yes, I thought Craft said that. I have been mistaken."

"It seems your father objects to your marriage, am I right?"

"Antonio," Paulina scolded, "we must not pry." And now it's Sandy who's being devoured, but by Paulina. My confidence was draining away like the proverbial. I cursed Craft, thinking he must still be playing the devil's advocate and giving us some kind of final test.

"My father does not approve of my choice of a wife. He has not met Sandy — despite many opportunities to do so — and so he disapproves of her because he doesn't know her." And that was the truth.

"I cannot believe," Paulina said. "She is an angel. I am sorry if I embarrass you Sandra, but Harry must be a fool. But what are your plans?"

I stood up. "Signor Contiorli, Signora Paulina, you must

excuse my manners, but I think my Uncle Craft has tricked us. You have been very kind to us and I know I'm being rude, but I came here only because Craft sent us and it was my impression that he had everything arranged for us. I see this is not so and you are just as embarrassed as we are. I'm very sorry, but I think we must leave. I hope you realize I'm very upset and I can't even apologize properly. Please forgive me." I took Sandy's hand. What I said was true, but I was crazy; we didn't have a lira to go anywhere. Then the woman Anna appeared, saying there was a call for the Signor, from Signor Rambulcek!

"You are not to worry, my dears," Paulina said when Antonio was gone. "I know Craft. He has some good plan in mind. My dear, you must not cry. Everything will be fine. I know it will. You shall see."

Antonio reappeared and again I stood up. "Signor Contiorli, I thank you for your hospitality, but I'm afraid we must leave now."

"No, you must wait a minute please." Then he was in the house again.

It pleased me to see Paulina comforting Sandy, but I knew the scene was doomed by the words of my father. How long till his words reach Paulina's ears and she too sees Sandy with new eyes? *"Corraggio,"* Paulina said to me, as if she'd heard my thoughts.

"You are very kind, but my father has spoken to Signor Contiorli and I know I can expect only a bad scene."

"If you are to be married, then you must not waste time. There will be much to prepare. Come, you must let me help you." She took Sandy's arm. "You must excuse us Jeffrey, but your bride has many preparations to make. There is much work to be done." I felt she was mad, but her madness was welcome. Sandy and I exchanged helpless smiles as Paulina led her away. It was a time for action but I didn't know what to do.

Again Antonio reappeared. "Jeffrey, your father is coming here. He asked me to have you remain until he comes." Sandy and Paulina were going down the terrace. Antonio and I watched them until they disappeared through the bronzed gates of a high wall above which I could see the roof of another house.

"But that's not all he told you, is it?"

He looked sad, as only parents can look sad when thinking of their children. "No, it wasn't all. He told me about the young lady."

"The young lady — what did he say about the young lady?"

Again the mournful look. "It's nineteen years since I've seen your father. I don't know if I can face him again. Jeffrey, I would do anything to help you; nothing could give me greater pleasure. I have so few pleasures in life anymore — though maybe more than I deserve. I don't see people anymore. You are the first visitor. But I'm vulnerable now. I've done your father a great insult. You know what I mean, don't you?"

"Yes, I think I do. Craft told me a little."

"A little. Yes. And now it's impossible that I should do anything further against your father. I have no hope we can meet as friends anymore, that is not possible, but I mustn't do anything against him. Do you understand?" I nodded. "Will you go to America?"

"I don't have any money, not even enough to leave this island."

"Jeffrey, I won't try to stop you from leaving. But that's a foolish statement. How could I? But I won't help you either. Can you forgive me?"

"I can understand, I don't know if forgiveness is important."

"That means you don't forgive me, doesn't it."

"Yes, Signor, I suppose that's what it means."

Two hours passed with no sign of my beloved father or uncle. Antonio showed me the grave of his son. "He would have been your age, a year younger" was all he said. Then he showed me Paulina's husband's grave. I looked across the garden toward the house where Sandy and Paulina had gone.

"Will Sandy be all right?"

"Oh, yes, certainly. Do you know, Sandra's the first person to set foot in Paulina's house in years." Then he asked what I did.

"I'm trying to be a pianist or a composer or both."

He sighed and again looked up for the helicopter that didn't appear. "When I was a very young man, I used to go to your mother's house to hear her play the piano. In the beginning I had to hide in the bushes so her family wouldn't see me. We have a piano here, but no one's played it in years. It will be out of tune, I suppose."

"Yes, it will."

We had a drink before lunch, and then another, but still there was no sign of my father. I didn't know what to do. I knew I should be doing something, but I didn't know what. Finally I stood up and said I must be going, that I'd given my father plenty of time to get there. Then I asked Antonio, "Will you help me Signor?"

"Jeffrey, Jeffrey, Jeffrey. I guess I must seem a sour old man, which is what I am, and not without reasons — and the reasons are my own fault. But in the past couple hours everything's been coming back to me — the good things, I mean. For the past couple hours I've almost been coming back — I *will* help you. We've given your father more than enough time."

In fiction as in life: Anna was in the doorway, behind her my father and Uncle Craft. They'd come over by boat.

Dad spoke first, then went up to Antonio and they shook hands. They smiled at each other, then spoke again, then stood looking at each other, but it didn't come off.

Even Craft's indomitable grin, for weeks a major source of approbation, faded in the short time it took him to cross the terrace and come up to Antonio. The grin faded like the proverbial. They shook hands, spoke, exchanged nervous smiles, etcetera, but etcetera.

Craft had said Paulina was a sort of mystic who could sometimes read people's minds and foresee events. She was in the archway and I was prepared to believe she was a sorceress as well. Behind her stood a princess in a white wedding gown, veil, the whole number. It took me a bit to identify the princess as Sandy. Someday as I lie dying, I think the last image I'll want to keep from this life is that manifestation of Sandy.

"Such greetings!" Paulina said as she stepped onto the terrace, leaving Sandy in the shadow of the archway. She kissed Craft and I think we all felt and welcomed the warmth and relief she'd brought to this strange confrontation. Then she kissed Dad on the cheek, turned to Antonio, then back to give Dad another kiss. "Two kisses. It should be two, *n'est-ce pas,* Antonio?"

The Signor gave a worried look.

"You see, Harry, I believe you may be the only person who does not know — if Craft had a middle name it would be Discretion — but once before I gave you two kisses. Ah! You don't even remember!"

"Paulina," the Signor said sternly.

But she ignored him. "Harry, one night on the beach down there I kissed you twice. Four people in their graves, and you don't remember. Two graves for each kiss. You see — ah, you remember now? — Antonio saw us and thought you were his good friend Harry and I his dear wife Helen."

"Why are you doing this Paulina?" The Signor was very disturbed.

But Dad cut in. "Craft! You knew this? You never told me?"

"Ten years later I found out. What purpose —"

"Paulina, why?"

"Why? Do you see this man? His name is Craft."

"Yes, Paulina, I know Craft."

"So you say, but I think not. When you came first to Consente, you both played tennis each morning. Sometimes it was difficult for you to stop the tennis and begin work because the games were so interesting. You told me this. And then you worked together and many times you told me how fortunate you were to have such a friend."

"Paulina —"

"Ah, but still why. Antonio, in the beginning you would ask me why time could not come back. You said you would give anything to see Helen again, to ask her forgiveness. Then in later years you often said you would like to see Harry and Craft. Why did you want these things Antonio? I saw this reunion with your old friends; you were worse than strangers. And if

Helen could come back, what greeting could she expect? To what purpose should she return?"

"You're right," the Signor said. "To what purpose? You know, Paulina, I have seen Helen. At least once each year I have been up here at night and saw her walking down there along the water's edge. It's true. Once I went down there, by those rocks, and waited as she came up the beach. She passed in front of me, not more than fifty or sixty feet away. I know she saw me; I could see the moment of recognition."

"You spoke to her?" Paulina asked quickly.

"I called her name."

"What did she say?"

"I knew she heard me, there's no mistaking that. But she didn't say anything and just continued up the beach as if I wasn't there. And I saw her again this spring. I was here, but she looked up and I knew she could see me and know it was me. Paulina, is this all in my mind? Or is it a real ghost? Or is Helen still alive at Sontern?"

It's difficult to know what Paulina's expression meant. She turned quickly to Dad and Craft, but they exchanged a look as if they were passers-by who had wandered too far within the grounds of an asylum. Paulina drew a deep breath. "What answer do you want Antonio?"

"You still offer choices? I know what I want, Paulina, but can you produce it? It appears you've 'produced' Craft and Harry today, and I have no doubt you could even produce my daughter." He gave a quick glance toward Sandy in the shadow of the archway, but Dad and Craft missed the significance of his look and seemed all the more convinced they had entered a madhouse. "So I suppose you could just as easily produce Helen. I do have faith in you, Paulina, but can you produce what I want?"

I have seen conductors during a performance who look as if the music or orchestra is escaping them, going on without them. Paulina had that look. "What do you want, Antonio?"

"I've lived with the guilt of my stupidity a long time. I know 'stupidity' seems too mild a word for my acts, and I don't mean to excuse myself or dismiss everything by calling it stupidity, but I'm afraid that's the word that seems to fit now. Do you know I feel there's almost humility in using that word? But anyway, what I want is more than forgiveness. I will ask Harry and Craft for their forgiveness and, as they are generous men, I think they might forgive me — if I'm not being too presumptuous. And if you could produce some ghost of Helen and I asked her forgiveness, I think she might forgive me. Maybe even the whole world could forgive me. It's more than I deserve, I know, but also less than I want.

"I've spent many years mourning Helen, Alexander, your Joachim and my daughter Antonia. But if I were to repeat those years and do the same again, I don't think it would do any good. My mourning won't make them live again.

"I guess I'm being arrogant, but I want to live again. Craft and Harry and even Helen can forgive me, but that won't change the look in their eyes. That's what I want Paulina, that someone see me as the man I once was. Can you do that Paulina? Can you take away pity from people's eyes?"

"Signor!" Sandy stepped into the sun and then quickly went halfway across the terrace toward Antonio. Of course it was because of all of us, only Sandy could truly understand his words. She'd started toward him on an impulse, but then the gasps from Craft and Dad (unaware of her presence until that moment) stopped her and her courage disappeared.

I saw the shock on my father's face as he finally realized who the princess in white must be, and God knows what he might have said when Antonio began to move.

He quickly crossed to Sandy and took her hand. It was the making or the breaking of the spell.

Then many things happened and I remember at one point Dad putting his arm round my shoulder and then we were all parading down the terrace with Sandy leading the Signor. We came to a small garden and the Signor said, "Paulina, the fountain's working," and I looked at the fountain as if it were some kind of miracle. Then going through a gate we came to Paulina's house where Sandy had spent most of the morning. At the door of the house an attractive woman was waiting, holding a small silver bell.